BRANDFIELD

by

JULIE GRIFFIN

Brandfield

For information about this title or to order other books and/or electronic media, contact the publisher:
Red Jasper Press
redjasperjulie@gmail.com

ISBN: 978-0-9838205-4-3 (softcover)
ISBN: 978-0-9838205-5-0 (eBook)

Printed in the United States of America
Cover and Interior design: 1106 Design

BRANDFIELD

Chapter One

There's the need for shelter.

There's the need to own a little land around that shelter.

Then there's the need to have your head examined.

Which is what I would do before I built a home where I had this appointment today. This place was too far east from Denver for me and further yet from the mountains. And it didn't take a degree in architectural design to see that it was ugly.

A monstrous, dark-brick structure hunched in the center of acres of dull, flat prairie, it climbed up and out over the top of a low rise in a heavy, brooding, bungalow-style-gone-mad sort of design. It had a name, Brandfield, but no trees or bushes out front to relieve the severity of the jutting angles or the sullenness of the deep overhangs. Just a wide, sloping lawn and a narrow ribbon of grayed, pebbly asphalt that snaked past the entrance in a silent, weathered strip.

The only thing ornamental I saw as I drove nearer were two raised flower beds that bracketed the bottom of the concrete front steps. Large and square, and made from the same dark brick as the house, the deep beds brimmed with blood-red geraniums but did nothing to soften the mansion's harsh façade. Although, given the reason for this meeting today, it was possible, I conceded, that no one here cared if the geraniums softened anything.

But I wasn't a judge from the garden club, so I pulled my eyes away from the flowers and drove on around and behind the mansion, as I had been instructed, to an expanse of pavement that looked to be about half the size of a football field and was bordered on two sides by buildings made from the same dark brick as the mansion.

The one to the north was a small, windowless building with a chimney puffing a dirty cloud of smoke that hung like a stain in the clear June sky above it. The one on the east edge was a long, low garage with four closed bays and attached rooms on either end that I figured to be chauffeur's quarters.

I didn't know if it was a slow day to be rich or siesta time at the money manor, but there was absolutely no activity or signs of life back there. Which made it easy to find a space and park in the area that I had been told was meant specifically for employees. Strangely, for a place as large as this, there were no other vehicles parked here.

Wondering about that, I left my SUV and followed a walkway that skirted the bottom edge of the back lawn. The sloping rise of grass here was split up the middle by another set of concrete steps that led to a wide, empty porch at the top. I noticed there were no flowers of any kind growing back here. Not even a lonely dandelion.

I continued along the walkway and around the back of the mansion—also as I had been instructed—to a garden-level side door that blended into the structure due to its location and the dark-stained wood that it was made from. Both gave me the impression that it was not meant to be easily found, which could have been done for security reasons but to me seemed weird—if not downright paranoid—given the isolation of this place.

But you took the clients as they came, so, putting that thought aside, I checked my watch, waited half a minute, and, at precisely one o'clock, I pressed the button that was set below a security camera's eye—once again, *exactly* as I had been instructed.

Right about now, you might be wondering if I'm one of those obsessive-compulsive people who always has to do a certain thing a certain way. Or maybe you think I'm a moron who is happy doing exactly what he is told to do. I can say truthfully that I'm neither. What you should know about me is that my name is Devon West, and I'm a finder.

And now I need to explain that a "finder," for lack of a better description, is the term my childhood guardian attached to me because of a unique tactile ability I have that allows me to do what I do—sometimes even when I shouldn't.

What I used to do for about six years after my college days was freelance photography and travel. But I have this appointment at Brandfield today because I now work for Mecklan Personal Services, the business my brother Jonah Mecklan started after he quit the cop shop in Denver. I was in Canada on a hiking trip with friends when Jonah called me out of the blue one day and announced that "recess was over." MPS was up and running, and it was time for me to come home and put my touchy talent to productive use.

Which I do when, like today, something about a potential case doesn't smell right to Jonah. He asks for my help on these occasions not because I have a better nose for these things, but because I have this unique ability.

And although Jonah has known about my unusual skill since we were kids, neither one of us understands it. So thank God I'd had his grandmother, Constance Mecklan. She had been my babysitter until the evening my drug-using parents dropped my four-year-old-self off at her house one day and never came back to get me. Then "Grandma Connie" became my guardian, my guide, and whatever else I needed when I needed it.

And damn, did I need it.

But right now, the nearly hidden door was opening, and I needed to focus.

"Mr. West?" said a lean, pale man framed in the dark entrance.

"Yes," I replied, recognizing the silky, deliberate voice that had given me all of the very specific instructions over the phone.

I knew instantly he was the assistant to the assistant—or, more accurately, I judged, the guard dog to the gatekeeper. I thought he looked like a normal, if a little pretentious-seeming, guy, except for his eyes. Those were a cold, piercing gray that put me in mind of twin ice chips even as they complemented his sandy-colored hair, a thick lock of which he had situated strategically over one eye.

Talk about vain.

But I figured I shouldn't and waited instead while he used his icy orbs to give me an arrogant once-over, along with a subtle sneer for my off-the-rack sport coat and inexpensive tie, the priggish snob. Still, I must have been what he expected because he stepped back and gestured for me to enter what I saw was a neatly furnished office.

His, I presumed.

"I'm Alexander," he identified himself in a quiet tone as he closed the door behind us. "Follow me, please," he added as he led the way past his desk, through an arched opening, and into the next room.

To the right in there was an alcove with a row of black metal filing cabinets and a door on the adjacent wall at the end. To the left was a waiting area with a couple of loveseats that faced each other from either side of a low, rectangular coffee table centered perfectly between them. All three pieces rested on a flat-woven rug patterned in a green, gold, and muddy-brown floral that covered most of the spotless, black terrazzo floor that led from Alexander's office into the room.

"If you would make yourself comfortable, Mr. West, Ms. Troy will be with you shortly," he said.

"Thanks," I said as he returned to his desk, and I sat down on the loveseat that faced a closed door opposite the archway. I assumed Ms. Troy's office was on the other side of that door. Not only would I be politely facing her when she opened it, but I would also have a shot at a quick first impression of her. And like I said, I'm not a detective, but when I help Jonah with one of these jobs, I am thorough.

I glanced down and saw a vintage issue of a magazine on the coffee table. Brandfield was on the cover. I was wondering who had written what about this dark, ugly place and why it deserved a cover story when Alexander reappeared.

I stood.

"Ms. Troy will see you now," he said as the door across from the archway opened.

"Hello, Mr. West," Lana Troy greeted me as I approached her.

She was Ellis J. Brandywine's personal assistant, and she spoke in a tone as quiet as Alexander had used.

Slender in build and average in height, Ms. Troy was dressed in a simple but sharply tailored navy-blue suit—a jacket-and-skirt combo—with a white blouse. A lack of any jewelry, combined with her stiff posture, projected a "no non-sense" attitude, while her light blond hair, gathered in a low bun at the nape of her neck, was pulled so tight it looked more like a punishment than a hairstyle to me. I waited while she appraised me with keen brown eyes and a hard-to-read look followed by a cool smile with what I thought was her best feature, her full and very distinctive lips.

"How do you do?" I said and extended my hand.

She gave it a glance as if I were offering her something that smelled bad and hesitated before shaking it. But when she did, her grip was firm and dry, although the skin-to-skin contact made my fingertips tingle.

"I'm fine, thank you. Come into my office, please," she said, keeping her voice low and conveying the words as more of a command than an invitation. Apparently uninterested in my well-being, Ms. Troy turned smoothly and retreated.

Not to be outdone, I followed smoothly, still feeling the slight tingle in my fingertips as I did.

Lana Troy's office was twice the size of Alexander's. All the furniture rested on thick, plush carpet that seemed to absorb not only the sound of our footsteps but any noise that might have the temerity to enter this room without permission. I took a seat in one of the chairs that faced her desk, as she walked around it to the other side and took hers.

"Mr. West," she began immediately, "I understand from Mr. Mecklan that you, rather than he, will be directly handling this matter. For this reason, I must also be sure you are clear on why my employer had me contact Mecklan Personal Services. Mr. Brandywine does not need to tire himself repeating details that have already been explained."

"Fair enough," I said and held her gaze that was easily as cool as those full, frosty lips. "Your employer is searching for the bodies of his murdered twin toddlers, and he would like to hire MPS to find them," I replied and waited to see if that was enough information to satisfy her.

"Well," she said after an assessing pause and a slight, sharp nod, "you do understand. But before I take you to Mr. Brandywine, I must also be sure you know how to comport yourself in his presence. My employer is not a well man. His maladies are many and quite severe. Do not offer to shake his hand or otherwise try to touch him. It could cause him excruciating pain. And no offense, Mr. West, but it could also introduce germs onto his skin that might cause infection and further exacerbate his suffering. Are we clear?" she said, sounding like a stern schoolteacher—and not the kind you wanted to be kept after class by, those lips notwithstanding.

"Yes," I assured her, biting off the sarcastic "ma'am" that was begging to be added.

"Then we're ready," she said.

We exited through another door at the back of her office. We made our way without making a sound down a carpeted hall to an elevator that floated us silently up two floors. When the elevator door opened, we entered directly into the private quarters of Ellis J. Brandywine.

My first impression was of stepping into a poorly lit chamber with a high vaulted ceiling that reigned like a melancholic monarch over a forest of dark, shiny timber—hardwood flooring, tall wood columns, high paneled walls, carved mahogany side tables, and, in the center of the room, an enormous black-walnut desk so big that, with the addition of an outboard motor, it could have doubled as a small boat. It looked to me like the captain of this ponderous vessel ran a tight ship, because there was a keyboard with a large monitor on the desk—and nothing else.

We turned right out of the elevator, and, as we proceeded, it struck me as odd that even though Ms. Troy was wearing two-inch heels, my footsteps were the only ones making noise on the polished hardwood floor.

We entered the next room. I assumed it to be Brandywine's personal sitting room, a place to rest, I supposed, after doing God knows what all day behind that barge of a desk in his office.

There was plenty of wood in this room, too, and one wall was covered floor to ceiling with bookshelves. And, of course, all the shelves held varying shades of unread leather-bound books, their smooth, perfect spines tattling their "decorator item" truth.

But that was no surprise. So far, what little I had seen in this place made me feel like I had stepped onto a stage instead of into a home, as if everything here had been carefully arranged to give an impression rather than a welcome, with every detail controlled down to the nth degree, including the inhabitants.

Unlike the office, the walls in this room were painted a deep shade of dusty green rather than paneled. Sunlight fought its way through tall, heavily curtained windows and gave the room light but no warmth. A massive limestone fireplace jutted from one wall like an oppressive, over-sized altar. Hanging above it in a heavy gilded frame and dominating everything in the room was a life-size portrait of Eleanora Richfield Brandywine, Ellis's mother and Brandfield's former mistress.

Eleanora appeared to be in her mid-forties in the painting. Looking at it, I could not decide if the artist was of mediocre ability and all of his paintings came out looking flat and hard or was a real talent who had captured the true nature of his subject. Either way, Mommy Brandywine came off as cold and imposing.

Kind of like her mansion.

"We'll wait here," Ms. Troy instructed and did not ask if I would like to sit down while we did. She also turned to face a set of double doors. They opened, and two men came through them, one being pushed in a wheelchair by the other.

The man in the wheelchair was tucked under a couple of heavy wool blankets. A disposable paper gown peeked out near his neck from beneath a plaid flannel robe. A rolling cadaver, he was the shrunken shell of a man who had once been tall and athletic but now looked like he belonged in an ICU ward rather than a sitting room and was way beyond what I would have called "not a well person."

Anemic wisps of feathery gray hair lay wan and fading on his mottled, paper-thin scalp. The skin on his hands and face was a sickly shade of pallid white, except for scattered patches left raw and inflamed from peeling. A portable oxygen tank was hanging on the back of the wheelchair. The clear tube that led from it snaked up and over the man's emaciated shoulder to his nose and was held in place by a loop of elastic that circled his gaunt, peeling head. The oxygen did what it could for the guy, but he still sucked in every breath like he might not get another.

This, or, at least, what was left of him, was Ellis J. Brandywine.

Jonah's background search had told me that the man was only sixty-five years old, but if I had seen this guy anywhere else, I would have pegged him for a hard-living, slow-dying eighty.

The man pushing the wheelchair was another story.

I put his stocky frame at five foot ten. I figured he must have spent most of his life indoors and out of the sun, or maybe he had a fondness for Botox, because his broad face was almost unlined, even though he was no kid. Regardless, he wore a spotless white lab coat over a crisply pressed shirt with a tie. His slacks and shoes looked comfortable and carefully chosen. He also had a large square head, a mane of snowy white hair, dispassionate dark eyes, and a smile of thick, livery lips that defined the word "smarmy."

"Sir," Lana Troy murmured the introduction, "Mr. West."

"Thank you, Lana," said Brandywine. "That will be all," he dismissed her in a weak, whispery voice.

She gave Brandywine her slight, sharp nod, executed a smooth heel-turn, and headed for the elevator, walking again, I could not help but notice, in her odd, soundless way.

"Hello, Mr. West," said Brandywine and gave me a small, feeble smile. "If you're wondering, the gentleman behind me is my physician, Dr. Laurence Glandon," he said, identifying the smooth-faced lab-coat guy.

The doctor and I nodded to each other.

"Laurence, if you would be so good ..." Brandywine said, letting his voice trail off.

Without further instruction, the doc pushed the wheelchair into Brandywine's sitting room to a place where another chair had been removed, it appeared, expressly for this purpose. Briefly, I wondered if *anything* happened around this place without previous study or planning, or with a hint of noise.

"Mr. West, please have a seat," Brandywine invited me, and I sat down on the sofa across from him.

Glandon bent down and threw the locks on the wheelchair. He straightened, nodded to me again, and, without a word, left through the doors by which he and Brandywine had entered. When they closed behind him, Brandywine spoke.

"First, thank you for coming, Mr. West. I can't tell you how much I appreciate your presence here. I have nowhere else to turn, and not many individuals are willing to take on the task of finding the bodies of two small children after so much time has elapsed," he said and stopped to breathe in some of the pure oxygen. "I'm dying, and I would like to go to my grave knowing that my children will rest beside me and that this painful chapter in the Brandywine family history will be closed once and for all."

"I understand," I said, "and I'm sorry it's come to this for you, Mr. Brandywine. But I'm not sure Mecklan Personal Services can help you. And even if we decide to try, I can't promise you that we'd be successful," I added, wanting to be upfront with him, already knowing the sad story behind the children's deaths.

"Don't sell your company short, Mr. West. Ms. Troy has done her homework on your private service, and you can believe me when I say that Lana is extremely thorough with all of her tasks. Other investigators have proved to be discreet but useless. You and Mr. Mecklan, on the other hand, appear to have a very successful track record of finding people, information, or things that no one else can," he replied.

All of which appeared to have been taxing for him to impart because his eyes slid shut and his head swayed back as if he needed a moment of rest from holding upright what little there was left of his wasting skull. And while my potential employer took a time-out, I took the time to mentally review the tragic Brandywine child murders.

Six years ago, while visiting her mother in Long Island, Ellis J. Brandywine's third wife and former New York socialite, Charlotte Fallwood, had gone sailing with her children, three-year old twins, Richfield and Eleanora. The boat had capsized in a sudden squall, and all that was ever found of the twins was a single, small life jacket that one of them had been pulled out of by the rough water. The crew of a passing deep-sea fishing boat had found Charlotte floating half drowned and almost ripped out of her own life vest. They pulled her out of the choppy waves and rushed her unconscious body to shore, where an ambulance whisked her off to a hospital.

The whole awful story was a terrible tragedy right up until the next day and the moment of shock and horror when tests showed that Charlotte had gulped more than seawater. As it turned out, she was also chock full of a toxic amount of sleeping pills. Immediately, the sailing accident had gone from heartbreaking tragedy to double-murder/suicide attempt, and a juicy new story for the press and the public.

I recalled that Charlotte Brandywine had never given a reason for what she had done, nor, as far as Jonah had been able to ascertain, had she spoken a single word in her own defense. There had not been a trial. Charlotte had admitted guilt, did not ask for mercy at her allocution, and was put away for life.

Case closed.

And yet, there I sat in a dark, eerily quiet mansion across from an enormously wealthy, slowly dying man who was willing to spend a bundle of his huge fortune in a last attempt to find the bodies of his two young children when it was legally established that they had been lost at sea.

So what was I really doing here?

As near as I could figure out, I was sent to satisfy Jonah's curiosity, which had been piqued when he had received the call from Lana Troy. Jo had obtained and read the record of the police interviews with Brandywine, and something had not sat right with him.

At the time of the tragedy, Ellis had insisted that, no matter how she was feeling about the worth of her *own* life, Charlotte would never have hurt their children. He was adamant that the boating accident had been staged and that the twins had been taken into hiding. Eventually, he had given up hope and conceded their probable deaths. But he had hung on to Charlotte and his belief that the twins had never been near the water that day and that Charlotte was keeping the locations of their bodies from him out of spite.

And I did not mean to think cruel thoughts as I watched the broken billionaire try to collect some strength, but this request made me wonder if Ellis J. Brandywine, for all of his money and resources, was losing his mind at a rate consistent with his diminishing health. I waited until he opened his eyes and lifted his head before I spoke.

"Have you considered talking to the authorities who were involved in this, Mr. Brandywine? Maybe they could interview your wife again. She's been in prison for six years. She's had a long time to think about what she did. If she knows how unwell you are, and, if things happened the way you think they did, she might have a change of heart about telling you," I suggested.

Brandywine gave me a sad look with his tired, watery eyes.

"I have consulted with these authorities from time to time over these past years, Mr. West. Each time, they insist that the circumstances of the case were thoroughly investigated and that the conclusion is accurate and final. As for the possibility of Charlotte having a change of heart, you must understand that she has no heart. She has been as cruelly intransigent on this matter as she has been despicable, and I assure you that Charlotte is quite despicable."

Which went without saying about a woman who would kill her own children, but it did not preclude this meeting from being a waste of his money and what little time he had left to live.

But I knew I would not be here if Jonah were not interested in this case. I also knew that he was already busy with a full workload. If I said "Yes" to Brandywine, not just the legwork but the lead on this job would be mine, a first for me. And even if being in this grim place made me want to be anywhere else, I didn't have the heart to turn down such a sick and dying old man.

"All right, Mr. Brandywine, we'll look into this," I said, "but obviously, we can't guarantee the outcome you hope for."

Brandywine's eyes closed again, and I couldn't decide if I heard him sigh or draw a deep breath. Or maybe it was the muted hiss of the oxygen tank I heard. But whatever it was, I did not hear the opening of the elevator door or Lana Troy's approach. When I noticed her, I saw that she was carrying a folder and a pen.

She handed me both and spoke.

"This is the employment contract Mr. Mecklan and I discussed before this meeting. It requires your signature at the bottom."

I opened the folder and glanced over the two-page document. Her signature as Brandywine's agent was already on it. I signed where indicated and handed the folder and pen back to her.

"Thank you, Mr. West," she murmured.

I stood up, ready to follow her and her odd, soundless walk back to the elevator when Brandywine rallied and spoke.

"Before you go, Mr. West, and because you are taking my case, I would ask one more thing of you," he said.

"What's that, sir?" I asked.

"Would you and Mr. Mecklan be so kind as to find out how the person who is murdering me is doing it?"

Chapter Two

"**S**ir?" I said and sat back down.

Lana Troy did not move, nor, I noticed, did her cool expression of professional attentiveness change. Ellis J. Brandywine smiled again but this time with more strength, and his watery eyes glinted with a hard light that suddenly made my skin crawl more than just the atmosphere did in this oversized mausoleum.

"You heard me, Mr. West. I was always healthy for a man my age. I played tennis and racquetball, ran the family corporation, and managed this estate. Two years ago, after a business trip to London, I became ill. And here you see me today, too weak to walk and with my skin literally shedding from what's left of my body.

"And although Laurence is an excellent physician, he's been unable to come to any other conclusion for the sad state you see me in except for murder. He believes, as do I, that I have been deliberately poisoned. The question is *how*."

Fortunately, while Brandywine talked, I'd had enough time to recover my wits and get over my shock.

"Excuse me, but don't you mean *who*?" I asked.

Brandywine and Lana Troy exchanged a look. His eyes flicked back to me.

"I know the *who*, Mr. West. As I said, the question is *how* did she arrange it."

"She?" I repeated, knowing as I said it that I must have sounded like a dumbfounded idiot, which, at the moment, I was.

"Yes. Charlotte. My third wife and the murderer of my children."

I was glad I was sitting down. Jonah believed that most people were never what they seemed to be, and, for as often as I'd helped him in this line of work, he felt I was a little too trusting. And this time, he was absolutely right.

Here I had been feeling sorry for what I thought was a sad, sickly old man with a tragic past when, in truth, I realized too late, it was only Brandywine's body that was failing and not his mind. He had led me along, clueless and docile until I had signed an agreement locking MPS into working for him before springing this information on me. And now, looking past that peeling skin and the façade of well-bred courtesy and manners, I could see by the hard gleam in his eyes that he was enjoying himself.

I should charge extra for making the bastard's day, I thought but went on.

"I hate to point out the obvious," I said, "but it seems unlikely that a woman who's been behind bars for the last six years would have access to anything that could be doing this to you, let alone the means to do it."

I watched another look pass between Brandywine and his assistant. It seemed designed to put me in my place, to make me feel like a dull schoolboy slow to catch on while the two of them were being graciously patient about my embarrassing thickheadedness.

I felt myself getting angry, and what Brandywine had to say next didn't improve that feeling.

"As you say, Mr. West, that would be the most likely consideration, but I'll not be paying you for facile statements. You've agreed to work for me, and as fond as you seem to be for noting the obvious, I would suggest that you start your investigation with a visit to Charlotte. Ms. Troy will give you the information you need about where she is imprisoned. Lana will also be your point of contact from this time forward. Good day," he said, dismissing me with an imperious flick from a bony-fingered hand.

The double doors opened again.

I stood as the doctor returned to his patient and released the locks on the wheelchair. The guy threw me one more smarmy smile and wheeled Brandywine from the room. I looked at Ms. Troy, who turned and led me to the elevator.

On the short ride down, I told her that if her boss had really been poisoned, he needed the police and not Mecklan Personal Services. She raked me with a cold, sideways glance and told me in a chilly tone that I needed to do the job I had just legally agreed to do or be sued out of existence.

Not much to say after that.

Back in her office, I managed to keep my temper in check while she made a copy of the contract I had signed and added it to a thick folder of documents. She handed the folder to me and assured me it contained all of the information I would need concerning Charlotte Brandywine's incarceration, along with the necessary contact numbers and prison protocols for visits.

"Goodbye, Mr. West," she said.

"If you please," said Alexander, he and his icy gray eyes silently appearing to escort me from the mansion.

This time as I drove around and away from the place, I saw a big, bulky-looking man in work clothes holding a rake and standing like a statue on the sloping front lawn. There wasn't a wayward leaf in sight or even a handful of grass clippings that appeared to need cleaning up, but there he stood, watching me as I drove by.

I pulled my eyes away and pressed harder on the accelerator, heading my vehicle in the direction of Denver and the mountains and still wondering why anyone would build a mansion, even an ugly one, way the hell out here, why Brandywine did not want the police involved, and how long it would take the tips of my fingers to stop tingling.

Chapter Three

It was an-hour-and-a-half drive back to Mecklan Personal Services, which Jonah had conveniently located on the main floor of the big Denver foursquare that we had grown up in and Connie had left us. Our neighborhood was part of a loosely knit, slowly gentrifying community where everybody had at least a waving knowledge of each other.

The area had recently begun attracting a young, upwardly mobile demographic who wanted a place in the good local schools for their current or future kiddies. They also liked the small-town vibe that this neighborhood, with its tree-lined streets, detached garages, and narrow alleys, still managed to project. We had boutique shops and a couple of restaurants within walking distance. A small grocery store was nearby, too, which was perfect for Jonah, since he was a biped who swore he did his best thinking on a run. He was also a guy who believed less was more and preferred two-wheel travel over four because he detested traffic and honestly hated to drive.

And like I said, I'm a finder. But if I were a shrink, I would probably tie my brother's distaste for motorized transportation back to the death of his father, Mike. Jonah was only eight years old when it happened, and I was seven. Up to that point, our boyhood lives could best be described as a series of rotating sleepovers and damn near idyllic. Jonah and I were already telling people we were brothers, and, when we were not in school, we were in each other's backyards. Connie was grateful for that because she knew I was a little different from other kids, and she figured me being around a healthy family with her son, Mike, as a solid male role model could only be good for me.

And as usual, Connie was right.

I have a lot of cherished memories from those days—Mike, Jonah, and I going to late-summer baseball games, Mike never being too tired after work to throw a football around with us or to toss us a few grounders, the three of us camping and fishing in the mountains or jeopardizing our Sunday-dinner appetites by slipping off for an early ice cream cone. But as special as these memories are to me, I don't recall them often because of the terrible pain that always follows their recollection.

Which is why I never blamed Jonah's mom, Alissa, for falling apart the way she did after Mike never came home again.

Jonah's parents were high-school sweethearts who had never wanted anyone but each other since they were both fifteen. I know that's a pretty way to start a story about two young people deeply in love. Unfortunately, there's a downside to that kind of love when something unforeseen and terrible happens to one of them.

The cold night in February that Mike did not come home, Alissa had been able to stay calm until after she sent Jonah to bed. Then she spent the lengthening hours calling Connie, the police, hospitals, friends, and anyone else she could think of who might know where her husband could be. By morning, she was glassy-eyed and frazzled.

She was completely distraught three days later, when Mike's truck—with his dead body in it—was found abandoned behind an old, shuttered factory in an empty part of town where he'd had no reason to be. He had been shot through the heart with a small-caliber gun, and his wallet was missing. His body was in the driver's seat, and it was surmised that he had given a ride to someone posing as needing a lift but whose real intent had been robbery and murder all along.

And a bouquet of flowers had also been found on the floor at Mike's feet.

But it was not the gunshot to his father's heart that Jonah dreamt about.

His terror involved chasing Mike's truck into darkness night after night and free-falling into his father's death over and over again, screaming a doomed warning and helpless to prevent it. It didn't help that it would be years before the killer was found and Jonah would be able to put an end to his nightmare, dissatisfying as that would be. Meanwhile, Alissa fell apart completely. When she did, Connie had had to step in. Holding her own grief at bay, Connie had buried her son, sold his house, and brought Jonah and Alissa home to ours to heal.

It took almost three weeks before Connie was able to coax Alissa out of bed in the morning and another two to get her to leave the bedroom itself. Even then, she would only shuffle as far as our living room couch, where she would sit in her robe and slippers all day, eating little and staring away into nothing. Often, Jonah sat beside his mother, holding her hand or stroking her arm. Sometimes, either Connie or I would find him asleep with his head in her lap.

"Honey, Jonah needs you," Connie would try to get through to her devastated daughter-in-law.

Alissa would look down at her sleeping son and smile as if surprised to see him there. But after touching his face or brushing a hand over his hair, she would lift her vacant eyes and go back to staring. Connie, with her own eyes full of sadness, would go back to whatever she had been doing, and I would go back to feeling lost and lonely.

In April, and during one of these lost moments after Mike's death, my loneliness got the best of me. Because we didn't understand my "gift," as Connie had called it, she had always urged me to be cautious with it.

Sure, it was a funny story now about the time when I was three and a social worker had been sent to check on me. While she and my mother had talked, I had touched my mother's hand, left the room, and innocently returned with the large stash of pills and a baggie of coke that my mother had lost when previously high. As you can imagine, there had been no cookie or a pat on the head for that find.

But this time was different. I had to know where Alissa and Jonah were drifting off to, believing that if I could find them and bring them back from wherever that place was, then maybe, just maybe, we could all have some sort of wholeness as a family again. I was not confident at seven years old, and I sure as hell did not know what I was doing, but I was determined. Still, it took all my courage to approach the two of them that day.

"Alissa?" I had whispered as she sat in her usual place with the same smile and the dreamy, faraway look in her eyes.

She didn't respond.

I waved my hand in front of her face.

No reaction.

I had turned and looked at Jonah, sleeping curled in a blanket at the other end of the couch.

This is for all of us, I remember thinking before placing my hand on the side of Alissa's face and closing my eyes.

It had taken only a moment, but there was Alissa on a bright, sunny day, happy and tending the garden in front of their house. She loved flowers, and she filled their yard, front and back, every summer with beautiful blooms. Now Mike was there, getting out of his truck and taking Alissa in his arms, and I could feel it all as real as if I were standing beside them. The love that flowed between them spread like a soft cloud as they melted into each other's arms. Mike bent to kiss Alissa, and, as he did, the summer light began to shimmer, glowing brighter and stronger the longer their lips touched. It became so intense that I had to look away. When I looked back, they were gone.

I opened my eyes, took my hand away from Alissa's face, and stepped over to Jonah.

I had watched him sleep wrapped in a blanket I knew he didn't need. The day was bright, and the house was warm. But since the cold, bitter night of Mike's death, it had not mattered how high Connie set the thermostat, Jonah complained of being cold. And there he had lain before me that day, cocooned so completely that only the side of his face was visible. I took a deep breath and placed my hand there.

I don't know how long I stood like that. All I can remember is the terrible darkness that engulfed me, a cold, black abyss through which I fell and fell and fell. On the way down, there were flashes of light and glimpses of favorite faces—Mike, Alissa, Connie, even me and Jonah, riding our bikes smiling and happy. They were beautiful, love-filled memories trying to break through the frightening emptiness and all the pain that slashed and tore at me as I continued to fall and fall and scream.

I woke up in my bed.

I had no idea how I had gotten there or how long I had been out. But Connie was sitting beside me placing a cool, wet cloth on my forehead.

"Please don't try that again, Dev. You're not ready," she had whispered, and I started to cry.

My tears had poured out like a roiling flash flood. I still remember how terrifying the sobs were as they rushed up and out from what felt like a split in my little-boy soul.

They must have frightened Connie, too, because she took the cloth from my forehead and pulled me from my bed onto her lap. She encircled me in her arms and wrapped me tight in her deep emotional strength and kept me safe with her powerful love until I had cried myself into numbness and all the way back to sleep. She woke me later with a tray of food.

It was dark in my room by then, and she had turned on my bedside lamp. Somehow, all of the pain that had poured into me from Jonah had poured back out as I had cried on Connie's lap. But the experience had left me weak, and she'd had to help me sit up, after which I ate like I had not had food in a month.

When I was done, I had dropped into another deep sleep. I awoke the next day on my own but groggy and stunned to see Alissa sitting on the edge of my bed. She was smiling, and her eyes were soft but focused.

I sat up, and she took my hand.

"Mike loves you very much," she had said, and I felt his love through her touch as much as I had through her words.

"I know," I had responded, my voice still weak. "I love him, too."

Alissa had smiled again.

"He knows that, Dev, and he knows that you have work to do. He just wants you to be careful," she had said, and her eyes had gone dreamy as she had looked beyond me to somewhere that made her happy.

And for a moment, because she was still holding my hand, I had felt myself get dreamy, too, floating in that blissful cloud of their lost love and drawing strength from it until the shimmering light came again and the cloud floated away.

Alissa let go of my hand.

"Mike wants me to be strong," she had said. "Will you help me be that, Dev?"

"Yes," I had promised, and, together, we had left my room.

Chapter Four

It was late afternoon when I got home from the Brandywine appointment. I found Jonah slouched in a chair at our backyard patio table with his eyes closed and his head tilted back, soaking up the day's slowly waning light. I removed my previously maligned sport coat, hung it on the back of a chair, loosened my tie, and sat down.

"Hey," I said.

"Hey," he said as he opened his eyes and drew himself up to face me.

"So?" he said.

"So," I replied and told him about signing the contract and then being hit with Brandywine's belief that he'd been poisoned two years ago and was slowly dying because of it, his desire for us to find out how it had been done, along with finding the bodies of the twins, and his insistence that we not involve the police.

Jonah chewed his lip for a second and then asked, "Did Brandywine look to you like he was dying?"

"In layers," I said.

"Maybe that's why there's been no mention of him in the media for the last couple of years," Jo said.

"Could be," I said and went on to tell him what an eerie, empty place Brandfield was and how Lana Troy's touch made my fingers tingle.

That brought a frown to his face, and I asked, "What about your afternoon?"

"On the chance that you might say 'Yes' to this guy, I tracked down one of the New York detectives who worked the murders on that end."

"Bad?" I asked.

Jonah shook his head.

"Not sure," he said, "but, at the very least, strange."

Jonah and I had lived off and on under the same roof for most of our lives, but it was not this long-term proximity that impacted our oral-communication skills. Ever since the day I had placed my hand on the side of his face and been pulled into his nightmare, something had changed between us. There was an understanding that could not be described, a connection that could not be put into words.

In a store, at the gym or just passing a neighbor on the street, we were both outgoing and friendly. But give us a certain kind of case, especially one involving a child or a damaged female, and all bets were off. We didn't exactly turn into grunting Neanderthals, but our vocabulary could become sharp or clipped. Sometimes, it was a look or a nod that said what needed to be said. Other times, it was a conversation shared in the yard where we used to play as kids.

Whatever it was, we each knew when the other was drawn to a case, even one that it might not be healthy for us to take. For me, it was a tingling in my fingertips that caused me to run them back and forth under my thumb. Jonah always noticed. For him, it was the words "not sure," because Jonah hated not being sure.

"The detective," I said. "Is he reliable?"

"Angie checked him out for me. Said he was."

What Jonah did not have to say was that he and Detective Angela Sanchez were more than friends or that she was an extremely smart woman. She had gone through the police academy two years ahead of Jonah and was his first partner after he had gotten his shield. They had always been attracted to each other but did not become occasional lovers until Jonah had quit the department to start the PI gig.

"Professional ethics," he had claimed.

"Intimidated," I'd said, because Angie was one tough lady. Their relationship was not exclusive, and they both dated other people. But in between those dates, they were always there for each other when a case got the emotional best of either of them, and they never let the sex screw that up.

Jonah went on.

"It was a couple of days before the doctor would allow anyone into Charlotte Brandywine's hospital room. When the detective did get in, he told me he was shocked. He expected to see a rich, spoiled brat with a pricey lawyer already at the bedside she was cuffed to, angling to get her out of what she had done. But he said when he finally got into her room, the third Mrs. Brandywine was alone and crying, devasted by the loss of her children."

Which didn't make sense.

When the tragedy had happened, tabloid magazines ran pictures of Charlotte taken at the time of her wedding. A tall, beautiful woman, she had long auburn hair and a knockout smile. When she and Brandywine had married, she was less than half her husband's age. The newspaper stories said she had a reputation for being one hell of a party girl, with some petty charges on a rap sheet to prove it. All the people who knew her—even her own mother—had expected the marriage to be over quickly. What none of them had expected was for Charlotte to get pregnant.

I thought for a moment.

"Scarlet O'Hara?" I said, which was our verbal shorthand for someone who, to quote Rhett Butler, was not sorry for what they had done but very sorry for getting caught.

Jonah shook his head.

"The detective didn't think so. He said he'd crossed paths with a lot of sociopaths, world-class liars who wouldn't tell the truth if you paid them. It goes with the job. He said Charlotte Brandywine never denied what she had been accused of doing. But at the same time, he believed she was truly inconsolable at the loss of her children."

"Shock, maybe?" I offered.

"Not sure," said Jonah.

"What about our new client? Did Angie know anything about him?"

"That's where it gets interesting," he said, and my fingertips began to tingle for the third time that day.

"Brandywine didn't rush to New York when it happened. Angie caught the case and was sent to interview him here in Colorado. She remembers him as a stiff, self-important asshole. For a guy who professed to be in a hurry to have his kids found, he had kept her waiting for half an hour when she first arrived at the mansion, which, to add to what you described, she also found dark and creepy as hell. She said it was like being invited into a professionally decorated dungeon. And when Brandywine did show, he had some smug bastard with him named 'Glennon' or 'Gleason' or something, and the guy never left his side."

"Had to be Glandon. The doctor I met," I said, and Jo continued.

"When she asked to see the twins' bedrooms, Brandywine 'summoned' a maid to show her to the nursery. When Angie pressed him, Brandywine could not tell her if either of the kids had a special blanket or a favorite stuffed animal. It was like he didn't know anything personal about his own children other than their given names."

Which didn't surprise me. Sick or healthy, Brandywine had not struck me as a *daddy* kind of guy.

"Nannies did the raising?" I suggested.

"No record of any I could find, and I checked out place-ment agencies all over the U.S. And that was the other odd thing, Dev. Angie said the New York detective was thorough. He had interviewed Charlotte's mother and several of her friends. They all said the same thing: Charlotte had been a hands-on mother and very protective of the twins."

"Yet, out of the blue, she drowns 'em." I shook my head. "Doesn't add up," I said.

"I know," Jo agreed. "And from what I've learned so far, Charlotte Brandywine had had no history of postpartum depression after the twins were born or any other mental-health issues. And there were no rumors of cheating or abuse or other marital problems that might have made her snap."

"So, what drove her to such an extreme?" I said.

"And what the hell is going on with Brandywine's assistant that set your radar off?" he said, and we fell silent, turning those questions over and around in our heads, and feeling the wrongness of them in our guts.

"By the way, Mrs. K called," Jonah said, changing the subject for a moment, I suspected, to put some distance between us and the unsettling vibe we were getting about this case. "She said Melvin is missing. She's hoping you might be able to find him."

"No problem," I said, both of us knowing I would find Melvin right where I had left him.

Mrs. Koselke, a widow who lived down the street from us, had been friends with Connie for as long as Jonah and I could remember, and she had watched us grow up. Mr. Koselke had already been dead for years when Connie had passed, but long before her death, she had let Mrs. K know that *her boys*, as Connie had always called us, would be happy to help her with anything she needed or find anything she might lose.

Jonah and I remained protective of Mrs. K and continued to check on her, because, no matter how much any of her four out-of-state kids pleaded with her to come and live with one of them, the old lady refused. She had been born and raised in Colorado, and she planned to die there and be planted next to her husband. End of conversation.

Melvin, on the other hand, was another story. The biggest, fattest cat Jonah or I had ever seen, he was the most recent addition to Mrs. K's menagerie of dogs, birds, cats, and, at one time, a raccoon.

"A feline Fatty Arbuckle," Jonah had called Melvin the first time we had set eyes on the giant gray tabby.

"A reincarnated sumo wrestler," had been my bet, minus the diaper, of course.

Melvin was the latest stray to have wandered into Mrs. K's yard, never to leave again. The food was plentiful, and the accommodations were safe and comfortable. But none of the Koselke kids were born stupid. There was only so much pet food they were willing to shell out for, and they did not want their stubborn mother getting raided by the board of health.

So, when a new dog or cat appeared, it would go missing for a few days while either Jonah or I whisked it off to the vet, where it would be groomed, given up-to-date vaccinations, and rendered powerless to reproduce. After that, I would "find" the animal and return it to Mrs. K. The vet would send the bill to her kids, and, once a year, her appreciative offspring would send us a set of tickets for fifty-yard-line seats to a Denver football home game.

Go, Broncos.

"What's today?" I needed to be reminded.

"Tuesday," said Jonah.

"Vet said he'd be good to go on Wednesday. I'll have him home sometime tomorrow."

Although given Melvin's size and disposition, Jonah and I had not been sure there had been an actual need for him to be neutered. I thought he was too fat to get cat-wood, no matter what was in heat, and Jonah thought he lacked the energy to do anything about it even if he did.

I squinted up at the late afternoon sun and asked, "Do you think he'll miss 'em?"

"Miss what?" asked Jonah.

"His balls," I said.

Jonah snorted.

"Not Melvin. He was too lazy to do anything with them when they were there. Bring him home, shove a dish of cat food under his pudgy nose, and he'll be fine."

I laughed as we both stood. I grabbed my sport coat, and we made our way inside, where Jonah became serious again.

"You're sure about taking the lead on this one, Dev?" he said, giving me one last chance to back out.

"I am," I said with the breezy confidence of someone who was still new at this and had no idea how wrong a case could go or how dangerous it could turn.

"Then I'm going for a run."

"Okay," I said and showed him the folder of information from Lana Troy that I had left on the kitchen table. "I wanted to get to work on this anyway."

I knew it was going to take some time to get the prison visit arranged and plan my flight to New York.

"All right," said Jonah and went upstairs to change into running clothes.

I carried my sport coat upstairs with me into the bathroom, peeled out of my clothes, and threw everything into the hamper as if it were all contaminated. I stepped into the shower, twisted the left faucet handle to "high," and stood under the steaming spray until the misgivings that had shadowed me home washed away and the tips of my fingers stopped tingling.

Chapter Five

Getting to Charlotte Brandywine's prison was going to be as easy as finding Melvin, for two reasons. First, I already knew where to look, and second, they were both nearby. Which was okay when it came to that fat, gray furball, but not when it came to Charlotte.

She had been arrested and convicted in the State of New York for the murders of her children. But with a glance at Lana Troy's paperwork and the reason my curiosity was piqued was that Charlotte was doing her time at the Denver Women's Correctional Facility. That was convenient for me because it meant a short drive for a visit instead of a few days of tedious travel. What was not convenient was any reason I could think of as to why she was moved to Colorado.

After my shower, I scrounged through the fridge and found enough leftovers to toss together for a passable dinner. When I finished eating, I poured a bourbon, grabbed the folder, and sat down in the living room to read. The folder contained, as Ellis J. Brandywine had assured me it would, all the information I needed to pay a visit to Charlotte. What it did not contain was any explanation for why his third wife was going to spend the rest of her natural life in a cell in Colorado and not at a prison in New York State.

I told Jonah about it after he returned from his run and was finishing his dinner. It left him as puzzled as I was. Later, we both went to bed wondering how and why Charlotte Brandywine had been moved to the women's prison in Denver.

I got up early on Wednesday and spent the morning at the gym. I stopped at the vet's office on my way home and "found" Melvin. I dropped him off with Mrs. K, and she sent me home with a plate of cookies. At seventy-eight years old, her hearing and eyesight were beginning to decline. But she could still bake without setting her kitchen on fire, and whatever came out of her oven melted in your mouth.

I took the cookies home, sat down at the kitchen table with my laptop and Ms. Troy's folder, and got to work. I spent the rest of the morning eating the cookies and trying to figure out how Charlotte Brandywine had become one of our incarcerated neighbors.

After several phone calls, most of them useless, along with countless internet searches, I took a break. My head ached, and my eyes burned from the strain of staring at my laptop screen, but I didn't know much more now than what I'd suspected when I started.

I could not prove it, but somehow, through his money and connections, Ellis Brandywine had gotten Charlotte out of the New York State penal system and into a "gated" community in Denver.

Along the way, the judge at her allocution had acquired an oceanside vacation home in Antigua, two senators—one from New York and one from Colorado—and a local con-gresswoman had had their re-elections secured by large donations from a Brandywine subsidiary called EJB Limited, and some New York Board of Prison officials' kids were able to attend expensive colleges that had been financially out of their reach prior to Charlotte's relocation.

So money talks. Big deal. You would have to be deaf, dumb, blind, under the age of ten, *and* from Mars not to know that. But after my meeting yesterday with Brandywine, along with the things Jonah was learning about him, I could not help but think there might be something more going on here. Maybe it was not money alone that had bought their cooperation.

I hit the phone again and got lucky.

This time, I was able to track down and talk to one of the ambulance guys who had transported Charlotte from the shore to the hospital six years ago. He seemed to still have a lot of sympathy for Charlotte but ended the call the minute I asked him if he knew anything about Ellis Brandywine.

I got stonewalled by everyone working for the two sena-tors, but I managed to get a low-level aide from the Colorado congresswoman's office to talk to me. All he did, though, was pass along the congresswoman's very sincere sentiment that she hoped Brandywine and anyone associated with him would roast in hell with their entrails nailed to a hot rock. Which is why I was surprised when someone in the judge's office took my call. At the mention of Brandywine's name, I was put straight through to him.

"Hello, Mr. West," Judge Daniel Halliday said. "How can I help you? I understand you're a friend of Ellis Brandywine."

"Not exactly," I said and went on to explain my employment, Brandywine's deteriorating health, and the purpose of my call. That brought silence from the judge. When he spoke again, his voice took loathing to a new level.

"So, you're working for that evil son of a bitch. Is he really dying?"

"He is," I confirmed, "although I don't understand why that matters."

"Oh, but you will," he said, with an undertone of something so ugly and knowing in his voice that it slithered from the phone, down my arm, and made the tips of my fingers tingle.

"I have to say I'm surprised by your attitude, your Honor, and I hope you'll excuse me for being … indelicate, but I was under the impression your dealings with my employer had been mutually beneficial," I said—and got a response I had not expected.

"Fuck you, Mr. West, and fuck Ellis Brandywine, and fuck the beach house in Antigua that I know you're *indelicately* referring to."

"You still own the place," I pushed back.

"Point of order, Mr. West. It's used as a rental, and the proceeds, after upkeep, are donated to a police fund. No member of my family has ever set foot in that house, nor have I. And I won't until the day that bastard dies. Then I'm going to fly there, walk in, and personally drop the match that burns it down to the beautiful ocean-view piece of ground that it sits on."

Now the silence was on my end.

The judge chuckled.

"I'm sorry, Mr. West. It appears I've left you speechless," he said.

"Yeah, you have," I admitted, and although I knew it was bad form to trash my own employer, I thought a little honesty might get the judge on my side. "Look, your Honor, just so you know, I met Brandywine only yesterday, but I came away with pretty much the same feelings he obviously gave you."

"But you agreed to work for him anyway," he said.

"I guess you had to be there, sir."

"I was. Six years ago."

"Then you understand," I said and heard him sigh.

"Mr. West, I've been threatened by many of the criminals I've sentenced, some of them psychopathically dangerous and fully capable of carrying out their threats once freed. It's the reason I maintain a strong security environment and keep my private life out of the papers as much as possible. You can imagine, then, my concern when a couple of months after Charlotte Brandywine's sentencing, Ellis Brandywine came to my home unannounced.

"My wife and I were helping our daughter and her fiancé with the plans for their wedding. Ellis and I went to my study, where he asked me to facilitate Charlotte's transfer to a prison in Colorado. I told him I couldn't do that. He then congratulated me on the upcoming nuptials. He also mentioned the church, the florist, and the reception venue we had decided on as excellent choices."

"I'm guessing he surprised you by having that information," I said.

"*Surprised* me?" said the judge. "More like *stunned* me. We had made those decisions only a few days before."

I pictured Ellis Brandywine long before he was ever ill, sitting in the judge's study, toying with him and enjoying every sadistic second of it. No wonder the judge loathed him.

Halliday went on.

"Believe me, I'm not a weak or stupid man. I've taught my family to be cautious and aware, and the security I surround them with is the best. As I said, I'm used to being threatened. But when he handed me the deed to the beach house, I changed my mind."

"Why was that?" I asked.

"Because the paper contained my signature."

I let out a low whistle.

"Neat trick. But couldn't you prove it was forged?"

"Not likely," he said. "Not even to myself. The work was that good."

"What about the day it was signed? Could you prove you were in court or somewhere else?"

"No. After the Brandywine sentencing, I needed some time alone. I told only my wife and my head of security that I was going to my hunting cabin, a place that has never been registered in my name or in the names of anyone in my family. For three days, I had no contact with anyone but Mother Nature."

"And the deed is dated on one of those days," I guessed. "Any chance you could retire or sell the beach house?"

"Brandywine covered those bases, too. I am to stay on the bench and keep the house. If anything changes, "Beach House

Bribe" hits the papers along with a disgusting, fabricated story about my wife, my daughter, and a male prostitute."

"I don't understand," I said. "Why the continued hold on you?"

"In case he needs my assistance in the future."

"But he got what he wanted," I said.

"But he didn't get *everything* that he wanted."

"What else is there?" I said.

"Charlotte," said the judge. "He never divorced her," he added, and I frowned.

"That's insane," I said. "Why would he want to stay married to the woman who killed his only children? He couldn't still be in love with her, could he?"

"Of course not. Ellis Brandywine is as deeply disturbed and dangerous as he is rich and powerful. The only thing he has ever loved are the games he plays with other peoples' lives. And no matter what he told you about his children, Mr. West, he's lying. He is convinced the twins are alive. He believes Charlotte staged everything and has the twins hidden with someone. He has never stopped hunting for them, and he will never stop haunting her."

"But what about Charlotte?" I asked. "What does she get out of this? Even if their deaths were staged, she still confessed to killing them. Whether she lived or died herself that day, Judge, Charlotte was never going to see them again. Could she hate the guy that much? Is she that spiteful of a person?"

"Not at all, but unless you've met her, Charlotte is not a woman who can be easily explained," he said. "I know, because, as her judge, and because she tried to kill herself, along with her children, I was concerned about her mental state. I had her brought to my chambers before her allocution. I wanted to know why she was doing nothing to help herself."

"And?"

"And you'll have to ask her yourself. But suffice it to say, it's more than disconcerting when a woman like Charlotte claims her children were better off after the boating accident and she was safer in prison than any of them ever were with Ellis Brandywine."

"I'm sorry, Judge, but I just don't get it," I said. "I agree that Brandywine is a twisted piece of work. But Charlotte drowned their three-year-old twins, for God's sake. Why does everyone I talk to make it sound like *she's* the victim?"

"You'll understand after you meet her. And Mr. West, for your own safety and the safety of anyone you care about, if you must continue with this case, don't ever again assume anything about your employer. At least not anything good. That's all I can tell you," he said, and the line went dead.

Chapter Six

I set my cell phone on the table and sat there trying to process what the judge had told me and waiting for my fingers to stop tingling. No matter how I looked at it, though, none of it made sense, and all of it left me uneasy.

What the hell did Brandywine really want from MPS? I wondered. To find the bodies of his long-dead children? Or was the judge right? Did Brandywine have some reason to believe the twins were alive and that, in our efforts to find their bodies, we would stumble onto them happy and healthy, and ready to go home to daddy and his ugly mansion?

And as for being poisoned, why, with all of Brandywine's money and resources, would he depend on one diagnosis? Why not get a second opinion? Or a third or a twenty-third? As slowly as he was dying, he'd had more than enough time to do that. Unless he was afraid his business empire would collapse if word of his illness got out. Could he be hiding that information from the outside world while he hoped for a miraculous cure? Or was he just hiding something in that eerie house?

I closed my laptop and stood. I stretched the tightness out of my back, and then I went looking for Jonah. I found him on the front porch, sitting in Connie's old rocking chair, the one neither of us could bring ourselves to get rid of.

"Got a minute?" I asked and parked myself and my worry on a section of porch railing across from him.

"Sure. What's up?" he said, and I told him about my phone call with the judge and that Ellis Brandywine had never divorced Charlotte.

Jo found that as odd as I had, and then he asked, "Did the judge know why Charlotte hasn't divorced him?"

"He didn't mention it, but I plan to ask when I meet with her," I replied and gave him a close look. "You okay?" I said.

Jonah shrugged.

"Just wrapping up the Barbie and Ken case," he answered.

Of course, Barbie and Ken were not the couple's real names, but that did not make them any less golden. Ken had played college baseball, and Barbie had been a tough competitor on the volleyball court. They were both blond, blue-eyed, and beautiful.

After college and marriage, he had worked hard and developed a thriving player-rep business, while she took care of the adorable daughter they'd had, threw parties, and socialized with anyone who could help further her husband's career. The business was going well, and the little girl was almost three now. By all accounts, Barbie and Ken were devoted to each other and were thinking of having another child.

But a month ago, mysterious phone calls had begun, and Ken was becoming distant. On his last business trip, Barbie had had trouble getting in touch with him. She was afraid to confront him about the possibility that he was having an affair and assumed he would deny it anyway, so she had asked around and gotten a recommendation from a friend of a friend for Mecklan Personal Services. She had hired Jonah to find out if Mr. College Baseball was sliding into someone else's home plate.

"And?" I prodded.

"And Barbie was right. Ken is seeing someone," Jonah said.

"Damn" was my response. "When are you going to tell her?"

"I'm not."

"But she hired you to—"

"She hired me to find out if he was cheating on her. She wasn't going to have another baby with him if he was."

"Smart lady. So, what's the issue?"

"The person he's seeing is an oncologist. The business trip was for a second opinion. He wanted all the facts before he told her."

This time my response was, "Shit."

Jonah looked away and back.

"Yeah, shit," he said.

"Are you going to tell her?"

"Don't have to. She called me. He told her this morning."

Jonah didn't have to say that Barbie had been crying when she called. The look on his face did.

"I'm going for a run," he said and stood. "After that, I'll be at Angie's. Maybe overnight."

"No problem," I said. "Tell her I said hello."

"I will," he said and left.

Chapter Seven

If you have never had the experience of visiting a prisoner at the Denver Women's Correctional Facility, then you might not know that you don't just drop by the Gray Bar Hotel on a sunny afternoon, knock on a big metal door, and say, "Hi, I'm here to see Suzy Inmate."

An application must be filled out, submitted, and approved. Visiting is on Fridays, Saturdays, and Sundays from 8:30 a.m. to 3 p.m. You must arrive by certain times for the morning and afternoon visiting hours, or the trip you made to the prison will be wasted. You will not be allowed in. No exceptions.

Prisoners can have two visits per week, but one of the visits must be on a Friday. If your inmate is allowed only non-contact visits, as Charlotte Brandywine was, that's another matter. You have to call a given number to schedule an appointment.

I called the number on Thursday to see about setting up a visit and to ask how long the approval process might take but ended up feeling as stunned as Judge Halliday had been by Brandywine's visit to him. Not only had my visitor's form been filled out, submitted, and approved, but I had a visit with Charlotte Brandywine set for 10 a.m. on Friday. The clerk reminded me to be early.

I was, although I had no idea what to expect. A low-lit room with Charlotte chained to a table perhaps? Or maybe a small enclosure with a thick plastic partition separating us, scarred black phone receivers to communicate with, and Charlotte looking hard and mean, and sporting a black eye for having given smack-talk to an inmate called *Helga the Horrible* by the other inmates *and* her own mother?

What I got was another shock. After showing identification and passing through several layers of security, I was ushered into a narrow gray room with a table and a chair on either side of it. There were two doors to this room—the one I'd entered through and one at the opposite end of the room. There was no two-way mirror or small ceiling camera to monitor the visit. Only Charlotte Brandywine, her hair a short, auburn bob now, wearing an orange jumpsuit, sitting at the table, and talking quietly with a female guard, who was standing near her. As I approached, I heard Charlotte say, "Thanks, Nell," and the guard stepped away.

Then Charlotte Brandywine looked up at me.

The gaze from her large blue eyes swept over me like a glowing force field and drew me forward like an unworthy supplicant to an elegant queen, instantly dissolving my intent, emptying my head of questions, and leaving me helpless to do anything but her bidding. I almost bowed before the magnetic spell that held me was broken by the shadow of deep pain that I saw claiming the edges of her gaze and dulling its glow with sadness.

Somehow, I made it to the table without tripping over my own feet, pulled the empty chair back, and sat down.

Charlotte Brandywine remained perfectly still, her hands resting in her lap. It made me wonder if she had always been this calm or if it was a defense mechanism developed over the years of dealing with the people her husband had sent before me. But looking at her now and into those hypnotic blue eyes, I had the feeling that old Ellis had met his match in this wife.

The question for me was, had I?

"Hello, Mrs. Brandywine. I'm Devon West. I work for Mecklan Personal Services," I began and, out of habit and nervousness, extended my hand.

The guard cleared her throat.

"Sorry," I said and pulled back my hand.

Charlotte watched me, moving nothing but her eyelids in a couple of slow, unnerving blinks, and I fumbled on.

"I'm, um, here because we've, uh, we've been hired by your husband on a personal matter. And, uh, I want you to know that I appreciate your willingness to meet with me and discuss a few things," I said, and her gaze sharpened.

"Willingness has nothing to do with this meeting, Mr. West," she said, her voice low and warm but firm. "And if you want me to discuss anything with you, the first thing you should know is that I don't like to be called 'Mrs. Brandywine.'"

"And if you don't like to be called 'Mrs. Brandywine,' you could have divorced your husband and taken back your maiden name," I said, forcing myself to remember that, beautiful or not, I was facing a woman who was sentenced to spend the rest of her life in prison for committing the cold-blooded murders of her own children.

"Why haven't you?" I pressed, and her voice stayed warm, but her gaze cooled.

"I have tried, Mr. West. Several times. But the paperwork always disappears. Ellis's reach is that long, and his touch is that powerful."

Which was a scary enough thought by itself. But when I added it to the ease with which that reach and power had gotten me into this meeting today, it was frightening on a whole other scale and made my fingertips tingle as Charlotte went on.

"You should also keep in mind that you're not the first investigator Ellis has sent to speak with me. I'm sure you won't be the last."

"That may not be true," I said and told her about my meeting at Brandfield—that I had seen him and he was dying.

That brought a flicker of interest from those glowing eyes but a wariness, too.

"Mr. West, as much as I would like to hope the world is going to be rid of Ellis, you need to be clear on something," she said and leaned toward me, bringing her arms up to rest on the table, laying one hand flat upon the other in front of her.

"I'm here because I'm a murderer, not a fool. If you think telling me Ellis is dying might soften my attitude about him, you're wasting your time. My rescue from the water on the day I lost Richie and Nora was an accident. My children and I were never meant to be found or ever near Ellis or Brandfield again. My life wasn't important back then, and, with my children gone, it's even less important now. Nothing you can say or do, no matter what trick you employ, will change that."

And as much as I believed that what she was saying was true, I was having have a hard time reconciling the deed and the words coming from the warm, beautiful woman speaking them. Even if she was wearing orange.

"Well, whatever your feelings are about him," I said, "he's convinced that, no matter what happened that day, the twins were never with you on the water."

"Ellis is cunning and dangerous," she said. "That doesn't mean he can't be wrong."

And for a split second, I wondered whether, for all of her calm and beauty, Charlotte Brandywine was just as cunning and dangerous—and playing me as her husband had. I mean, there had to be a reason these two had been attracted to each other in the first place.

The poker face that I didn't have must have been projecting my thoughts across the table like a satellite beam, because Charlotte leaned back and rested her hands in her lap again. There was also an adorable smirk on her face—a slight, sweet rise of the corners of her lovely lips.

"It's okay. You can ask me, Mr. West," she said, and I stopped her.

"Please … just … call me 'Dev,'" I said, fighting a blush as her smirk became a smile.

I was betting it was not her biggest or her best smile, but it was enough to light up the plain gray room we were in and almost make me forget my question.

But I had to know.

"You were already rich, Charlotte, so why marry Ellis Brandywine? A man more than twice your age?"

"Because, back then, I *was* a fool," she said. "Shallow and selfish. Never caring about anything or anyone except finding the next high or lining up the next party. I looked at marriage to anyone as a lark. Something I hadn't tried. A party I hadn't been to."

I considered that and shook my head.

"Hard to picture Brandywine at a party," I said.

"Ellis was a different person when I met him," she said.

"How so?" I said, and she studied me in a way that made me hope I didn't fall short.

"You've heard the term 'handsome devil,' haven't you?"

I nodded.

"Well," she went on, "Ellis was a handsome devil. Handsome and charming enough to hide the devil that he was until after we were married."

I stayed quiet, weighing her words, knowing that she had not been the first young woman who had fallen prey to a bastard like Ellis Brandywine and that she would not be the last. But by her own admission, she had become a different person after the marriage, too.

Which made me wonder what kind of person that was and why it had convinced Ellis Brandywine that she had not just the vindictive desire but also the capability to set his death into motion. And what would make him believe that she had the power and the connections to get the job done—from a prison cell, no less?

"And remember," Charlotte cut into my musings, "you've seen him only with whatever this illness is that he has," she said, and I corrected her.

"He isn't just ill, Charlotte. He's dying. Slowly and painfully. And there doesn't seem to be anything his doctor can do about it."

"His doctor?" she said.

"A guy named 'Glandon,'" I said—and everything changed.

The warm glow that had been emanating from her instantly crystalized into a harsh, cold light, and the look in her eyes turned into fear. The tips of my fingers tingled hard as she leaned forward, and her hands came up again. This time, they gripped the edge of the table.

"Dev, listen to me. Drop this case. Drop it *now.* It doesn't matter what Ellis is paying you. Drop it for your own safety and the safety of anyone you care about," she warned.

It could have been my imagination, but it seemed that even the guard in the room had stiffened.

"You sound like Judge Halliday," I said.

"You've met Daniel?"

"We had a long phone conversation. He also warned me about working for Ellis Brandywine," I said, and her eyes softened.

"Daniel Halliday is a good man. He's honest and fair, and very wise. If you won't listen to me, please listen to him," she said and lowered her hands back to her lap.

When she did, my fingers stopped tingling, but the level indicator on my guilt meter soared like a rocket up into the red zone from knowing I was about to disappoint her.

"I'm sorry, Charlotte. I can't do that," I said, and we sat in silence until she gave a wistful smile that, for all of its sadness, still lit up the room.

She took a breath—slow and even—and the calm and the warmth returned to her. She slid back her chair and rose. I did the same.

"Goodbye, then, Dev. I truly hope you stay safe. If you do, maybe we'll talk again."

"Goodbye," I said, and Nell opened the far door for Charlotte to leave through. When she was gone, Nell closed the door and came around the table to escort me from the room.

"I know what you're thinking," she said as we walked.

"Do you?" I said, and she smiled.

Her smile, however, didn't light up shit.

"You're thinking she doesn't belong here, that it has to be a giant mistake. That she was set up. But she's a murderer. You heard it from her yourself. And as hard as he tries, that old man of hers can't get to her in here, no matter how many guys like you he sends," she said and stopped walking. At the same time, she put an iron-fingered grip on my forearm and yanked me around to face her.

I'm almost six feet tall and work out enough to be considered strong. Nell was a head shorter than me and had a solid, wiry build. I've got a good grip, but there was a painful amount of strength in the hold she had on my arm. I had no doubt that she could have me on my knees in an instant, with me begging her not to break the arm she would have twisted up behind my back to do it. During the interview, I had barely noticed she was there. Now, she had my full attention, as she looked me hard in the eyes in straight-up *don't-fuck-with-me* mode.

I didn't.

"Look," I tried to explain.

"No, you look," she said and let go of my arm.

It took all my male pride not to wince and rub the spot where she had half-crushed it.

"Tell that piece of shit you work for that this is as far as Charlotte goes. She isn't getting moved to Sunridge, and he should stop trying to put her there. Otherwise, I'll be paying him a visit, and it won't be pretty."

Before I could respond, she called out to another guard, who escorted me the rest of the way from the prison. Outside, I took my time getting to my SUV, thinking about Charlotte and how right Judge Halliday had been about her.

I drove away flexing the pain from my arm and wondering why Ellis Brandywine would want Charlotte in Sunridge—a mental hospital in the foothills—and what a visit from a pissed-off Nell might look like.

Chapter Eight

When I got home, I found Jonah back from Angie's and at work in the office. He swiveled his chair around and handed me a note. It was a message from Alexander.

Ms. Troy expects an email summary of Mr. West's prison visit within the hour, it read.

"What's this about?" he said as I took a seat across from his desk.

I filled him in on the pre-filled-out paperwork and the pre-arranged prison visit. When I was done, his mouth was a tight line.

I waited for a comment or a question, but all he gave was a hard-sounding "Huh," so I went on to tell him about Charlotte Brandywine, which was hard to do without sounding like an adolescent kid talking about his first crush. Then I told him about "Nell the Grip" and her curious statement that Charlotte was not going to be moved to Sunridge.

"If you went back and talked to Nell, do you think you could get her to tell you what she meant by that?" Jo asked.

"I think if I went back and talked to Nell about anything, she'd twist me into a fuckin' pretzel," I said, and he laughed.

"So, what's your next move?" he asked, and, because my head was still swirling with thoughts of Charlotte Brandywine, I didn't have one.

I knew I should just admit that I didn't and ask Jonah what he would do, but my ego and inexperience overrode my sense. And my feelings about Charlotte Brandywine added an embarrassing complication that I didn't want to talk about—a red-flag warning if there ever was one.

But ignoring any color of a warning flag is one of my knot-headed specialties, and I did it by flashing the email at Jo and said, "Taking care of this."

"Okay," he said, "and I'll try and find some time to dig deeper into Brandywine's background for you. Unless Charlotte told you of anyone besides herself who might be glad to see her husband dead."

"I had to meet Ellis Brandywine only once to know he's the kind of guy that *plenty* of people would like to see dead. But I don't think Charlotte's the one trying to kill him."

"You're sure?" Jonah said.

"Maybe not a hundred percent. At least not yet. And to be honest, I didn't ask her if she was. I never told her that Ellis believes he was poisoned. I only said that Ellis was sick and dying. She was okay with that until the end of the visit. That's when something … something odd happened," I said and stopped to organize my thoughts. Or maybe I was waiting for Jonah to cut in or to ask me something else, but he stayed quiet.

Cop Quiet, I called it, and Jonah had an instinct and a special patience for it. I had seen him do it with perps *and* clients. He always knew when to talk, or when to shut up and let the other person do the talking, or the lying, or the confessing. And now he was doing it with me. It worked just like it had when we were kids.

I spilled my guts.

"My conversation with Charlotte was going well until I mentioned Glandon," I said. "Then she changed. Got upset. She told me to walk away and drop the case. She warned me never to go back to Brandfield again."

"What did you tell her?" Jonah asked.

"That I couldn't," I said and felt guilty again for disappointing her.

"How did she react to that?"

I thought a moment.

"She seemed sad. Honestly sad."

"Not surprising," Jonah said. "The little I've found in print about Brandywine makes him seem like a great guy. He's a big philanthropist and supports plenty of charities. He also donated a lot of money to medical research after his mother died in her late fifties from a stroke."

"But?"

Jonah shook his head and turned back to me.

"But it got weird when I talked to people who'd had actual, direct dealings with him. Some said he was kind and generous. A perfect gentleman. Others insisted he was arrogant and dictatorial. A real bastard. A few said he was creepy and cold, and one woman insisted he was the personification of evil. She said if the charity she was working for hadn't desperately needed the money he made her beg for, she would have told him to shove his ten thousand dollars up his self-important ass."

"In other words, they had the same reaction to Brandywine that I had," I said and remembered how smoothly the guy had gone from one personality to another on the day I met him—helpless old man to imperious, commanding prick, without batting either one of his sick, watery eyes. "It's almost like he's two people."

"Uh, huh," said Jonah. "And if he has enough money and power to get a murderer moved around the federal penal system, maybe he's also the kind of guy who could leave a young wife feeling that death was the only way out of her unhappy marriage."

Which made me curious.

"What happened to the first two wives? Death or divorce?"

"Divorce," said Jonah. "The papers are filed here in Denver."

"What grounds did the first two wives give?" I asked, and Jonah shook his head.

"Other way around. *He* dumped *them*."

"So why hang on to Charlotte?" I said.

"Beats me. Did Charlotte tell you why she hasn't divorced him?"

"She told me she's tried, but the paperwork always disappears," I said.

"All of which puts us almost back where we started," Jonah said, "except for that," he added with a nod at the message from Alexander that was still in my hand. "What are you going to tell them in your email?"

I looked at the message and thought about how exact and rigid everything seemed to be at the ugly mansion, how precisely the people there had behaved, and how Brandywine had pissed me off. Call it childish, but it gave me the urge to grab their exact, rigid world, shake it up like a snow globe, and slam it back down to see how it settled.

"I'm not going to email anybody, Jo. I'm going to call Lana Troy, tell her it's not Charlotte who's trying to kill Ellis Brandywine, and that we're still investigating. I wasn't kidding when I told you how strange everyone at Brandfield is. I think nothing—and I mean *nothing*—goes on in that oversized crypt without a lot of thought and pre-planning."

"So?" he said.

"So, I'll call my point-of-contact tomorrow," I said, rising to leave. "And while I'm talking to her, I'll ask about the two previous wives."

"Sounds good. I've got a couple of things to wrap up today, but I'll have some time after that to delve deeper into Brandywine's business dealings. I'll see if I can find anything else on the other two wives, too," said Jonah, already turned back to his keyboard and typing away.

I went upstairs to change into shorts, a tee shirt, and old sneakers. I left the house and headed down the street to Mrs. K's. I had passed her place on my way home and noticed her grass needed cutting. I figured I could take care of that and maybe say hello to Melvin, too.

And who knows? Maybe Mrs. K had been baking today.

Chapter Nine

I waited until ten o'clock the next morning to make my call. Alexander answered, and I did not have to see those icy gray eyes of his to know how angry he was about me not sending the email that had been demanded the previous day. The restrained fury in his voice brightened further for me the sunny Colorado morning I had awoken to.

When I asked to speak to Lana Troy, his voice got so hard you could have split rock—or my head—with it. Jonah has warned me that being a smart-ass was going to catch up with me someday and land me in a hospital or the morgue. I know he's right, but the opportunity to ruffle the composure of a guy like Alexander was just a little too sweet for me to pass up.

And if aggravating Alexander was like having one of Mrs. K's cakes for breakfast, talking to Lana Troy was the buttercream frosting that covered it.

"Good morning, Mr. West. It seems we've had our first misunderstanding," she said, and the cold in her voice bit so hard through the phone I half expected frostbite to form on my ear.

God, this was going great.

"Good morning," I said in an obnoxiously cheerful tone and went straight into the summary of my visit with Charlotte. Not detail for detail, only the assurance that I did not believe the third Mrs. Brandywine was behind Ellis's illness.

"And along those lines, I was wondering if you had any information about his first and second wives," I said and got a short silence that crackled in my ear colder than her voice had.

"We have no knowledge of the location of Mr. Brandywine's second wife, Aubrey. As for the first, she and my employer have been divorced for three decades. That matter is settled. It isn't necessary for you to speak with Rebecca Brandywine," she said.

"Why not?" I pressed, feeling like I had touched a nerve or something. "He dumped her. Maybe she's held a grudge all of these years and decided it was time to get some revenge," I suggested and got another icy reply.

"If you must know, Mr. West, Rebecca Brandywine is so mentally incompetent that she is almost incapable of dressing herself. She can barely hold a thought, let alone a grudge. Mr. Brandywine has already ruled her out as a possible perpetrator."

"And I need to do the same," I said, but the reference to mental illness made me think of Nell's statement about Charlotte and Sunridge. It was a shot in the dark that Rebecca Brandywine—"B1," as Jonah had dubbed her—might be there. Regardless, I was curious to see what reaction a mention of the place would get me. "Let someone at Sunridge know I'll be coming."

What it got me was another crackling silence, and that was enough. Now more than ever, I was determined to meet

Rebecca Brandywine and check out the mental asylum with or without permission from anyone at Brandfield.

"I repeat, it is not necessary for you to speak with Rebecca Brandywine," she said.

"And *I* repeat …" I began, but she cut me off.

"Please don't, Mr. West. You've already wasted enough of my time this morning. The director's name at Sunridge is Dr. Morley. I will call and tell him to be expecting you."

"Thanks," I said.

"Don't thank me, Mr. West, because I'm also going to call Mr. Mecklan today and report your lack of discipline," she said, sounding like the stern schoolteacher again.

I had to stop myself from laughing at her threat or telling her that she would only be wasting more of her time. Jonah never grounds me or takes away my electronics, and he never sends me to bed without supper. I was about to chalk up a win and say goodbye when she added, in her iciest tone yet, "And, Mr. West, I want you to know that there will be an appropriate-level punishment for your juvenile behavior."

I pulled the cell away from my ear and the deep vein of menace in her voice. I looked at the screen. Lana Troy had ended the call but had once again left the tips of my fingers tingling.

Chapter Ten

When my fingers got back to feeling normal and the swell of anxiety I had felt from her threat had rippled away, I got on my laptop to find an address for Sunridge. As I typed, I realized that, although I had always known what Sunridge was in that vague way any person picks up and stores incidental information, I had no idea exactly where it was. But I was surprised when my search turned up so little information. There were no pictures or history of the place, or any reference at all to it being a mental facility. Just "private institution" and a location.

That didn't bother me because I didn't care what it looked like, didn't give a damn how it got started, and I already knew what it was—a mental hospital for extremely rich patients. The location, however, put it on the edge of Evergreen, one of my favorite towns in the foothills, and anything that puts me heading west toward any part of the Rocky Mountains makes my day.

I closed my laptop and grabbed my camera bag. I found Jonah in the office and stopped to tell him that I was off to Sunridge to talk to the first Mrs. Brandywine.

"Did you find out anything about the second wife?" he asked, frowning at his computer screen.

"No," I said. "Lana Troy told me they didn't know where she was."

"That could be true, Dev. B2 isn't coming up on any search I've run," he said.

Which was surprising because whenever Jonah got on the trail of anything or anyone, he put bloodhounds to shame. It was what had made him a good detective for the Denver PD and now an excellent PI.

But sometimes a case like this one came along that aroused a different level of curiosity in Jo and tapped into a deeper need to understand the motivation behind the crime. Nailing *who* did it and figuring out *how* they did it were not enough. He had to keep digging to try to understand *why* the perpetrator did it, as if that would somehow make the criminal act less senseless.

I knew it was because of losing his dad like he did, a random, senseless act if there ever was one. Mike Mecklan's funeral was barely over when Jonah had decided that there were bad people in this world and when he grew up, he was going to make it his mission to find and stop them. And whenever he becomes "mission directed," as I call it, I think the old tapes play in his head, and he is secretly trying to find his dad and stop Mike's killer before, well … before.

And that's the problem.

No matter who Jonah helps, when the case is over, Mike is still dead. And if the outcome of the case is bad, Jonah re-experiences the crushing sadness of losing him. Sometimes, too, there is a dangerous physical component. Like the time that I'd had to rush him to the emergency room with chest pains.

Jonah had been working with the authorities on a kidnapping case—a young mother and her infant son being held for ransom—and he figured out in fifty-two hours from the time of the snatch where the kidnapper had stashed them. They were rescued safely, but, for Jonah, it had been a straight fifty-two hours of no sleep, no food, no water. Just black coffee, frustration, and pressure. Afterwards, when it turned out to be a close family friend behind the kidnapping, Jonah's exhausted mind had snapped. He went into a tirade about all the evil and deception loose in the world. I'd been trying to calm him down when he had clutched his chest and collapsed.

And then there was his personal life.

Jonah tried hard for balance between work and women. He was always upfront about what he did for a living, and most of the ladies he dated were interested and initially understanding. But after two or three broken or forgotten dates while he turned into a glassy-eyed recluse slamming away at his computer or slipping off to follow someone, they all eventually dumped him. Only Angie remained true.

Well, Angie and me.

And I remained more worried than true.

Like I was now standing in his office and picking up that *mission-directed* vibe.

But Jonah was a grown man, as strong and stocky as a bull, and as stubborn as a bulldog. Even Connie used to comment about it. She said that stubbornness was evident in Jonah from the time he'd been a little boy. She also reminded him regularly that, if it was his greatest strength, it was also his greatest weakness, and that, like *my* ability, he needed to use it wisely.

"I'll be gone all day," I said, trying to break his concentration.

"Sure," he replied, still scrolling through something on the screen in front of him.

"From what Lana Troy said, it doesn't sound like Rebecca Brandywine will be much help with the case, but you know me, Jo. I can't pass up an excuse to spend time in the foothills with my camera."

"Uh, huh," he said and continued scrolling.

"Well, then," I said, still unable to get him to look at me, "I guess I'll—"

"—get out or stand there and keep nagging?" he said, making me want to knock some sense into his head with a swing from my camera bag.

"Listen," I snapped at him instead, "you want to get rid of me? Promise me you'll remember to eat something today, and I'm gone. And drink some goddamn water, too."

"I'll do better than that, Dev," he said and punched a square on his keyboard.

The printer kicked into life and started spitting out pages. Jo got up, walked across the room, and collected them. He returned to his desk, tapped the pages into a neat stack, and slipped them into a folder.

"I'm going to lunch with a new client," he said and waved the folder of papers at me before tucking them into his backpack. "Small-businessman. Thinks his bookkeeper might be embezzling from him."

"Is he?" I asked.

"She," he said. "And it's worse. She's not."

"How can that be worse?" I said.

"Because I interviewed her. She's young, eager, and hard-working but in over her head. She doesn't really know what she's doing, but she's managed to do enough of whatever to misplace a lot of money *and* catch the attention of the IRS.

"You're right," I agreed. "That's worse."

"No," said Jonah. "That's bad."

"Then what the hell is *worse?*" I said.

"She's his wife's baby sister," said Jonah. "The one the whole family loves and dotes on. The one they all pressured him to hire. The one he has to now fire."

"Damn," I said, feeling sorry for a guy I had never met.

"Yeah," said Jonah as we left the office and went outside together.

"Wouldn't want to be him at the next family dinner," I said.

"Me, neither," said Jonah, "but if he's smart, he won't tell the family. He'll either keep her and throw himself on the mercy of the IRS or go out and throw himself in front of a bus before the gravy is passed."

Laughing, we made our way to the garage. I hit the button to raise the garage door while Jonah slipped his arms into the straps of the backpack and put his helmet on. Jo straddled his ten-speed, and I slid behind the wheel of my SUV. I was about to back out when he rolled up beside me. I put my window down.

"Yeah?" I said.

"I'm fine, Dev," he said, and we stared at each other for a moment.

"Okay," I said. "I believe you."

"Good," he said, "because I don't want another lecture from Nanny West when you get home later and find me working."

Our eyes held for another few seconds.

"Mecklan?" I said.

"Yeah?" he replied.

"Fuck you," I said, and he laughed.

"Fuck you, too, West," he said and pedaled away.

Chapter Eleven

According to my GPS map, it was a forty-five-minute drive to Sunridge. I made it in an easy hour and a half. What can I say? I'm a careful driver, especially when it's a beautiful Mile High day—plenty of sun, temp in the low eighties, and a nearly cloudless blue sky. Perfect for putting the windows down, turning the music up, and cruising.

Traffic on I-70 was light. The small, family-owned Mexican restaurant where I stopped for lunch smelled heavenly, and the chicken enchiladas I ordered were *muy delicioso*. I said a reluctant "No" to the flan and the sopapillas and tucked my copy of the check into my wallet, along with a gasoline receipt for the expense account. I was sure that Alexander would appreciate my meticulous record-keeping and that Ms. Troy would be happy to see I was staying well-nourished, too.

Or not.

I took the exit off the highway at Evergreen and drove through the town to a narrow two-lane road so densely edged by trees that it took me a minute to realize that, off to my right, a high red-brick wall was paralleling the road. A black ribbon of decorative iron that scrolled along the top of the intimidating structure brought it up to at least fourteen feet high, ensuring that nobody was getting over that wall easily from either side. And even if someone made it to the top, they would still have to contend with the vicious-looking spear heads that tipped the decorative scrollwork in twelve-inch increments.

I drove until I reached a break in the trees and came to a set of huge iron gates. The scrollwork on the gates matched the iron on the top of the wall, right down to the vicious-looking spear heads. There must have been electronic surveillance some-where, because, as I made the turn onto the paved entrance, the gates swung slowly open before me. I eased my vehicle on through, feeling unsettled by the sensation of being watched. Maybe that's why I experienced a moment of claustrophobia when the gates clanged shut behind me, trapping me inside.

But met by open, rolling lawn on this side of the gates and the intimidating wall, the claustrophobia passed as fast as it came. I drove on through park-like grounds past neatly trimmed bushes, trees, and hedges. Large beds of colorful mixed flowers dotted the landscape here and there, gently breaking up the expanse of the manicured lawn.

Up ahead loomed a tall, white Georgian-style building with a columned front porch. I had never considered what a mental hospital for the rich and addled might look like, and even if I had, I'm sure I would not have pictured Tara.

I found parking concealed behind a berm and made my way to the front door. A decorative lion's head with hard, shiny eyes and a loop of gleaming brass through its mouth stared at me like it wanted to bite my head off. I stared back, daring it to try. I pressed the doorbell, only to be disappointed when neither a liveried butler nor Scarlet O'Hara opened it.

"Hello," I said to a fifty-something-looking woman with shoulder-length, honey-blond hair and a sunny smile.

"May I help you?" she said.

"I'm Devon West," I said. "I'm here to see Rebecca Brandywine."

"Of course, Mr. West. Please come in. I'm Annalee Morley. I was about to leave for an appointment, but if you don't mind waiting a minute, I'll get my husband for you," she said as I followed her inside.

She floated away while I waited in the high-ceilinged foyer that was as big as a normal living room. The foyer opened into a room four times as large and tastefully furnished with groupings of upholstered chairs and love seats for people to gather or rest. Wood-spindled staircases on either side of this area gently curved, like beckoning arms, up to the second level. A wide balustraded landing stretched between the top of the staircases. There were two doors up there, one each directly across from where the stairs ended. Both doors were heavy and wooden, and neither one, I noticed, had a doorknob—only a small, numbered keypad on the wall beside it.

On the ground floor and in the center of the room, a large, round pedestal table hosted a huge bouquet of bright, freshly cut flowers. Several feet beyond the table, a set of double doors were winged by single doors that lined up directly below the doors at the top of the stairs. All the doors on this level had knobs *and* keypads, making me wonder if they took security and privacy here seriously, or, if coupled with the imposing wall, they were making sure no one, including me, went anywhere they were not wanted to go.

Mrs. Morley had made her way around the table to the set of double doors. She knocked lightly on one of them and disappeared inside what I assumed was her husband's office. It took only a moment for the door to open again and for her husband to appear. Graying at the temples of his brown hair and much taller than his wife, he wore a dark suit and a distracted expression. Together, the couple approached, and his wife made the introductions.

"Dear, this is Mr. West," she said and gave me another sunny smile. "Mr. West, this is my husband, Dr. John Morley."

"Hello," I said, and we shook hands.

"Hello, Mr. West. And thank you, Annalee," he said to his wife. "Be careful driving."

"I will be," she said and raised on tiptoe to plant a quick kiss on his cheek. He patted her shoulder, and she turned to me.

"It was nice to meet you, Mr. West. Have a good day," she said and left through the front door.

Dr. Morley watched his wife leave before turning back to me.

"Shall we go to my office?" he said.

"Sure," I said, and we did.

"Where are you from, Mr. West?" he asked.

"Denver," I said as he shut the door behind us.

He offered me a seat as he walked around his desk to his.

"Then not too long a drive for you," he said as he got comfortable. "How was the traffic?"

"Light," was all I said, hoping he would take the hint and realize that I had not driven here to make small talk.

"Well," he said, "well, that's um … that's fortunate, isn't it?"

I nodded, and he picked up a pencil, tapped it on his desk a few times, and set it back down. He straightened some papers in front of him that didn't need straightening, after which his eyes flicked around the room and back to me. He looked like he was about to ask me something but changed his mind.

"Rebeca Brandywine. I'm here to see her," I reminded him.

"Oh, yes. Yes, of course," he said. "Ms. Troy phoned me about your visit."

"I'm sure she did," I said, guessing that was the source of his nervousness.

"Well," he said, coming to some sort of a decision, "let's, um, let's go find Rebecca."

We stood, and I followed him as he turned left out of his office. He punched in a code on the keypad for the door, turned the knob, and led us into a wide hallway bright with sunshine that flooded in through a row of curtained windows on our right. Doors lined the left side of the hallway, and a few of them were standing open. I glanced into each room as we passed by them and saw a mix of male and female employees busy at their desks doing office things. Some of them looked up and acknowledged us with a smile or a nod as we passed. To me, everyone seemed relaxed and happy, except for their boss.

As we made our way down the hall, I glanced outside through the windows on the right to see more well-tended grass, colorful flower beds, and large, leafy trees that provided plenty of restful shade.

A flowing sidewalk meandered in a leisurely design over the lawn. Cushioned benches and outdoor chairs had been placed where it passed through the shady spots. A blanket was spread in one area where several, what I assumed to be patients, were sitting around its edges, sharing food from a picnic hamper. Everyone seemed calm and happy, and nowhere did I see a nurse or a white-clad orderly standing guard over or attending to these people. I was about to mention this to Dr. Morley when a question occurred to me.

"Does Rebecca Brandywine have many visitors?" I asked as we continued down the quiet, sunny hallway.

"Only one," he said. "Once every three months. Like clockwork."

"'Like clockwork'?" I repeated at the oddness of that statement.

"Yes. Same person, same day of the week, and arriving at exactly the same time," he said, but before I could ask him more, we had reached the door at the end of the long hall. He was about to knock on it when his hand stopped in mid-air. We both leaned forward and listened to what sounded like someone flitting about the room, mumbling and crying. Dr. Morley's brow wrinkled. He rapped gently on the door and turned the knob.

"Rebecca, it's Dr. Morley," he called out. "You have a guest. We're coming in, dear."

When he pushed the door open, we stepped into what looked to me like a high-end hotel suite rather than a bed in a ward at a mental hospital.

A large window centered in the far wall overlooked the beautiful grounds and allowed in plenty of light. In front of it, a settee and two small club chairs were clustered around a low coffee table. The walls here and in the bedroom that I could see through an open door off to our left were all painted a soft shade of yellow that added to the sunniness of the room.

Altogether, I thought it made an appealing place to live, whether you were in or out of your mind, or being deliberately hidden from the world by a rich and devious ex-spouse.

"Oh, dear, oh, dear," I heard a woman say and was startled when she popped up from behind the settee.

She had darting brown eyes and a cap of light-brown hair woven throughout with strands of gray. She also had a delicate build that, along with her quick, fluttery movements, made her seem birdlike and fragile.

"Don't worry. Mommy will find you," she cried as tears streaked down what had once been a very beautiful face, and flitted off into the bedroom.

I turned to Dr. Morley, who looked angry.

"Rebecca Brandywine?" I said.

"Yes," he said.

He marched over to the door and pressed a button on the wall located next to a light switch. In seconds, a young man and woman entered the room.

"Rebecca has lost her baby, and she is very upset. You're her neighbors, and your job is to prevent such things from hap- pening," he said, his tone holding a note of steel I had not expected him to have.

The couple looked embarrassed as they stuttered their apologies, but, for the doctor, it was not enough.

"Bring her another, and get to work finding the missing one," he ordered, and they slipped shamefacedly from the room.

I could feel the shock and surprise from witnessing this peculiar little drama spreading all over my face. But before I had a chance to ask the doctor what the hell was going on, Rebecca Brandywine flew back into the room and clutched my right hand in both of her small, delicate ones.

"My baby," she cried, and, when she did, the overwhelming pain and desperation I registered through her touch almost knocked me down.

Whatever had happened to Rebecca Brandywine in the past had left her mind as torn and jumbled as an Alzheimer's victim's. I whipped my left hand up and wrapped it over her two small ones, and, in a split second of concentration, I saw the image of a young Rebecca in bed, crying and begging as a baby was being disentangled from her grasp. Whether the memory was real or not, her suffering was. But before I could see more, I was interrupted by the soothing sound of Dr. Morley, speaking in a gentle voice.

"Rebecca, dear, let's sit down," he said as he slipped her hands from mine and led her to the settee. "The sitter will be back any moment, and you don't want to be upset when she returns. It might frighten your baby," he said as they both sat down.

Rebecca stopped crying and frowned.

"The sitter?" she said and gave the doctor a confused look.

"Yes, dear. She took your baby out for some fresh air. And look, Rebecca, here she is now," he said, and, with that, we all turned to watch as the female neighbor entered the room carrying a baby wrapped in a fuzzy pink-and-blue-patterned blanket.

At which point I began wondering if everything I knew about human biology was wrong, or if I was losing my mind and needed to reserve a room here.

At Rebecca Brandywine's age, there was no way in hell, I knew, that she could have produced a baby. But here came the neighbor with the precious bundle. I didn't understand what was going on until she handed the baby to Rebecca, and I saw its little face. It was round and sweet and appeared to be sleeping. It was also one of those incredibly life-like replicas of a baby that creep me out so badly, I thought they should be outlawed.

I still do.

"My baby," chirped Rebecca and hugged the doll to her chest.

Dr. Morley smiled.

"Thank you, Gayle," he said to the neighbor, who nodded and left the room. He turned back to Rebecca. "Now, dear, you look tired. Why don't you and the baby lie down for a nap," he suggested.

He stood and helped Rebecca with her baby up to her feet.

"Yes, I think that's a good idea," she said, and, cooing to the doll, she went to her bedroom, lay down on the bed with it, and closed her eyes.

Dr. Morley sighed as he walked over and closed the door behind her. He turned back to me.

"Well, Mr. West, you can't help but have questions after seeing all that," he said.

I nodded.

"Then let's go back to my office. We might as well be comfortable while we talk, and I have a few questions, too."

Chapter Twelve

We left Rebecca Brandywine's room and retraced our path back down the airy hall. We stopped at one of the offices, and I waited while Dr. Morley stepped in and let someone know that Rebecca should be checked on before dinner. Then we went to the doctor's office. I took the same seat I had before, as he closed the door behind us. He went to his desk chair and sat down. Whether I was being rude or not, I didn't waste any time.

"Who in your family was mentally ill, Dr. Morley?" I said.

"What makes you ask?" he said.

"Because there has to be a reason you care so much about your patients," I said, and he corrected me.

"Not 'patients,' Mr. West, 'guests.' To call them 'patients' implies their illnesses are curable and, with treatment, will get better. Our guests will never be well, but they can be well-cared for," he said. "And as to your question, it was my older sister, Melinda, who was mentally damaged."

He leaned forward, reached across his desk, and turned a small, framed picture toward me. The subject in the picture was a pretty teenaged girl with soft brown hair and eyes. Her smile was lovely, and there was a delicateness about her that reminded me of Rebecca Brandywine.

"That was taken after high school, a short time before she went away to college, where she was gang-raped by at least three boys at a frat party. She wasn't drunk or high. Just small, naive, and easily overpowered. We think that's why the bastards didn't even bother to drug her, which left her conscious through every second of the ugly ordeal. The whole dirty business shattered her innocent mind. Afterwards, she couldn't identify with certainty the animals who had done it, and the ones she could name claimed it was consensual sex. They went back to their classes, while she left the college by ambulance and in a near-catatonic state."

He turned the picture to face him again and looked at it sadly.

"Did she ever recover?" I asked as gently as I could.

He shook his head and returned his gaze to me.

"Not fully. She had to be placed in a state mental hospital."

"Not Sunridge?" I said and got another headshake from him.

"We weren't a wealthy family, Mr. West. My parents were hardworking, middle-class people. I was in high school at the time, and we all took extra jobs to get enough money together to get Melinda moved to a better facility. And besides, the old Sunridge was not what you see today. We would not have wanted her here then."

"Where is your sister now?"

"Dead," he told me quietly, his voice tinged with sorrow. "After a year, she had recovered enough to slip away from the mental ward staff and throw herself down a stairwell. I think my mother was relieved that Melinda was no longer suffering, but my father went to his grave full of guilt for having let her go away to college in the first place."

"And you found your purpose in life," I said, and he nodded. "How did Sunridge become part of that purpose?"

"I had interned here while working on my psychiatric degree. It's how I met Annalee. She was employed here as a nurse. So, I guess you could say some good did come out of the tragedy," he said and sighed from the weight of the old pain.

"Your wife seems like a very nice person," I said.

"Oh, she's way more than nice, Mr. West. Without her strength and goodness, I might have left Sunridge long ago."

"Why is that?"

"Because, as I said, Sunridge was not always what it is today. When I first came here, it wasn't much more than a dumping place for wealthy embarrassments. I treated mostly addicts and alcoholics. There were Down Syndrome adults being hidden here, along with nymphomaniacs and kleptomaniacs and teenaged sex offenders. All of them mixed dangerously together and rather than being helped, they were being controlled with mind-numbing drugs and the threat or actual use of physical violence from employees who were nothing more than white-coated sadists or felons who couldn't find employment elsewhere."

"So why didn't you leave?"

"For two reasons. First, because Annalee convinced me that I had to stay and help the people who could be helped."

"And the second reason?" I asked.

"Gloria Brite, the director at that time," he began, and his face and voice both hardened. "She was a nasty, venal woman whose treatment of the people in her charge was criminal. It was she who turned Sunridge from a refuge into a warehouse and for no other reason than financial gain. When I think of the damage and suffering she caused, I shudder. Then I pray there's a hell because she belongs in its lowest ring forever."

"Wasn't there anyone you could have reported her to, Dr. Morley?"

"I tried," he said. "But I was young and wasn't taken seriously, partly, I believe, because of my inexperience but also because mental illness is a topic no one seems to want to address. Not now and certainly not back then."

I couldn't disagree with that sad fact, but now he had me wondering.

"With your admitted lack of experience, how did you become the director?" I asked, and he shrugged.

"Happenstance? Attrition? Fate, maybe?" he said. "Whatever the reason, my advance to the directorship was set in motion the day Gloria Brite left Sundridge unexpectedly."

"When was this?"

"About a year after Rebecca Brandywine arrived here," he said, and I found that curious.

"You must have dealt with a lot of guests over the years, Dr. Morley. Why do you associate the timing of Gloria Brite's departure specifically with Rebecca Brandywine's arrival?"

"Because of something that happened early on when I tried to report the director's reprehensible behavior. At that time, there were a dozen people who sat on a board that governed Sunridge. They comprised the only authority over-seeing Ms. Brite's actions. I contacted them all, but only one person returned my call. A member by the name of Eleanora Brandywine," he said, and my fingertips tingled at the mention of her name.

"Rebecca Brandywine's mother-in-law?" I said, and a chill began working its way up my spine, too.

"Yes, but Rebecca didn't arrive here until long after that phone call," he said as the chill peaked between my shoulder blades.

"That must have been an interesting conversation," I said, fighting off a shiver. But my fingertips were still tingling, and I had to focus hard to keep my mind on his words as the doctor continued.

"Short but memorable. She laughed off my concerns and made it clear that if I continued to complain, not only could she put me out of my job here, but she could also arrange for me to lose my psychiatric license permanently."

All of which rang true based on the interaction I'd had with her son.

I thought for a moment and asked, "I know the Brandy-wine name is powerful now, but could she really have man-aged that back then?"

"At the time, I didn't think she could, and, not only was I naïve enough to challenge her on that, I told her I would not be threatened. Her response was some of the ugliest laughter I have ever heard and her assurance that she could, with no trouble at all, produce evidence that I was the person mistreat-ing the patients here."

"And every bit of it, I'm betting, faked and forged to such a degree that it couldn't be disputed," I said, thinking of the papers Judge Halliday had received from Ellis Brandywine.

Like mother, like son. Damn.

"I was afraid so, Mr. West. She was quite convincing. And because of that, I became determined to leave Sunridge once and for all."

My eyebrows went up.

"But?" I said, and he smiled.

"You can't guess?" he asked.

I could.

"Your wife," I said, and the tingling in my fingertips faded away.

"Yes. Annalee," he said and sat back in his chair. "I told her about the phone call and my decision to leave. We were engaged by then, and she said she loved me and would follow me anywhere—as long as my path led us both back to Sunridge. She insisted our work was here."

"Rock and a hard place," I said, thinking of Charlotte— her warmth, clarity, and emotional strength—and if I could put my foot down with a woman like her or Annalee once their minds were made up. As for Jonah's Angie, I knew I wouldn't even try.

I know, I know. Tough guy, right?

"And then?" I said.

"And then I began taking on more responsibility here while Annalee went immediately to work on her medical degree. Eventually, Rebecca arrived. Months later, Eleanora

Brandywine had a stroke and died. The board started losing other members over the next couple of years, and better ones took their places. Gloria Brite had left, and directorship candidates came and went, and I stayed. By the time I assumed the job, Annalee had finished medical school, and we were free to run Sunridge as you see it now."

We were both quiet for a moment until I reminded him, "You said you had questions, too, Doctor."

"I do," he said and paused. "I guess I should start with the most important one."

"Which is?" I said.

"Well, what exactly are you doing here?"

"Didn't Lana Troy tell you?"

"I received a phone call from her, but all she told me was your name and surprised me with the information that you would be coming here to speak to Rebecca."

"Why was that surprising?" I said.

"Because, Mr. West, up until a few years ago, Rebecca Brandywine had never had a visitor."

"Never?" I said. "No family? Not even her former husband?"

"Not until Lana Troy began showing up here. As I mentioned before, she is the person who comes here every three months. And even then, I wouldn't call it a visit. They don't go for a walk on the grounds or have lunch together. She doesn't hold Rebecca's hand or make any physical contact with her at all. It's more like a visual inspection of Rebecca and her room, and, when she's satisfied that nothing has changed, Ms. Troy leaves."

I considered that and said, "When I first arrived, Dr. Morley, you seemed bothered that I was here to see Rebecca. Why was that?"

"Because Sunridge is her whole world. One day thirty years ago, Gloria Brite was gushing about an extremely large donation to Sunridge that Ellis Brandywine had made. A week later, Rebecca was brought here. Since then, no one has seemed to care if Rebecca was alive or dead. I was concerned that your visit meant Brandywine was planning to regain guardianship over her and possibly move her to another facility. He isn't, is he? A change like that would be disastrous for Rebecca."

"Not that I know of."

"That's good," he said. "But then I have to ask again about the purpose of your visit today."

"Fair enough," I said and told him about Mecklan Personal Services. I explained that we had been hired to handle a personal matter for Ellis Brandywine and had hoped Rebecca might be well enough to help us. As I finished, another question occurred to me.

"You're a psychiatrist, and your wife was a medical nurse. But it seemed important to you that she studied to become a doctor. Why was that?"

"Because we both knew that, if our guests were to be completely safe, we had to replace the doctor who had been put on staff here by Eleanora Brandywine. He was another nasty piece of work by the name of Glandon," he said, and the name hit me like a quick jab to the gut does—not painful enough to drop you to your knees but sharp enough to catch your attention and make your breath come a little short.

I was able to make myself breathe, but I could not make my fingers stop the tingling that had come back so sharply it made them sting. I knew he could not be talking about Ellis Brandywine's doctor. Laurence Glandon would have been too young back then. But I also knew the odds were astronomically against the possibility of the Brandywines employing two doctors with the same last name not being blood related.

"Tell me about him," I said, deciding to wait for the moment on that connection.

"Merrick Glandon was cold and imperious, and without true concern for the well-being of anyone he treated here. But that wasn't the worst of it. After he died, my wife and I went through the medical files in his office. I'll never forget the sickening moment when we realized that he had been using the guests here, mostly women, as guinea pigs, experimenting on them with drugs and surgeries. I thanked God that Annalee was ready to step into his position once he was gone."

I found that information sickening and frightening, too. But, at least, at the mention of Annalee's name again, my fingers stopped tingling.

"Dr. Morley," I said, "the day I met Ellis Brandywine, I met his doctor, who is also named Glandon. Laurence Glandon. Have you ever met or spoken to him?"

"Never," he said, which, assuming they were related, struck me as odd.

"No contact at all?" I said. "No interest from him or anyone else at Brandfield concerning Rebecca or even a letter asking for any of the medical records left here?"

Dr. Morley shook his head "No," and I thought of another question.

"What about Rebecca Brandywine's records? Did you ever get a look at those?"

He shifted in his chair before answering.

"I didn't because I never found any. Either Merrick never treated her, or, if he had, he didn't move any of her records with her. Then he died, shortly after Rebecca came here. And at the beginning of Rebecca's stay, I saw her only once or twice before she disappeared. I thought Rebecca had been moved to another facility until she reappeared several months later, as suddenly as she had originally vanished.

"Didn't that strike you as strange, Doctor?"

"Not really. Guests seemed to come and go regularly back then. And as I said, Gloria left soon after that. That's when I looked but couldn't find any records on Rebecca. I don't know if Ms. Brite destroyed the information—if it had ever been here—or took it with her. She may not have even bothered to keep a file on Rebecca. Especially not financial ones, if, as I suspect, she had helped herself to some of Ellis Brandywine's original donation."

Which fits with his description of the frightening way this place used to be run, I thought, and then spoke.

"As sketchy as her arrival was, Dr. Morley, you still must have been told something about Rebecca's background when she came to Sunridge," I said, and his look held equal amounts of anger and sadness.

"The only thing I was told about Rebecca on her return was that she'd had several miscarriages and that her mind had deteriorated with each one. After she'd had a stillborn baby, she had a complete mental collapse and could no longer take care of herself."

"Did you ever try to get in touch with Gloria Brite after you became director?" I said.

"I wanted to, but she left here without any contact information. And a short time later, she was dead—a victim of a violent rape and murder. I found out about it only because two Denver detectives came to see if anyone here could help shed light on a possible suspect. I don't know if the crime was ever solved, and, frankly, at the time, I didn't care. Annalee and I had made our plan. We were determined to find a way to weed out the dangerous elements here and turn Sunridge into the care facility it should have always been."

"And you take care of Rebecca," I said.

"As well as if she were my own sister," he replied, and the anger and sadness left him.

"Well, Dr. Morley, I think I've taken enough of your time. Thank you for seeing me," I said, and we both stood.

He came around his desk and opened the door. We left his office together, and, as we passed through the quiet lobby, I had another question.

"Doctor, do you ever worry about who will run Sunridge after you retire?"

"Not at all, Mr. West. Our son is working on his doctoral degree in psychiatry. He and his partner will be the next generation to welcome guests to Sunridge when Annalee and I are gone."

For whatever reason, I found that comforting. But as we reached the foyer, I wondered about something.

"Dr. Morley, does it ever make you bitter that, because of money, the guests here get better care than your sister ever had a chance of receiving?"

Dr. Morley smiled and opened the front door. We stepped outside and into a flood of sunshine.

"Mental illness doesn't recognize financial disparity, Mr. West. And everyone who suffers from it deserves the care we give here. It's true that the families of our guests pay very well for that care. But because they do, and, along with the generous bequests we receive from these families after their loved ones have passed, Sunridge provides care for many who could never afford to be here otherwise," he said and drew my attention to a car that was approaching up the drive.

I looked and saw that Annalee was driving. There was a dark-haired young man huddled beneath a blanket beside her in the front seat. He seemed listless, and his face was blank.

"This is Rodrigo. At least he thinks that's his name. His mind goes in and out of reality. His drug-addicted mother sold him to a pornographer when he was probably four or five years old. He guesses he's about seventeen now. The only thing he's sure of is that his life has been hell and that he's dying of AIDS. A policeman, one of our contacts, found him sleeping behind a dumpster in an alley. He took him to a hospital and got in touch with us."

"And now Rodrigo is here," I said, watching the car go by and around behind the building.

"Yes. We have our own clinic. Rodrigo will be safe and cared for, and what is left of his life and thoughts will be peaceful and secure. We don't accept any violent guests, and we don't allow violence by our staff toward anyone," he said and looked beyond me toward the gates.

"That wall, Mr. West, wasn't put up to keep our guests in. It's there to keep the cruel degradations and the harsh realities of life out."

I looked around at the wall, the rolling lawn, and the beautiful flowers. It made me think of Alissa and that she would have been safe and content here. It also made me think how happy Jonah would have been to visit his mother here instead of at the grave she had been lowered into beside Mike a year after he had been murdered. I felt the burden of all that old sadness begin to weigh me down as it always had the power to do. It must have shown because Dr. Morley gave me a close look.

"Are you all right, Mr. West?" he asked.

I shook off the sadness and answered.

"Sure," I said but with the sudden feeling that finding the truth about what happened to the twins and Ellis Brandywine's slow demise in the present were somehow linked with something hidden in Rebecca's past. "Thanks again for your time, Doctor," I added and extended my hand, ready to leave.

Dr. Morley took my hand. When he did, I felt a soothing calm wash over me, and I could sense the inner peace that fortified him for the work he did here.

"Goodbye, Mr. West," he said. "Drive safely."

"Goodbye," I said and left him at the door.

I got in my SUV and turned the engine on. I dropped the windows and flipped my AC to high. I sat thinking while the cold air pushed out the hot air along with, I hoped, the dark feeling that had settled on me. Normally, a few minutes of summer warmth and sunshine did the job, but, this time, it was not working.

I put the windows up, lowered the AC, and drove around to the huge wrought-iron gates. While they swung slowly open before me again, I thought about Evergreen Lake, the beautiful mountain views here, and the camera I had brought. But I knew I would not be stopping to take pictures when I thought about the Brandywines—mother and son—and the trail of tortured and broken lives they left in their wakes.

"Call Jonah," I told my hands-free phone as I headed for I-70 and Denver.

Chapter Thirteen

I awoke late Saturday morning with a dirt-dry mouth, a skull-splitting headache, and a yellow sticky note in my hand that I had plucked from my hair.

Check your email, the note said.

Which I would have gratefully done if I could get downstairs before experiencing a fatal brain aneurism.

I took a careful breath and pulled myself up against the headboard. I attempted a slow head-turn toward the nightstand, but my nasty hangover asserted itself, and my stomach flipped. For a minute, I thought I was going to hurl. I stopped for another breath and then settled for sliding my gritty eyes the rest of the way in that direction. I saw a bottle of water there with another sticky note attached to it.

Check your email.

I picked up the bottle, peeled the note from it, and stuck it to the one from my hair. I opened the water and chugged half the bottle. After another breath, I noticed that my bedroom door was open and that another yellow sticky note was waving cheerfully to me from the jamb.

The little fucker.

Although I had no one to blame but myself. And the Brandywines. And the anxiety that I had not been able to shake on my drive home from Sunridge. After the call to Jonah and filling him in about all I had learned there, I had hit Denver and my favorite bar. I thought a couple of drinks might help ease the anxiety while Jonah dug up everything he could on our malevolent client and his dead Mommy Dearest.

It had, unfortunately, taken more than a couple to do the trick, but, luckily, my favorite bartender, Doni, had been working. Whip-smart and with a wicked sense of humor, Doni's warm, smooth skin registered a shade darker than the color of rich, creamy milk chocolate. She had a killer smile to go with a soft, bouncy 'fro that, coupled with the large, gold-hoop earrings she always wore, made a delightful distraction from the observant intelligence in her alluring brown eyes.

Doni and I had gone to a few concerts together and had spent a couple of long weekends in the mountains. It never went further than that, but we were always glad to see each other. And on evenings like last night, she knew (with my blessing and while laughing heartily at me) to slip a twenty from my wallet to cover the cost of the cab she would eventually pour me into.

What I knew about Doni that nobody else at the bar did was that she had a bachelor's degree in Cultural Anthropology and was working on her master's with a plan to go into teaching. Whenever I got drunk enough to ask what a beautiful woman like her was doing wasting her time working in a bar like this, she would laugh and remind me that the tips were good, it didn't interfere with her class schedule, and it was great people-watching.

Then she would call that cab.

I closed my eyes and tried to recall more about last night. I remembered a soft, sweet kiss and hoped to God that it was from Doni saying "Goodnight" and not a sloppy snog from the cab driver, who had reeked of grease, garlic, and stale cigarette smoke.

I opened my eyes, finished the water, and tossed the empty bottle in the general direction of the small trash can next to the dresser. I slowly hauled myself out of bed, pulled on a pair of sweatpants, and followed the trail of sticky notes to the stairs.

I always knew when Jo had worked all night, because, like today, I woke up with a sticky note in my hair or stuck to my forehead. I measure the depth and the importance of that information by how many sticky notes I collect on my way to the kitchen and a first cup of life-saving black gold.

Yawning, I fumbled my way down the stairs and through the hallway to the kitchen, collecting the notes as I went. This morning, I had a fistful of them by the time I hit the button on the brewer. While it went to work, I went to the head. I knew Jonah was on to something besides learning where Ellis Brandywine had gone to grade school when I saw another note with exclamation points stuck to the upraised toilet seat.

Back in the kitchen, I threw away all the notes I had collected. I filled a mug with coffee, took it to the table, eased out a chair, and sat down. I pulled one last sticky note off my laptop, which Jonah had left open on the table for me. I brought it to life with a light tap and logged in. I touched the sticky note icon, took a deep breath, and read.

Eleanora Richfield Brandywine is a descendant of Romanian immigrants. I found records of twin brothers, Garridan and Costache Raiciulescu, who came to New York as teenagers in 1858, where they immediately changed their last name to something easier for Americans to pronounce, Richmont. They both married on the same day in 1870 (maybe it was a twin thing), when they were thirty years old. They were financially set by then, having established themselves selling gold and gems they had brought with them and using the money to branch out into buying other businesses.

Garridan had five children, although only two of them survived to adulthood. Costache's marital luck was worse. His first wife died during the birth of their second baby, as did the baby. After this, Costache took his first child, a son, and moved to Chicago. Maybe in an attempt at a fresh start, Costache changed his name to Christopher and the family surname to Richfield. It gets murky after that. There appears to have been at least two more wives, another son, and a daughter who joined a convent.

There also appears to have been some bad blood that developed between the twin brothers that spilled over onto both families. The later generations were always fighting about money and property, and suing each other over one issue or another. Also, neither side of the family seems to be a hardy bunch, a condition attributed to "the family curse." None of the members that I found records on survived into anything near old age, Eleanora being a current example.

All of which brings us closer to the present.

Eleanora's paternal grandfather, Charles Richfield, came to Denver from Chicago as a young man, and he didn't come broke. He had enough money to buy a small hotel, improve it, grow it into a large hotel, and sell it. Nothing seemed to slow him down, not even the suicide of his first wife after only eight months of marriage. Five years later, he remarried and had a son they named Harrison. Charles kept right on buying, improving, and selling small businesses until he had an impressively large fortune before he turned fifty and right up to the day his second wife shredded his heart with a large-caliber slug at the breakfast table.

The maid who had been serving their poached eggs and toast points said there had been no argument. Mrs. Richfield had simply pulled out the gun, calmly told her husband, "It's time for you to go to hell, Charles, and to take your black soul with you," and fired.

After the missus had plugged him, she began laughing and laughing, and when she stopped, she sang, "Happy birthday to me," put the gun to her head, and popped herself.

Harrison was away at college when he was so violently orphaned. About half of the servants quit before he returned to bury his parents and take over managing the family home and all the businesses. The reason given was that he was a spoiled, self-important brat with a wide mean streak and absolutely unlikable.

Regardless, being young, single, somewhat handsome, and without any siblings to have to share all that money with, he was still considered a catch. Several years later, Harrison married a woman the remaining servants referred to as "a quiet, pretty little thing," and, eventually, our employer's mother was born.

Eleanora Richfield was an only child. She was born here in Denver but attended a small private college in New York. Merrick Glandon was a scholarship student there. Everything I found on him indicates he was extremely intelligent (graduated high-school valedictorian at sixteen) and single-mindedly ambitious but financially strapped. It appears that he and Eleanora became close friends, and the Richfield family, in a philanthropically motivated gesture, paid for his undergraduate and medical degrees.

"Appears" is the operative word here, Dev. I found newspaper stories about a dorm fire during Eleanora's junior year that killed her roommate. It was shortly after that blaze that the Richfields began paying Merrick Glandon's tuition. Police records indicate the fire was highly suspicious for arson.

Eleanora was the main suspect.

Merrick Glandon was the only witness.

Of course, neither of them was talking, so all the frustrated arson inspector could do was document his suspicions and include statements in his report about a rivalry over a guy between the highly competitive Eleanora and the dead roommate.

The guy's name was Jeremy Ellis Brandywine.

Eleanora's family had money, but the Brandywines had old money and connections to all the best families. They also inhabited a circle of society ordinarily closed to "newcomers" like the Richfields. But shortly after college and what may have been the commission of murder with that fire (we can only guess if it was her first), Eleanora married Jeremy and his larger fortune. Merrick Glandon—financially set now with money from Eleanora—finished his medical degree in New York while Jeremy and Eleanora set up housekeeping in Southampton. But if there had been any marital bliss for the newlyweds, it didn't last long.

Coffee Break

Did Jonah know me, or what?

I got up, refilled my cup, placed it on the table, and went to the fridge. My stomach was growling, and I knew I needed food, but I wasn't sure what to put in it. I didn't want to eat anything that might make me throw up on my laptop. Or my feet. Or, hell, I didn't want to throw up at all, afraid my pounding head would explode from the reverse motion if I did.

I opened the fridge and looked inside, but no rummaging was necessary. Jonah had left me a large container of green chili, along with flour tortillas wrapped in foil. My favorite hangover food. I didn't bother with hot sauce because I knew Jonah would have bought this ambrosia of the Mexican gods already as hot as I could stand it.

I grabbed the green chili from the fridge, poured some into a bowl, and stuck the bowl in the microwave. I turned on a stove burner and warmed the tortillas over the gas flame into puffed perfection. The microwave dinged as I finished the last one. I stacked up the tortillas on a small plate, found a spoon, grabbed the bowl from the microwave, and took it all to the table. I sat back down and ate while I continued to read.

Maybe beach life wasn't for Eleanora. Maybe she missed the mountains. Maybe marriage to Jeremy Brandywine was less exciting than the pursuit of him. I spoke with Jeremy's younger brother, James, last night, and, after apologizing for "speaking ill of the dead," he said it was as if Eleanora became another person before the ink on the marriage certificate was dry. It had been a shock to the whole family, he told me, to see a woman who had been warm, witty, and loving during the engagement become suddenly cold, bitchy, and controlling after the nuptials.

Nor did it help the relationship when Eleanora miscarried shortly after their first anniversary due to a fall while horseback riding. She claimed she hadn't realized she was pregnant when she went riding that day, but Jeremy had confided to his brother that he didn't believe her. And he wasn't sure the fall was an accident.

Regardless, she and Jeremy had a baby girl fifteen months later. Elea-nora had been home alone when she found the baby dead in her crib six weeks after her birth. The baby had been perfectly healthy up to that point, so cause of death was ruled SIDS. Jeremy was devastated by the baby's death, while his family was frightened by how unaffected Eleanora had been by the loss. Jeremy had become extremely depressed and was openly speaking of divorce. But Eleanora had suddenly become kind and gentle and pregnant again four months later.

This time the baby was a boy (and our future employer), and Jeremy hired a battery of nurses to watch the newborn 24/7. Which appeared to be fine with Eleanora since, according to her brother-in-law, she showed little or no interest in Ellis. He said he had visited Jeremy and Eleanora not long after his nephew was born. A nurse brought the baby to them, but Eleanora made no move to take him from her. Jeremy had held Ellis instead, and, where he was delighted and loving with his son, the brother-in-law said Eleanora looked at the baby as if she were observing a stray puppy that had wandered into their home that she had no desire to pet or care for. She had looked more, James had felt, as if she had wanted to pick it up and toss into oncoming traffic.

Not long after this, she reconnected with Merrick Glandon and began spending time with him in New York. Whether she was sleeping with him or not, either Jeremy didn't know or didn't care if she was. The younger brother said everyone—especially Jeremy—was happier when Eleanora was not around and he was free to dote on Ellis.

But as Ellis grew up, Jeremy grew concerned.

As an infant, Ellis was never a problem. Even with a cold or cutting teeth, he cried little, ate well, and slept soundly. He was a quiet toddler and didn't need much attention from the adults who surrounded him, no matter how much they were willing to interact with him. He always had plenty of toys but had played with them only one at a time until he had broken the one he had selected. But it was as a preschooler that family and teachers began noticing something distinctly odd about little Ellis Brandywine.

It was not that he didn't get along well with other children. It was that, one minute he would be playing with a group of kids, and the next he would be outside the group watching them play whatever game he had set in motion. Halfway through grade school, his teachers reported that he had a strange habit of drawing classmates to him and then turning on them, leaving them confused and hurt.

And it was at this point in Jonah's narrative that the tips of my fingers began tingling. I rolled them back and forth under my thumbs as I thought about Charlotte and what she had said about Ellis's personality change. I was also reminded of my own unsettling experience with him. This was obviously a family trait, and I thought it was frightening how young Ellis was when it had first manifested in him.

Jeremy Brandywine spent as much time as he could with Ellis, trying to change his son's behavior. Maybe if Jeremy had had more time, it would have made a difference. But shortly after Ellis turned eleven, Eleanora once again turned sweet and loving toward her husband. She even gave Jeremy a flashy new sports car for his birthday. But two weeks later, while zipping along in fast-moving highway traffic, the engine malfunctioned, and Jeremy was killed in the multi-car pile-up that followed. Eleanora, the not-so-grieving widow, promptly sold the home in Southampton and moved back to Denver.

The following school term, Ellis was packed off to a preppy boarding academy. Not long after, Merrick Glandon took up residence in Denver. After a large donation toward the cause of mental-health improvement, Eleanora took control of the board that oversaw Sunridge, and Merrick

Glandon became the staff doctor. Six months later, she bought a large parcel of land well east of Denver and began building a new home.

It took a full year to construct Brandfield and another couple of months to furnish and decorate the place and hire the staff to run it. When it was done, Eleanora closed the house in Denver, moved into her new digs with Merrick Glandon, and threw a huge party. A magazine did a cover story on the party and the mansion. And that was it. No other parties were given. Eleanora immersed herself in her businesses and attended no other public social functions. Whatever she and the doctor were doing way the hell out there at Brandfield, everybody guessed, but nobody knew.

Over time, people lost interest in Brandfield and its occupants. Ellis grew up and went on to college. When he graduated, he returned home but not to Brandfield. Instead, he took up residence at the house in Denver. He also took up partying between Denver and New York. But he did make occasional trips to Brandfield, and, on one of these trips, he met Merrick Glandon's nephew, Laurence, who was spending some time there after having graduated from medical school. Laurence got along well with Ellis, but, more importantly, Laurence seemed to have made friends with Eleanora. So much so that, when Rebecca was later institutionalized and his uncle Merrick died suddenly thereafter, Eleanora hired Laurence to take Merrick's place.

Eleanora sold the house in Denver after Merrick's death, and Ellis moved to Brandfield permanently. He was thirty years old when he married Rebecca, and she was twenty-two.

We know how sadly that marriage ended for Rebecca Brandywine, Dev. We also know how things went for Charlotte. What we still don't know are the things we were hired to learn—the location of the twins' bodies if they really didn't end up in the ocean and who poisoned Ellis

J. Brandywine. Rebecca can't help us, and Charlotte won't help us. That leaves staff, business associates, or the second wife as help or possible suspects, and I'm going to go to work finding her—whether she's alive or dead—when I get up later today.

In the meantime, if you come up with any other leads or go anywhere, leave me a note or something because this case is beginning to worry me. I think Judge Halliday and Charlotte are right. We need to be careful.

I knew Jonah was right about that, just as I knew that I needed to find some aspirin to relieve the pain of my still-pounding head. But first, I needed to find out who was knocking on the front door. I closed my laptop and left the kitchen. I went to the front door and opened it to find Mrs. Koselke on the porch, crying.

Hank Spitball was dead.

Chapter Fourteen

brought Mrs. K in and consoled her with a hug. I sat her down on the living-room couch and went upstairs to change into jeans and a tee shirt. I splashed some cold water on my face and rinsed my mouth. The combination of minty mouthwash and green chili aftertaste made my queasy stomach go for the hurl again, but I was able to calm it and even get a couple of aspirins down. I remembered to put on deodorant, swiped a comb through my matted hair, and went back downstairs. I gave Mrs. K another hug, and we walked to her home while I thought about her loss.

Hank Spitball was already an old dog when he had limped into Mrs. K's yard three or four years ago. He was short-haired—filthy white fur with reddish-brown markings—and it didn't take a dog breeder's eye to see that Hank was just another medium-sized, abandoned mutt. He was also malnourished, wheezing, and favoring his left rear leg. Mrs. K had carefully approached him with water and food and had then called me and Jonah. Hank had needed the vet, and she had needed our help getting him there.

Hank had been wearing a worn red collar with his name engraved on a silver, dog-bone-shaped medallion that hung from it. Because Hank had been collared and named, the vet thought the owner may have had him chipped, too, but no dice. Nor had there been any flyers recently tacked to light poles or trees in the neighborhood by anyone searching for a missing Mr. Spitball.

So, after a week with the vet (wheezing cured, no broken bones in the favored left hip, but deeply bruised from what was probably a vicious kick), Hank Spitball, with his new collar and dog-bone-shaped name tag had come home to the Koselke menagerie to heal and live out his doggy days.

Mrs. K and I reached her house and turned into her driveway. We went to the backyard, and there was Hank, stretched out on his belly, head on his front paws, eyes closed, and looking like he was only asleep. He was lying in a patch of shade beneath a big cottonwood tree. *Not a bad way to go*, I thought, until I got close enough to see there was something off about the angle of Hank's head. "Mrs. K," I said, "would you get me a blanket to wrap him in, please?"

"Of course, dear," she said and went into her house.

When she was gone, I squatted down and put my hand on Hank's head. I tried to move it, but rigor had set in, although it was mild, due to the lack of muscle tissue left on the old pup. I brushed my hand down to his neck and squeezed. I felt broken bones there and knew someone had slipped into the yard during the night and snapped Hank's neck.

And the medallion from his collar was gone.

My stomach lurched. When it did, I knew it had nothing to do with my hangover and everything to do with Lana Troy's promise to punish me. I had to take a couple of deep breaths to get rid of the fear that sliced down my spine seeing the petty lengths she was willing to go to in order to do it. What I didn't have to do was find the thick lock of sandy-colored hair beneath one of Hank's front paws to know who she had sent to do it.

I stood up when I heard Mrs. K returning.

"Here, Dev," she said and handed me an old, red blanket. "It was Hank's favorite."

"He'd like that," I said and hoped she didn't notice that my hand was shaking when I took it from her. And if she did, I hoped she would think I was just upset for her loss and not dangerously close to losing control of my temper.

"Why don't you go inside, Mrs. K," I said. "I'll take care of Hank now."

She sniffed and bent to stroke Hank's old head a last time.

"Goodbye, Hank. And thank you, Dev," she said and ambled away.

I waited until I heard her back door close, and then I looked up into the tree.

"It's okay, Melvin. You can come down now," I said, but the furry, gray lard-ass didn't move.

Melvin was perched above Hank on a low branch of the cottonwood tree, lazily cleaning himself. He stopped to stare at me and held up a messy paw as if waiting for my inspection.

I had to step around Hank to get a closer look, but I saw it clearly—the blood that was on Melvin's paw and spattered on his chubby body. I knew Melvin was too disinterested to chase birds and too well-fed to bother with mice. And Hank's neck had been broken, not slit. The blood looked relatively fresh, and there was only one place it could have come from. As surprised as I was that Melvin had expended the energy to climb up into the cottonwood, I was amazed that he had first used some of that energy to attack Hank's killer.

"Good one, buddy," I said. "I owe you some catnip."

Melvin looked at me as if he were cataloguing that promise and then went back to cleaning himself.

I wrapped Hank in his blanket and cradled him like a baby as I quick-marched home. By the time I got there, my anger had muscled aside my hangover, and my mind was laser-focused on vengeance. I knew Jonah would still be sleeping, and I had no intention of waking him up. Partly because he needed the sleep but mainly because I did not want to come clean about Hank Spitball right now.

It was not that I was afraid that Jonah would say he had warned me about the results of my smart-ass tendencies or my adolescent need to poke the Brandywine bear. It was because I knew that, as soon as I told him what had happened down the street, he would shift into protection mode and remove me from this case.

I also knew we would have a hell of a fight over that, because, inexperienced or not, no way was I stepping aside now. Not until I figured out what the hell was going on with those twisted freak-jobs at Brandfield, what had really happened to the Brandywine twins—or I was dead.

I left Hank behind the lilac bushes that grew alongside the house. I whipped around the back and into the kitchen to grab my wallet and keys. Then I was out the door, on Jonah's ten-speed, and pedaling like an Olympic racer to collect my SUV for a fast drive to Brandfield.

Somebody there was going to pay for Hank Spitball's death.

Chapter Fifteen

By the time I roared up to Brandfield and slammed to a stop in front of the ugly place, my jaws ached from clenching my teeth, the muscles in my shoulders felt like burning knots, and I was consumed with the need to punch someone at Brandfield into next week.

And fuck that side-door shit.

I pried my fingers from the steering wheel, flung open my door, and lunged out like the lead villager with a pitchfork on his way to storm the monster's castle.

I took the concrete stairs two at a time. But when I hit the landing at the top, my sleepy lizard brain woke up, called me an asshole, and told me to slow down, reminding me that morphing into a monster myself was not the way to deal with this.

I got a rein on my anger with a few deep breaths and some pacing back and forth. Then I rang the bell and waited, betting that since Eleanora's big party decades ago, no one had ever used this door again. I figured somebody was scrambling around in there right now, trying to find it.

And, man, was I shocked when that somebody did.

"What do you want?" she snapped.

My mouth dropped open, and, for a fractured moment, my mind went blank because I felt like I was standing in Ellis Brandywine's study, looking at the painting of his mother. This woman's coloring and facial features were a near-perfect copy of Eleanora's. But my mouth closed when I realized she had about ten years and thirty pounds on the portrait, and this charmer's dark hair was laced with strands of wiry gray. Her black dress and white apron finally registered with me, and her familial features, combined with her surly attitude, made me think that Ellis had given a humbling servant's job to a distant and disliked relative.

"I'm here to see Lana Troy," I said, and she glared at me.

"Go around to the side. You can't come in through here."

"Wanna bet?" I said and pushed past her.

When she made a grab for my arm to stop me, the skin-to-skin contact sent a zap like an electrical charge zinging down to my fingertips. I jerked a look at her hand and saw that it was red and chafed, and the nails were bitten and broken. There were also what looked like old burn scars on the back of her hand and up her forearm. Her grip was strong, but she was no Nell. I yanked my arm away, and she started yelling as I shoved my way further into the house.

I don't know who the architect was for Brandfield, but fulfilling Eleanora's design must have been a nightmare. Like the façade, the interior was blocky and jumbled, and the rooms were dark and mazelike. I stormed around them in the half-gloom like a crazed lab rat looking for a researcher to bite while the world's crappiest servant scurried behind me, cursing at my back and threatening me with violence and dire consequences.

I found a staircase and was about to start up it when Laurence Glandon appeared like an oily specter at the top.

"Hello, Mr. West. We've been waiting for you," he said and dismissed the housekeeper with a glance.

And in the short second it took for her to shut up and turn away, my stomach went hollow, my anger turned flat, and the adrenaline that had fueled my actions up to now was replaced with a cold dose of fear, knowing I had raced impulsively into a set-up. My conscious mind blanked for a second time, but my lizard brain, still on alert, sprang back into action and told me to bolt.

My ego, unfortunately, came to the fore at the same time. It remembered poor, dead Hank Spitball and said, "Screw it," and goaded me to put one foot after the other until I reached the top of the stairs.

"This way," said Glandon and gave me that smarmy smile of his.

I followed his confident footsteps with my uncertain ones, feeling disoriented in the gloom and by the bizarreness of him chatting on as if we were old friends.

"I see you've met our housekeeper. Noreena has some interesting quirks, but we know how to deal with them. She's also a very good cook, by the way," he said and led me down to the end of the hall and to a door.

He opened it, and I followed him into a bedroom. I was pretty sure it was Ellis Brandywine's because there was an empty hospital bed in the middle of the room, flanked on both sides by long tables covered in enough medical supplies and equipment to stock a third-world hospital for a year.

"Come, come," Glandon said as if I were a small child with a wandering mind and had to be encouraged to pick up the pace.

He opened a set of double doors that I recognized as the ones that separated Brandywine's bedroom from his sitting room.

We walked through the sitting room and on into the wood-paneled office, where my employer was burrowed into a pile of blankets in his wheelchair and rolled into place behind his enormous desk. He was watching something on the large computer monitor there.

Ellis slid his watery eyes from the screen as we entered. He laid his haughty glare on me before drifting his gaze to his doctor and raising the few wispy hairs that comprised what was left of his eyebrows.

Glandon stepped forward, drew a twenty from his pocket and placed it on the desk.

Brandywine smiled.

"Thank you, Laurence," said Ellis and brought his gloating, watery eyes to mine. "A small wager, Mr. West, at your expense, I'm afraid. You see, I was informed by Ms. Troy that she had sent Alexander to do a little chore for her last night, the completion of which would most likely result in you paying us an unannounced visit today. Laurence was sure you would go around to the side entrance to confront Lana and Alexander first. But I said, no, you were too young and brash for that. I *knew* the front door would be your entry of choice," he added with a triumphant little smile.

My hands balled into fists at the sound of his smooth, slithery voice. His arrogance reignited my anger and sent it ripping through me again. It took monumental effort for me not to leap across the desk, grab the disintegrating old bastard's scrawny neck, and wring it like wet laundry.

I held his gloating look and said, "And?"

"And," he continued, his tone sharp now, "Ms. Troy does not have the patience for your insubordination, and I do not have the time. I want your assurance that this will be the end of it."

I stood throbbing with frustration, knowing the only assurance I wanted to give him was the kind delivered to the head in a hard shot straight from the shoulder. But as angry as I was, I knew I would probably punch right through his face, so I gritted my teeth and said, "Done."

"Good," he said, not sounding as sick as he looked to be.

Maybe winning a twenty from Glandon had made him feel strong. Or maybe being a move ahead of me had done the trick. Either way, it was obvious he was in control and moving on to the next item on his agenda.

"Now, gentlemen, if you would step around the desk, please," he said.

Glandon walked around and stood behind Brandywine's wheelchair. I took the few steps necessary to stand near—but not *too* near—either of them.

We all had a clear view of the large monitor screen, which was sectioned into four even rectangles. The upper right corner was blank. The views in the other three were of different angles showing the same thing—a thin, pale man, shirtless, and with his pants down around his ankles, leaving him naked from his neck down to the crumpled trousers. He was bent forward, bracing himself with his hands on a table.

His head came up and I saw three things—a black rubber ball held securely in his mouth by leather straps, deep scratches covering his face and neck, and the strategically located thick lock of sandy colored hair missing from above one eye.

"What the *fuck*," I said, repulsed as my point-of-contact came into view wearing one of her perfectly tailored suits and carrying a quirt.

Lana Troy, the epitome of office efficiency, the woman who did not have the patience for my insubordination, took a position behind Alexander and began to mete out slow, measured strokes to his bare ass as I stood shocked and disgusted.

I spun away from the screen. I didn't need my lizard brain now to tell me to get the hell out of here, but I didn't get more than a few steps before Ellis Brandywine spoke.

"Don't leave yet, Mr. West. I haven't given you permission," he said.

I turned and threw him a hard look.

"I'm not going to stay and watch this sick shit," I said, about to turn away again.

"Oh, but you are," he assured me. "Either you will stay and watch, or Alexander will make another trip to your neighborhood and introduce himself to your dear friend, Mrs. Koselke."

My body went rigid. My fingertips went crazy.

Charlotte was right. I needed to get free from these freaks, out of Brandfield fast, and never go back, no matter how angry anyone here made me.

"I quit," I snapped.

"Same conditions if you do, Mr. West, but they will include Mr. Mecklan, too," he said with a glint of something so evil in his eyes that my soul went cold.

The bastard had me, and he knew it.

Disgusted with myself for each heavy, obedient footstep, I returned to a spot behind the desk where Brandywine indicated he wanted me to stand. Lana Troy was no longer in view on the monitor, but Alexander had not moved. I locked my arms over my chest and waited for whatever was coming next.

Glandon looked at me and cleared his throat.

"You rest, Ellis. I'll explain," he said with the relish of a necrophiliac left alone in a morgue for his birthday.

"It seems, Devon—you don't mind if I call you Devon, do you—our Alexander is quite a unique person. He has no emotions. He is neither happy nor sad. If he performs poorly for Ms. Troy, he is impervious to a tongue lashing or her disappointment, which can be quite severe. When he does well on a little task for her, say, as he did last night, praise means nothing to him. It's only been through diligent trial and error that Lana has found the only thing Alexander can feel. And that's what she uses to reward him," he said, and a slimy light brightened his ghoulish eyes.

I waited for him to go on, but Glandon waited for me to ask.

Seething, I dropped my hands to my sides, where they waited, balled again and aching to take a swing at him. But even more than wanting to smash that big, smug face, I wanted to be done with whatever game these two were playing with me.

"I'll bite," I said. "What's the only thing that chicken-shit-dog-killer can feel?"

"Humiliation," said Glandon. "Abject humiliation."

"And what does that have to do with me?" I said.

Brandywine rallied and spoke.

"Why you, Mr. West, are the cherry on top of Alexander's congratulatory sundae, so to speak. The abject part of his humiliation. Look," he said as he raised an emaciated hand and pointed a bony finger to draw my attention to the monitor again.

This time, all four screens were running. Lana Troy was back in action, lashing away with her quirt in three of them, stopping only to grab Alexander by the hair to pull his head back. And in the fourth screen, there was what Lana Troy and Alexander could see from their side, Brandywine, Glandon—and me.

If it was humanly possible to scream with your eyes, Alexander did. He never lifted his hands from the desk, but now his body strained against every new lash of the quirt. Lana Troy stopped and set the quirt aside for a moment to hold up Hank's dog-bone medallion and smirk. Then she got back on task.

My stomach dropped.

My throat tightened.

My heart went into a Gene Krupa solo.

Two birds. One humiliation.

Abject. Complete.

Suddenly, I felt dizzy and sick. Hot bile gushed like a geyser of acid up into my throat. I fought down the urge to vomit but had to place a hand on Brandywine's desk to steady myself.

And that's when Brandywine did it—brought his wasted hand to mine and patted the back of it like he would a naughty child's. His touch had no strength, but I was nevertheless pinned in place with the weight of the inner rot and evil that came through it.

My breath came short. My legs turned to rubber. My vision clouded as figures flooded my sight like a horror movie whizzing by in fast forward, swirling with images of children who were lost and frightened and wailing in terror. Women crying and begging not to be hurt. Infants stillborn. Babies deformed. Eleanora Brandywine laughing and laughing. Rebecca, fragile and broken. Charlotte, defeated and drowning. The twins terrified and screaming, reaching for their mother. And not just pain, but walls of suffering. Mountains of agony. Until finally, mercifully, complete blackness.

The light returned, and my vision cleared. When it did, I found myself behind the wheel of my SUV, engine running, AC on, and a vent angled to blast a cold stream of air directly into my face. Too weak to reach out and direct the icy jet of air away, I turned my head toward the driver's side window and saw someone standing there.

A man.

Something familiar about him.

Big. Blocky.

The gardener?

Yeah, the gardener.

He tapped on the window, and I put it down.

"Goodbye," he said.

An excellent suggestion.

I sat up, threw the engine into gear, and drove away, hoping I had enough strength to make it back to Denver without causing an accident or my own death.

Chapter Sixteen

The mountains were backlit by the yellowy glow of the half-set sun before I made it home and parked in the driveway. My legs still felt like rubber, while my arms felt so numb and heavy, I was afraid I would have to call Jonah on my cell to come out and help me inside. But I managed to leave the SUV on my own and make it through the front door and into the living room.

I collapsed onto the couch, where, only hours earlier, I had left Mrs. Koselke to sit while I had cleaned myself up. Or was that a day ago? I wasn't sure. Time and reality felt disconnected and floating. I closed my eyes and heard myself moan loud enough to bring Jonah from his office.

"Jesus Christ, Dev. What the hell happened?" he said as he rushed into the room.

I opened my eyes and told him. All of it. From Mrs. K knocking at the door, to Hank Spitball's death, to the degrading incident at Brandfield, and Brandywine's threats. I only interrupted myself to clarify with him the day or the time, to figure out if I was awake or dreaming, and finally, to ask for something to drink.

Jonah went to the kitchen. He returned with a bottle of water and a look that would have made me cringe if I'd had the strength.

I didn't.

He opened the bottle, handed it to me, and said, "You should have left me a note or a voice message, Dev."

"I know," I said and chugged down about half the water.

The dizziness slowed, and I was able to draw a long breath that left me feeling better but still weak.

"Where did you stash Hank?" he asked.

"Alongside the house. Behind Connie's lilac bushes," I said, as the dizziness ended, and my head began to clear.

"All right. You rest. I'll take care of him," he said and turned to leave.

"Jo," I said, and he turned back to me.

"What?"

"I fucked up," I said.

He responded with the same look as before.

I had recovered enough strength to cringe this time, and I did. I probably should have left it at that, but I had to know.

"Are you going to take this case away from me?" I asked.

"Would you let me?" he said.

I scrunched my eyes shut. I got one back open and looked at him.

"I'll take that as a 'No,'" he said and left to take care of Hank.

I finished the water and set the empty bottle on the coffee table. I kicked off my shoes and stretched out on the couch. I closed my eyes and drifted off into sleep, hoping I would not dream.

But later, I did.

Chapter Seventeen

onday morning slipped clear and bright into my room, but I still woke up late and exhausted. I had managed to make it upstairs from the couch to my bed but had spent the night tossing and turning and moving from one nightmare into another, all of them ugly replays of the suffering and pain I had seen yesterday, when Brandywine had patted the back of my hand. I was grateful when my eyes finally opened.

I pushed the bedclothes back, got up, and pulled on my sweats. I made it down the stairs without falling to my death and checked in the office.

No Jonah.

I dragged myself to the kitchen to start my coffee and found a note from him.

Back soon. Wait for me.

He hadn't added, *or I'll break your neck,* so I figured he had forgiven me for yesterday.

I glanced at the clock as I started the brewer and saw that it was almost noon. I had slept way longer than I thought I had, but that was no reason not to drink coffee.

Which I did in the backyard at the patio table, where Jonah found me with my head back, eyes closed, letting the bright rays burn away all the horrible images from yesterday at Brandfield and the terrifying ones in my dreams last night. I opened my eyes and straightened in my chair.

"Hey," I said.

"Hey," he said and sat down. He looked me over and asked, "How are you feeling?"

"Like hammered shit," I said and told him about the dreams. Then I asked, "Where've you been?"

He looked at my empty mug.

"Let me get you a refill, and we'll talk," he said.

When he returned and sat down again, I said, "So?"

"So, I've been thinking," he said, and I had to stop myself from groaning.

Jonah was nothing if not methodical, while I was the furthest thing from it, even when I was not feeling as lousy as I felt today. All I wanted was a straight answer to a simple question. What I was about to get, I knew, was a slow, step-by-step analysis of where we were in this case and where we were going with it, the recitation of which was only going to add to how lousy I was already feeling.

But I sipped my coffee and pretended to be patient and listening closely. After yesterday's screwup, I knew I deserved this punishment and should take it like a man rather than a bored, obnoxious teenager. So I stuffed a passive-aggressive sigh, stifled an eye-roll, and did the best I could to look interested as Jo began ticking items off an organized mental list.

"I'm going to begin with what we know, Dev, and the first thing is that Brandywine has been deceptive with us from the beginning. Then there are the employees you've encountered, who are twisted at best and criminal at worst. We've been on this case for a week, with nothing to show for it other than getting a poor old dog killed. The honest thing for us to do is quit. But after what happened yesterday and what we've learned about Brandywine so far, we can't be sure what the consequences might be if we do or how far they would extend. If I had to gamble, I'd say it's not worth the risk right now.

"At the same time, for as much as Ellis Brandywine seems unhappy with us, he would rather intimidate than fire us. Why? What's his game here?

"Next there's the background work I've done that says he's made some business enemies but none who hate him enough to want to kill him. And Brandywine, himself, is adamant that it's his third wife who is doing him in. Why? And if it's true, why the hell stay married to her? What does he get out of that?

"And why so little interest in the second wife as a suspect? What do they know about her that they aren't telling us? Why hasn't she shown up on any of my searches if she isn't actually hiding? Granted, I haven't had time to do any in-depth searches on her, but even googling her name should have turned up something," he said.

"So?" I repeated and drank some coffee to wash down another groan.

"So I decided that, before we spent any more time looking for B2, I wanted to be sure we weren't spinning our wheels."

"What do you mean?" I said.

"I mean we've been employed to find the bodies of the Brandywine twins. But we learn Brandywine really believes they're alive. Why? He also wants us to find out who is slowly killing him—a job he should have the police do but apparently doesn't want them involved. Why? We ask Lana Troy about the second wife, Aubrey, and get shut down. Why? What are they hiding about her? Did B2 leave Colorado? The country? Is she dead? Buried out there at Brandfield in the middle of nowhere?"

Which made me think of the big-headed, empty-faced gardener. Yeah, that was a job I could see him doing.

I could also see all of those "whys" piling up behind Jonah's eyes and taking his level of determination from normal to mission-focused.

"We don't have time for ghost hunting," he said.

"We don't, but that doesn't tell me where you've been this morning," I said, lifting my cup for another sip when he told me.

"Denver Women's," he said, and I set my cup down.

I stared at him, looking for the reason on his face, but "cop quiet" isn't readable or forthcoming.

I knew the surprise on my face was both, but I asked anyway.

"Why?" I said.

"To get a feel for Charlotte Brandywine myself, Dev."

"And?" I said.

"And I can see why you had a tough time trying to explain her to me."

And although the corroboration was nice to have, it was no help with how I was feeling or the doubt that had been plaguing me since I woke up.

But I had to know.

"Now that you've met her, Jo, do you think I was wrong? Could she have done it? Faked the twins' drowning and had Brandywine poisoned, like he believes?"

Jonah thought for a moment.

"I think it's like you said before, Dev—no, but not a-hundred-percent-sure no. My gut says there's something more to Brandywine's insistence that Charlotte is his murderer and more to his obsession with finding the bodies of his children."

"And more with whatever the hell is going on inside that creepy mansion," I added, remembering Charlotte's sudden fear at the mention of Glandon's name and her warning to me to stay away from Brandfield. "But how do we find out what's really going on without going back and confronting him?"

"By finding the second wife and talking to her," he said. "Because even if her marriage to Brandywine was short, I think she knows something about him and Brandfield that we need to know, too."

"Does that mean Charlotte told you B2 is alive?" I said, and Jonah shook his head.

"I didn't ask her," he said, and I gave him a look that, roughly translated, meant, "What the hell?"

Before I could translate that verbally into something more vulgar, Jonah held up a hand like a stop sign.

"Hear me out," he said and continued on in that slow, grating pace. "I didn't go there to grill Charlotte for information. I went for confirmation that B2 might be alive."

"Which I'm guessing you got," I said. "How?"

"I asked her if Ellis Brandywine had ever talked about his second wife. Charlotte said 'No.' I asked if she had any reason to believe that Aubrey was dead. She said 'No.'"

"How does that help us?" I said, tamping down another groan.

"Because, as strange as it sounds," said Jonah, "Charlotte Brandywine may be a murderer, but I don't think she's a liar. Remember, she never said she *didn't* kill her twins. And this morning she *didn't* say that she believed Aubrey Brandywine was dead."

"So we're going to keep looking for B2," I said.

"We are," Jo said. "Because I've never known a live person to disappear this cleanly unless they were hiding from the law or they knew something they were afraid would get them killed if it came out. Either way, I think we need to know the *why* and the *what* B2 knows if we're going to figure out *why* Ellis Brandywine *really* hired us and *how* he was poisoned."

"Then, what's next?" I asked.

"Hank's funeral is on Wednesday afternoon," said Jonah.

"What's Mrs. K going to do with the ashes?" I said, flushing with anger as the ugly memory of Lana Troy holding up Hank's name tag slammed into my mind.

"She wants to bury the ashes where she found Hank. She said it was his favorite spot in the yard."

"Makes sense," I said, glad that something in this convoluted mess did.

"In the meantime, I'm going to start looking for B2."

"I can help," I offered, but Jonah shook his head.

"You need more rest," he said as he stood up and started for the house.

"Oh, by the way," he tossed over his shoulder as he left, "Charlotte said to tell you 'Hi.'"

I was about to smile until he added, with a laugh, "Nell did, too."

Chapter Eighteen

I finished the coffee Jonah had brought me, questioning my ability to run this case and wondering if I was letting him down.

As a cop, he had faced his share of dangerous situations—domestic violence calls with an armed perp, drunks with bats and grievances, and once a charging Rottweiler with an owner more rabid than the dog.

He had been able to diffuse most of the instances with patience and calm words, or, in the case of the Rottweiler, a zap from a taser and a shot of pepper spray for the owner. Other times, he had taken some punches, and twice he had needed stitches, but he had never gone down.

I, on the other hand, had fainted from nothing more than a malevolent bastard's touch.

I wandered my eyes around the yard while I chewed my lip and worried if Jonah's faith in me was misplaced. Maybe I was not the one who should be dealing with Ellis Brandywine and handling a job I had agreed to take out of emotion rather than sense, a job growing with danger at every turn.

My stomach growled. I got up and carried my empty coffee cup inside to find that Jonah had brought home a couple of deli sandwiches for lunch. We ate them standing in the kitchen and discussing the baseball season. Afterwards, he went to his desk and back to his computer search, and I went to the living room. I sat down on the couch and switched the flat screen on and my doubts off for a while.

Neither Jonah nor I watched much television, but I did like old movies. It was a good thing I had already seen (many times) the one I'd put on, because I kept dozing off. But I did not dream, and I woke up feeling better.

Late in the day, I poked around in the fridge and was reminded why Jonah was a good PI and a great roommate. He always thought ahead. Like now, for instance.

When Jonah had returned from the prison visit, he had not just brought lunch from the deli. He had brought home dinner, too—steaks and a Greek salad. I fired up the grill and seared the steaks. He opened a beer, and I went with ice water. We ate in the backyard and talked about how his search was going and how much better I was feeling. What we did not talk about was the demand for an update that we both knew would be coming from Brandfield in a few days. But that would be my problem, and I had time to decide how I would handle it.

Jonah and I were up early on Tuesday. We spent the day electronically scouring public government databases and private school records for leads on Aubrey Brandywine.

Nothing.

We went to Hank's funeral on Wednesday. I brought Melvin his promised catnip, and Jo and I went straight back to the search afterwards. But at the end of the day, no trace of B2.

Mrs. Koselke dropped off a plate of thick fudgy brownies around lunchtime on Thursday. They were almost gone before dinner.

And still not a hint of B2.

Alexander sent an email Friday morning looking for that week's update. I gritted my teeth and called Lana Troy.

I told her that we were reconsidering Charlotte as the possible poisoner and about Jonah's visit to the prison, sure that Ellis Brandywine had people at the women's facility on his payroll and that he would know anyway.

I said we still had nothing on the twins but lied and said we were looking at the backgrounds of any prison employees who had regular contact with Charlotte. It made sense, I said, that she had to have had help if she was the one behind the poisoning of our mutual (if highly psychotic and deeply deserving) boss. What I did not tell Ms. Troy was that Jonah and I had decided to downplay to her our search for Aubrey Brandywine.

During the call, I'd had to choke down the bitter pill of having to admit to Lana Troy that she had been right about Brandywine's first wife not having the mental wherewithal to harm her ex-husband.

Ms. Troy, cold and as aloof as ever, said we needed to stop wasting our employer's dwindling time and concentrate on what we were hired to do. Namely, find the bodies of the twins and find out how Charlotte had him poisoned.

I was grateful when she ended the call as she always did—abruptly—but was left wondering why, with that dwindling time Ms. Troy had referenced, did Ellis Brandywine continue to be fixated on Charlotte as his murderer and finding the twins? Even if he was right about Charlotte having him poisoned, she was already in prison for the rest of her life for murder. And even if the twins were alive, it was not like he was going to have a sudden return to good health or time for a quick game of hide the meds or polish the oxygen bottle.

Like Jonah, I could not help but believe there was something else going on here, that Brandywine had involved us in a game he was playing, a variation of the one he had been playing since childhood.

And maybe that was why, if B2 was alive, she did not want to be found by him or anyone else connected to Brandfield. With Ellis Brandywine being what he had always been, it was a safe bet that Aubrey had been a victim of his sadistic psychological games, too. If so, it was possible she had been left as mentally broken by them as Rebecca. Or maybe she was functional but lived in fear of being made a Brandywine toy again.

Maybe, I considered, finding Aubrey Brandywine and pressing her for answers would help us with our case. Maybe it would be a huge and expensive waste of time. Either way, there were too many questions surrounding this woman, and Jonah and I were not going to leave them unanswered. But we had, by mutual agreement, decided that we were not necessarily going to share all the answers with anyone at Brandfield.

And so we moved on.

When Jonah was a cop, he was a good one. When he was a detective, he was better. He was relentless in his pursuit of a perp, and what had made him successful in closing cases was that he knew when to drop a line of investigation that was not working, open his mind to other possibilities, and look in a different direction. In this case, it took the form of going back to go forward.

The young Aubrey Guinevere Phelps had graduated from the University of Denver with honors and a master's degree in Child, Family, and School Psychology. Her parents had split their time between the States and Europe. But Aubrey's father had recently passed away, and her mother had moved to London permanently. Her older sister lived in Italy with her family, her brother in Washington, DC. All of them had refused Jonah's calls. He had already been in touch with as many of Aubrey's sorority sisters and classmates as he could find. None of them had heard from her in years.

Dead end.

On Saturday morning, I still had no useful ideas percolating and decided I needed to take a break. I put an overnight bag and a couple of camaras in the SUV and headed for Vail. Jonah was already up and gone for a long bike ride when I left. I came home Sunday afternoon to find that Jonah and Mrs. K had been to the animal shelter. They had returned with Mutt and Jeff.

Jeff was an undersized, geriatric pit bull scheduled to be euthanized, and Mutt was just that—a small, surrendered mutt but Jeff's inseparable buddy at the shelter. Mrs. K would not have dreamed of splitting up the pair when she met them, and, besides, she said, her backyard was big enough for them both. How Melvin would react to the new family members was going to be the wildcard.

And Jonah's inspiration.

Jo got up Monday morning thinking about Aubrey's degree. He printed out the list of sorority sisters and their phone numbers. He split the list between us, and we began calling them, this time not to ask where Aubrey might be, but to ask *about* her, the kind of person she was.

They all said the same thing.

Aubrey Phelps was a hard worker, a loyal friend, always fun to be with, and she loved Colorado and the mountains. That was why it was surprising that she had pretty much dropped off the map after she had gotten married. She had been very outgoing and dedicated to everything involving children. She volunteered with Special Olympics. She helped in classrooms and with after-school programs when she had the time. She looked forward to having her own babies and maybe adopting special-needs children or opening her home to older, harder-to-place kids. Everything about her screamed *family and a bright future*.

And then she had met Ellis Brandywine at a fundraiser for a children's shelter.

He was more than twenty years older than Aubrey, and the sorority sisters who had been to the event with her had not only been unimpressed with him—they had been repulsed. They said they felt as if he were watching them, sizing them up as if shopping for a good brood mare. One even said she thought he should be on a sex-offender's list for the way he looked at them.

But Aubrey could not see it, and the next thing any of them knew, she was married to him and gone. No one was really surprised when she had called a couple of them three months later to tell them she was pregnant. They just wondered what kind of a father Ellis Brandywine would be. She had also shared some lunch dates in Denver after that with a few of her other college friends. Other than that contact, she had disappeared so completely, none of them had realized the relationship had ended until Brandywine's marriage to Charlotte had hit the society news a few years later.

And it was those memories that gave Jonah the new direction he needed.

He reasoned that, since Ellis Brandywine had ostensibly hired Mecklan Personal Services to find the bodies of his dead twins, Jonah could not see Brandywine easily giving up custody of a living child. But there were no records of Aubrey's pregnancy ending in a live birth. And no matter what had happened during her marriage to Ellis, Jonah could not believe a person like Aubrey would have changed drastically enough to stop loving children or end her desire to have or adopt them.

That's when Jonah stopped looking for Aubrey Brandywine and started looking for her children.

Thinking it was a safe bet that, even if B2 had had biological children of her own, Jonah believed Aubrey, much like Mrs. Koselke and her animal menagerie, would have also made room in her heart and her home for other kids who would have needed a family, too. And this is where Jonah's past came into play.

In his capacity as a DPD detective, his career had overlapped by a couple of years with a Denver district attorney named Randall Stevens. DA Stevens, much like Jonah, was relentless in his prosecution of criminals—especially pedophiles and child abusers. But he also had young children of his own who would eventually go to college.

So, after twelve years of cases, trials, and convictions, and with future tuition bills in mind, Randall Stevens had left the DA's office and gone into private practice. And when he learned that Jonah had left the DPD, Randall often hired Mecklan Personal Services to locate deadbeat parents and do background checks on potential clients who he thought to be a little shady. Once, Jo had even been needed to hide a battered wife until her soon-to-be-ex's case went to trial and the violent asshole was convicted, sentenced, and out of her life permanently.

Stevens also handled private adoptions.

Tuesday morning, Jonah made a call to Randall Stevens. Tuesday afternoon, they met for lunch, and Jonah explained why he was looking for her. Wednesday afternoon, Randall Stevens called Jonah. Thursday morning, I was on I-25 north to the home of Gwen Smith, aka Aubrey Guinevere Phelps Brandywine.

Chapter Nineteen

It was short notice, but Jonah had prepared me as well as he could for this meeting. That was why I knew when I parked in front of her house that Gwen Smith lived in a five-bedroom, four-and-a half-bathroom, three-car-garage, quad-level home in the upscale Huntington Hills neighborhood of Fort Collins, Colorado. Clubhouse. Pool. Excellent schools. Close to parks and running trails.

Had to admit, the place had curb appeal.

I also knew as I made my way up the flower-lined walk to her front door that Gwen Smith was a stay-at-home mother of four and that her African-American husband, Quinn, was also Professor Smith, who taught in the college of agricultural sciences at Colorado State University.

What I did not know as I took the three steps up to the covered front porch was the kind of reception I would get from Mrs. Smith.

In his call-back to Jonah on Wednesday afternoon, Randall Stevens explained that he had permission to tell him that Aubrey Brandywine was now Gwen Smith. He also said that he had handled her third adoption eight years ago—a little girl who had lost her hearing as a victim of shaken-baby syndrome and had needed more help than foster care could provide—and that he had checked out Gwen and Quinn thoroughly at the time. That's why he believed Jonah to be completely off-base about her. But Gwen had told him that she had nothing to hide and would be happy to meet with anyone from Mecklan Personal Services. Randall warned Jonah that she was a woman who spoke bluntly and to be prepared for direct, intimidating eye contact from her.

And while I would be spending most of my day on the Aubrey/Gwen field trip, Jonah would be looking into the backgrounds of the staff at the Denver Women's Corrections Facility. I had told Lana Troy we were doing that, so she would be expecting a report about it soon anyway. It was time consuming, but the plus was that it would give us cover while we also looked for anyone who might be keeping tabs on Charlotte and reporting to Brandywine. While Charlotte, Jonah, and I knew her husband well enough to be sure he was doing just that, it would be satisfying to know that Nell would have specific identities to go with any arms she might need to crush.

Standing on the porch, I gathered my thoughts together and rang the bell.

The door opened, and I was pleasantly surprised to be greeted by an athletically trim woman in denim shorts and a bright yellow tank top. Her smile was warm and welcoming, and her large eyes were almost as dark as her lustrous black hair that she had captured high on the back of her head in a thick, wavy ponytail.

"Hello," she said in a voice that was as warm as her smile and touched, I couldn't help but notice, with a hint of sultry.

"Mrs. Smith?" I checked, having expected, I guess, a woman who looked harried or bothered or more obviously on her way to forty instead of someone so relaxed and calm and, um, fit. But she nodded, and I continued, "My name is Devon West. I'm from Mecklan Personal Services."

"Oh, yes," she said, opening the door further and better revealing her long, tanned, and well-toned legs. "Randall said you'd be dropping by. Please come in."

"Thank you," I said and stepped into a wide, tiled foyer centered between a large dining room to my left and a formal living room on my right, where a young girl with strawberry-blond hair was lounging on a couch, reading a book. She seemed so deeply engrossed in the story that she had not noticed my arrival.

Gwen shut the door behind me.

"If you'd excuse me for a moment, Mr. West, this is my daughter, Ellie. I need to speak with her."

She went to the girl and tapped her on the shoulder. Ellie looked up and waited while Gwen's hands moved in a flurry of signed words. The girl nodded, closed her book, and placed it on the coffee table. She stood to leave the room, and, as she passed me, she smiled, bobbed her head in a quick greeting, and left. Somewhere from the back of the house, I heard the sound of a sliding glass door swish open and closed, and then Gwen spoke again.

"Would you mind if we talked in the kitchen while I make sandwiches? I'm babysitting some of the neighbor kids, and I promised everyone lunch was almost ready."

I followed her through to the bright, sunny kitchen that stretched almost the complete width across the house back here. I looked out to see a yard full of kids who ranged in age from a toddler up to middle-schoolers. Ellie was pushing the toddler, a little girl wearing a bandage that covered her left eye and much of the facial area surrounding it, on a swing.

"Wow," I said, counting eight kids and all of them in motion.

Gwen laughed.

"Have a seat," she said and pointed to a high stool at the end of the island, where she had been preparing the sandwiches. "Can I get you anything? Water? Coffee?"

"Ice water would be great," I told her.

She fixed a tall glass of it and brought it to me.

"Thanks," I said and drank some while she got busy making the rest of the sandwiches.

And this is where Jonah had me beat hands down. He would not have set foot on the porch of the Smith homestead without a complete mental plan of approach, a list of questions he would ask, and the order he would ask them in.

I, on the other hand, was looking around and thinking about asking to use the bathroom when I noticed a smile playing around the edges of Gwen's lips.

She cut the sandwich she was making in half and set the pieces on a platter stacked with other halves. She pulled two more slices of bread from a package and started another sandwich.

"You don't know where to start, do you?" she said.

"Well," I said and cleared my throat, feeling embarrassed and a little turned on.

I know. I know.

Sick, right?

But there is something about smart, assertive women that I find intensely sensual, and Gwen Smith was all that. What can I say? I'm a guy. Or maybe I was born with a few strands of pig DNA. And as much as I hated to give Ellis Brandywine credit for anything, I had to admit that he had great taste in women.

I was trying to figure out what to say or do next when Gwen smiled and asked, "Did you have troubling finding me?"

"No," I said. "GPS did all the work."

She laughed again and said, "Not my house, Mr. West, *me.*"

I felt my face turn red and had to stop myself from smacking my forehead for being the obtuse idiot that I was.

"As a matter of fact, yes," I said, hoping to recover a little dignity with a shot of honesty. "And please call me 'Dev.'"

"I will, which means it's only fair that you call me 'Gwen.' And I want you to know I'm glad that you found me, Dev."

That brought my eyebrows up.

"It's true," she said. "Besides my parents and my therapist, my husband is the only person who knows what happened to me during my marriage to Ellis Brandywine. I told Quinn everything when he proposed to me. I thought he should know what a mess of a woman I was before he committed to spending the rest of his life with me."

She finished the last sandwich, sliced it in half, and put the two pieces on the platter with the others. While she went to an over-sized refrigerator, I glanced out to the large backyard again.

The activity out there struck me as chaos—but safe, organized chaos. And other than Ellie, I had no idea which kids out there were Gwen's other three, although I was guessing that the bandaged toddler was one of them. The rest seemed to be grouped by friendship. There was a scrum-like game of tag going on with some kids in the six-to-nine age range, and two tall, thin boys—one black, one white—standing apart, kicking a soccer ball back and forth between them.

I shook my head.

"I don't think a mess of a woman could run an operation like this, Gwen. At least not this smoothly."

That got me another smile as she closed the fridge and returned to the work island with a pitcher of lemonade. She placed it on a tray with plastic tumblers, paper plates, and napkins.

"I said *was*, Dev. And would you mind giving me a hand?" she asked with a glance at the sandwiches.

"Not at all," I said and picked up the tray, prepared to carry it out to the backyard or barefoot over hot coals for her.

God, I'm easy.

Outside, a long picnic table stood near the swing-set in the yard, and a large, round patio table with cushioned chairs sat tucked under the awninged back porch. We set the platter and tray on the patio table next to a bowl piled with apples, bananas, and oranges, and Gwen filled tumblers with lemonade. I stepped back and watched the kids help themselves to sandwiches, fruit, and drinks. They were all polite and patient, and each said their thanks before separating themselves into groups between the two tables. After she reminded them to clean up when they were done and their promises that they would, Gwen and I went back inside.

She refilled my glass of ice water and fixed herself a glass of iced tea. She carried her glass to the kitchen table, and I picked up mine and followed.

"I hope you don't mind if we sit here to talk, Dev. The older kids are good about helping with the younger ones, but I still like to keep an eye on them."

Gwen took a place at the table that allowed her a clear view of the backyard through the sliding glass door. I chose a chair across from her and sat down. I drank some of my ice water and watched Gwen over the rim of my glass.

Her warm, maternal gaze floated over the yard and her happy brood. She honest-to-God glowed with her love for them. I set my glass down and wondered if she was a woman at peace with whatever had gone on in her past or one so fiercely protective that she would kill to keep her loved ones safe.

Probably both, I thought, and realized I had the questions I needed answered.

Did Gwen Smith, the former B2, have some reason to consider Ellis Brandywine a threat to her or to her family? And if she did, what would she be willing to do to protect them, or, worse, what might she have done already?

"Gwen," I said, and she pulled her gaze away from the children.

There was a soft smile on her face, but tears were glistening in her dark eyes now. I guessed she was steeling herself for the conversation to come, but it didn't make me feel like any less of a dirtbag for being the person who was there to make her have it.

I waited while she readied herself, recalling while I did, delicate, broken Rebecca Brandywine searching for her lost baby and the excruciating pain I had experienced when she had clutched my hand in hers. I thought of Charlotte in depressing prison garb, controlling her fear but radiating emotional pain for the loss of her twins as she sat across the table from me, concerned for my safety and warning me to end this case and never to go back to Brandfield.

And here I sat now making another woman, one who had wanted only to love and help the most vulnerable beings that life produced, dredge up a part of her personal history that she had escaped from, the smallest memory of which still caused her immense and obvious pain.

For a moment, I considered getting up and walking out, apologizing while I did for being the insensitive schmuck who was making her relive the anguish and not caring if she was the person doing the world a favor by removing Ellis Brandywine from this earth.

But then I thought of that prick teamed with Laurence Glandon, Lana Troy, and Alexander. I pictured Mrs. K and her tears for Hank Spitball and the old dog's unnecessary, spiteful death. I also thought of Jonah—and anyone else important to me—and Brandywine's threats to hurt them all. It was enough to keep me seated, but I needed a deep breath to steel myself, too.

I was about to speak when Gwen surprised me.

"Before we start," she said, "I have something for you."

Chapter Twenty

Two and a half hours later, I merged onto I-25 south on my way back to Denver. That "something" that Gwen had had for me—a large, worn manila envelope containing the information Gwen's father had gathered on Ellis Brandywine more than a decade ago—lay on the seat beside me. The sinking feeling I had lay wedged with the weight of an anvil in my gut.

Gwen's history of her first marriage should not have taken long to tell, but there had been interruptions—Ellie bringing in the bandaged toddler, Carmella, for her nap before returning to her book in the living room—little Carmella, who had been in her biological mother's arms when the pleading, terrified woman had been shot in the head by her insanely jealous husband.

The father had used his second shot to blow apart his own head and avoid justice, but the damage had been done. High-velocity bone fragments from her mother's skull had destroyed the sight in Carmella's left eye. She had been with the Smiths for only eight months when a last small shard had worked its way to the surface and had needed to be removed surgically. The bandage the toddler was wearing now would come off in a few days, but the Smiths would love Carmella for the rest of her life.

And Embende—he went by Ben—had stepped inside to ask Gwen a question. Ben had been born in Uganda, orphaned by disease, abandoned by relatives because of his club feet, and was a year old when Quinn had begun his Peace Corps time there. Quinn had become attached to him and was able to adopt Ben and bring him home to Colorado. Gwen had been volunteering on the children's floor at the hospital where Quinn had brought Ben to have his feet fixed. It was how the three of them had met, fallen in love, and become the nucleus of the Smith family.

So there were starts and stops in Gwen's recounting but none in her strength or honesty. The beginning of her story was a repetition of Charlotte's—young, happy, and swept off her feet by a warm, dashing (if much older than her) Ellis Brandywine. Ignoring her family's concerns, Gwen was married and pregnant almost immediately, after which the real EJB began to show flashes of his cold, sadistic self.

It was at this point in her story that Ellie had brought Carmella in for her nap. Gwen had taken the sleepy toddler from Ellie's arms and upstairs to her crib. While she was gone, I thought about Rebecca and what it must have been like for her living in the dark, depressing atmosphere of Brandfield, at the mercy of Ellis and his cruel mental games, helpless in the hands of Merrick Glandon, and watched with laughing disdain by the cold, domineering Eleanora. My anger had burned, my temper had risen, and I had shaken my head in disgust for the gentle Rebecca, whose fragile mind, I was sure, had not had a snowball's chance in hell against a triumvirate of evil and darkness like that.

And again, I thought of getting up and walking out before causing Gwen any more pain, but what stopped me this time was every reason I had given myself before, plus the determination to learn everything I could about Ellis Brandywine in order to find an edge or a weakness or a way to deliver justice—or, hell, just some plain, damn payback for Rebecca, Charlotte, and every other innocent person damaged or destroyed by either Brandywine or their dangerous employees. My face must have once again betrayed me, because, when Gwen returned to the kitchen, she had stopped a moment before sitting down and asked if I was okay.

I had lied and said that I was, and she had continued.

I never liked Brandfield, Dev. It was dark and dreary and so far east. In a house full of servants, I always felt alone. I missed Denver and my friends, and seeing the mountains every day. But I was quickly pregnant and deliriously happy about becoming a mother, even though Ellis's attitude toward me had already begun to change. I excused the behavior, put it down to a natural period of adjustment or the difference in our ages. But I could not excuse Laurence Glandon's constant, hovering presence. I felt like I was under a microscope whenever he was around.

To make matters worse, Ellis insisted that I get all of my obstetrical care from Glandon.

We had a terrible, screaming fight about that. I threatened to jump off the roof rather than let Glandon touch me. We compromised that I would get my own doctor in Denver, but I would allow Glandon to do the first ultrasound to determine the sex of the baby. I didn't know it then, of course, but that ultrasound would be the end of my marriage and almost my sanity.

Gwen needed to stop for a moment at that point in her recounting, and that's when Ben had tapped on the patio door before sliding it open. She introduced me, and Ben greeted me respectfully; then he asked for permission to go to the park with Jimmy to play soccer with friends. She gave it, but like any good mother, she reminded him to check in with her and told him how late they could stay.

Before they left, Jimmy, who had been welcomed into the Smith home after his mother, a woman who had fallen into a suicidal depression and given up custody of Jimmy when he was a little guy, waved from the patio and gave his adoptive mother a beautiful smile that seemed to brighten even more the bustling, sunny backyard. Gwen had smiled back, and a quick conversation in sign language had taken place. Gwen laughed and seemed centered again. But she noticed my quizzical look and explained that Jimmy was not hearing impaired. The whole family had learned sign language in order to better communicate with Ellie.

Jimmy had, however, gone through a spy phase when he was eight. Signing had been his form of secret communication, and Gwen had been his handler, who sent him on his missions. She said she had lost track of how many times Jimmy had saved the world from destruction and told me that even if she could remember, she could not tell me. That information was classified. I laughed at that, and, with the mood lightened, she went on.

I found an OB in Denver that I trusted and was comfortable with. Ellis always accompanied me to my checkups, and I was naïve enough to find that touching rather than controlling. But at eighteen weeks, less than five months into my pregnancy, Ellis insisted that I fulfill my end of the bargain and allow Glandon to do the promised ultrasound. I was still sickened at the thought of that ghoul touching me, but Ellis had kept his word, so we picked the afternoon when I would keep mine.

I had interrupted Gwen there because, in all of Jonah's background research, it occurred to me that I had not seen an address listed for an office or a clinic anywhere in Colorado where either of the two Glandons had practiced. Dr. Morley had said Merrick Glandon's records proved he had been operating on some of his patients from Sunridge, but I knew for sure I had not seen the name of any hospital where uncle or nephew had had medical privileges. I was curious as to where the ultrasound had been done. Gwen's answer had left her hugging herself as if from a sudden chill and the tips of my fingers tingling.

He did it there. Right there in the basement at Brandfield. There is a single-purpose elevator hidden behind a panel in Ellis's office. I was shaking as I stepped into it with him. He had shown me the upper rooms in Brandfield but never the basement. He had always referred to it as Laurence's domain and said no one ever went down there without his or Laurence's permission.

Looking back, I think Ellis knew how much I was dreading the ultrasound that afternoon, and, rather than wanting to comfort me, he was enjoying my dread. But I didn't have time to dwell on that because the ride down was quick and soundless. I told myself I would be fine until the elevator stopped, the doors opened, and I saw what looked like the lobby of any doctor's office. The area was large, and the ceiling was high. I knew I was in the basement of the dark, gloomy mansion, but, down there, the lighting was done in such a way as to give the impression of bright sunlight flooding in.

I was already anxious, and now I was frightened and disoriented, too. Up was down, and down was up. I was hit by a wave of vertigo. I remember reaching for Ellis's hand to steady myself. I gripped it, but he didn't squeeze mine back, leaving me holding nothing but hard bone and thin, cold flesh. I couldn't think what to do other than get the ultrasound over with and get back upstairs as quickly as possible. I let go of Ellis's hand and stepped out of the elevator.

I was moving along smoothly in the left lane of traffic when I checked my rearview mirror and saw a jerk in a big, black pickup truck flying up on my tail. I have never been a guy who thought any roadway, particularly one filled with speeding, two-ton boxes of steel, was the appropriate venue to launch into a duel over dick size. Irritated, I put my blinker on, eased into the right lane and let him bully his way by wishing there was a cop around to nail his reckless ass.

But truthfully, I knew I was irritated more by his interrupting my recollection of Gwen's narrative than by his dangerous driving, because I was getting the itchy feeling that I was close to something important, something floating in the back of my mind just out of reach and understanding.

All three women, Rebecca, Charlotte, and Gwen, were part of a sick, psychological puzzle, I was sure, but were there pieces missing, or was I putting the pieces I had together wrong?

And how much time did Jonah and I have to figure this out? Could we chase dead ends until Ellis Brandywine became one himself and was no longer a threat? Or would there be another dead-pet reminder before then, an injured Mrs. K, a battered Jonah, or a dead me?

I was betting that Ellis had never been a patient man when it came to employees. It was obvious that he liked giving orders and having them obeyed instantly by any gender. But it seemed to be women specifically that he most enjoyed tormenting, toying with them, slowly destroying their self-worth and their minds. I felt rather than knew that I was close to an answer tied to his victims, although that feeling was nothing compared to the tangle of emotions beginning to burn inside me like a glowing pile of smoldering embers.

I put my blinker on again and eased back into the left lane. I picked up speed and continued with my recall of Gwen's story and the angst that filled her voice all of these years later, as she had shared the dread of stepping out of that elevator without any emotional support. I was reaching for Gwen's hand in a belated offer of comfort and protection when there had been a knock at the front door.

A woman had come to claim the last four kids in the backyard. Two were hers, and the other two were their cousins. She was a neighborhood friend who'd had a hair appointment that morning, and Gwen had been happy to babysit for her. After the woman had wrangled the noisy, eight-armed squad of giggling, squirming energy out the door, the house had fallen silent. Gwen had needed a moment to gather herself but had been able to finish her story.

I had braced myself physically and mentally to get through the ultrasound. What I had not braced myself for were the results. Ellis and I were going to have a daughter, which was wonderful. But during the procedure, my budding little girl had moved. The left side of her tiny head could be seen clearly, and it was completely smooth. It was a terrible shock for me. I had loved that baby from the moment I knew I was pregnant and hadn't thought I could love her more than I already did. But in that moment, my love swelled, along with a fierce resolve to help and protect her.

Fool that I was, I had again looked to Ellis for support. What I got from him was a look of disgust while that toad, Glandon, shook his big, square head and "tsk-tsked" about the deformity being "a shame but interesting." I was left to clean myself up and straighten my clothes while the two of them stepped away to talk.

I was too upset to catch more than a few sentences of their discussion, but it wasn't until much later that I realized I should have paid close attention. Glandon was saying something about waiting, but Ellis's face looked hard, and he was shaking his head "No." I was already crying, but now I was angry, too. Their backs were turned to me while they argued about "timing" and Glandon needing "a couple of days to prepare." They didn't notice me leave the room. I was looking for the elevator but feeling like I was making an escape.

As I said, stepping out of that elevator earlier had been disorienting. Now everything became bizarre. I made a wrong turn into a short, wide corridor. There were four doors set two and two across from each other. The two on the right were open, and I saw they were fully furnished hospital rooms. The other two doors were closed, but I was sure I heard whimpering coming from behind the one nearest to me. I put my hand on the door and was about to push it open when I heard Ellis shout for me to stop.

I looked over my shoulder, and Ellis and Glandon were right on me. Ellis looked furious, and Glandon had a sickening sneer on his face. He slipped behind me while Ellis put an arm around my shoulders and turned me away from the hospital-room door. I will never forget the sound of Ellis's voice or what happened next.

"You've had a terrible shock, Aubrey. You need to rest now," he said, and there was something so smooth, so evil in his tone that I felt as if I were wrapped in the arms of Satan himself. Then I felt a sharp jab in my neck. Hours later, I woke up in our bedroom with a note on my nightstand from Ellis. It said he had been called to New York on a business emergency but would be home in a few days.

I didn't care that he was gone, partly because I was so devastated by his behavior at the ultrasound and partly because of whatever they had drugged me with had left me woozy.

But I should have cared, Dev. I should have cared deeply.

Chapter Twenty-One

Gwen was right. She should have cared but, at the time, she had not recognized the vein of misogyny in Ellis's behavior or known any of the long, ugly Brandywine history well enough to understand what kind of danger she and her unborn baby were in.

I had known Ellis Brandywine for only a couple of weeks myself but, at that point in Gwen's story, my fingertips were stinging, and the hot knot in my stomach had swelled into a searing ball of avenging anger. The recollection of her story as I drove was enough to upset me again, along with the growing traffic that was slowing everything to a crawl on the highway. I was as far as Johnstown now and saw the billboard advertising Johnson's Corner.

I moved back into the right lane and took the exit to the service road and around to the parking lot of the truck stop that served "good food and plenty of it." I wasn't hungry, but I needed coffee and could have used a sugar rush, and they served cinnamon rolls as big as dinner plates.

I parked and grabbed the envelope from Gwen off the empty passenger seat. I went inside, got a booth, and ordered.

I sipped my coffee while I shuffled through the papers and waited for my roll. I was trying to concentrate on the info in front of me, but my mind kept drifting to the end of Gwen's story. How she had lain in bed for two days listless and sad, and barely eating. Ellis had returned the morning of the third day. When he found her there, he had berated her for being "selfish and pitiful and a terrible disappointment."

She had gotten angry enough to force herself out of bed with her mind made up. She was going to pull herself together, pack some things, and go back to Denver for a while. She told him she needed time to think, to figure out how this was going to affect their marriage. The last thing she remembered was starting for the bathroom when something hit her on the side of her head, and she collapsed.

I looked up and saw my waitress approaching with my giant roll. I pushed the papers aside to make room for the plate she set down in front of me. I stared at it with my mouth hanging open while she refilled my coffee cup and laughed.

"We get that reaction a lot," she said and walked away.

I shook off my momentary paralysis and attacked the pile of warm, sugary calories with a knife and fork. I devoured a third of the doughy bliss while my memory continued on with the rest of Gwen's ordeal.

I woke up in one of Glandon's hospital beds, not knowing how many hours or days I had lain there. I was groggy, and it took a bit for my head to clear and realize that Ellis was standing beside me. There was an odd gleam in his eyes and a look of pure satisfaction on his face, as if he had gotten the better of someone in a big financial deal or was in the afterglow of something sexual. He said I had slipped in the shower and that the fall had caused me to miscarry. He watched as I started to cry. Then he smiled a horrible, cruel smile.

He said, "Goodbye, Aubrey," and left.

The next time I woke up, a housemaid was there with some of my clothes. Once I was dressed, an odd-looking man I sometimes saw standing outside in the yard came into the room with a wheelchair. The two of them took me up to the main level and put me into the back seat of a car waiting to take me away from Brandfield. Their treatment of me was like everything else at Brandfield—neat, efficient, and cold. The last thing anyone there said to me came from the housemaid.

"Here," she had mumbled and dropped a legal-sized envelope in my lap.

I had been riding for quite a while before I cared enough to open it, and, when I did, I received another shock. It contained divorce papers with my signature on them. When or how I could have signed them, Dev, I don't know. But rather than cry again, a flood of relief washed over me, and I began laughing instead. But I had to get a grip on myself because that laughter turned hysterical and drew the attention of the driver, a young man who watched me in the rearview mirror with the iciest gray eyes I have ever seen.

The papers said I had agreed to leave the marriage with only the clothes and personal items I had brought to it. That may sound unfair, but it didn't matter to me. All I wanted was to be done with Ellis, away from Brandfield and its darkness, and back in Denver, where I would awake to the sight of the mountains every day. But then I remembered I was also leaving without my baby. I felt hollow and empty. But I would have no idea how empty Ellis had actually left me, not for several weeks.

I was a little better than halfway through my roll now, and, with my sugar jones sated, I placed the knife and fork on the plate and pushed it away, making a mental note to hit the gym tomorrow to mitigate the carb and caloric damage.

I sat back in the booth, picked up my coffee, and sipped it while I thought about the young Aubrey Guinevere Phelps Brandywine returning to Denver and her parents. They had tried to talk her out of marrying Ellis in the first place, but as Gwen had admitted, she was headstrong and foolish, and had ignored their concerns. But in the aftermath, they had welcomed her home with love and relief—and no recriminations.

I recalled some of the information Jonah had gathered on Aubrey/Gwen and her family. He had learned that her father was American and that her mother was British. They were both lawyers and worked for an international oil company. They split much of their time between Denver and London. Two weeks after the alleged fall and miscarriage, Gwen said her parents had her in London and deep into therapy. But it was at least a month after that before she could stand the thought of another doctor touching her.

Once again, Dev, the results were a shock. One of my ovaries had been damaged, and my fallopian tubes had been severed. I would never have a baby. And that's when I remembered that sick gleam in Ellis's eyes as I had lain in the hospital bed at Brandfield. When I learned in London what had been done to me, I knew Ellis had broken me beyond physical repair and was done playing with me. I hadn't been divorced. I had been discarded.

And in that moment, the real reason Ellis Brandywine had hired Mecklan Personal Services presented itself to me so bright and clearly that I had to stop myself from squinting against a light that went on only in my head. There were no angels singing, but in that state of mind, I thought for a second that one had landed beside me. I shook my head and looked up to see my waitress smiling down at me.

"Not bad," she said with a nod at the remains of my roll. "Can I get you anything else?"

"Thanks, but no," I said, and she laughed.

"Just the check then?" she asked.

I thought for a minute.

"Mind if I stay? I don't want to tie up your table, but I'd like to go over these papers before I get back on the highway."

"Which way you headed?" she asked.

"South to Denver," I said.

"Then you take your time, honey. A trucker just came in and said some idiot hopping lanes in a black pickup had spun out and rolled his truck into a median. It's got traffic snarled up for miles. Even the ambulance had trouble getting to him. It's going to be a while before you get back to Denver. Might as well sit here and be comfortable until things are moving again."

I thanked her as she topped off my coffee. She picked up the plate holding the last of the cinnamon roll, winked, and walked away.

I spread the papers from Gwen's envelope on the table.

Gwen had said that, because she had fallen for Ellis so quickly, the people who had put the file together for her father had had to gather the information fast. She had refused to look at it before she married Ellis. But her parents had obviously saved it, and, later, after moving from London back to Denver, she had seen no point in looking through it when she found it among her things. Even now she was not sure why she had kept it and could not vouch for the quality of the information.

She didn't need to. A quick perusal was enough to tell me the report was detailed and well-organized. And if this was an example of average work, I couldn't imagine what this company's best would consist of.

Maybe DNA samples from a third cousin twice removed?

A great, great, great aunt's complete medical history?

A grandfather's toenail clippings wrapped in a sample of his belly-button lint?

I went to the first page of the first section and the name of the service that had compiled the info:

Deckard and Drew

Worldwide Consultants

There was a website address and an email given for contact but no phone number. The company name didn't ring any bells for me, so I went to the next page. It contained a neatly typed and indexed list of people, their names placed in order by date. I scanned the page. Some of the names I recognized, but there were many I didn't. I picked one of the unfamiliar women's names and flipped to the page indicated.

This name went way back. It was a girl Ellis had dated during the summer between his junior and senior years of high school. She was described as pretty, petite, gentle, and well mannered. She was also dead from a sleeping-pill overdose shortly after Ellis dumped her. The story did not surprise me. I knew that Brandywine had been sowing a path of emotional destruction for decades. But it still made my heart ache for the girl and her family, even now.

It also made me think about the jerk in the black truck. Some bullies are just assholes who eventually get their due because of their narcissism and stupidity. You can only hope that most people are alert enough to see them coming and can get out of their way before any collateral damage is done to them.

But the ones like Ellis Brandywine were in a class by themselves. Too smooth and polished to see them coming. Too powerful to break free from once within their grasp. Not finished with their chosen victims until they were left broken beyond repair.

And that was the missing piece.

Aubrey/Gwen had been a toy as surely as Rebecca had been, as was Charlotte even now. Ellis had had no need to find his second wife, because he knew that, like Rebecca, there was no fixing the kind of damage he had inflicted.

But Charlotte?

Ellis had broken her, but she had not *stayed* broken. That was why he had not divorced her and why he continued to use his power and money to keep her from divorcing him. He was not done playing with her. She had eluded him and his game six years ago, but she had not won. And using guys like me in a hunt for the bodies of the twins was his diabolical way of keeping pressure on her, making every prison visit—*his* suggestion where the investigation should start—a devious reminder to Charlotte that the game was not over until he decided it was.

And the twins themselves?

My guess was that, after their birth, Ellis had been as surprised as everyone else by the maternal change that had taken place in the beautiful, audacious party girl he had married. He probably saw Charlotte's love for Nora and Richie as a weakness or a deformity, or in Laurence Glandon's words, "a shame but interesting." And being the monster of mental cruelty that he was, Ellis would also see that love as a vulnerability, a weapon for him to use against her—a frightening skill, as it was, that he had perfected.

Yet somehow during the short marriage, under the steady pressure from Ellis's insidious mind games and the lurking presence of the ghoulish Dr. Glandon, Charlotte had kept enough of her wits to devise and implement a plan to spirit herself and her children away from Brandfield, on to New York, and out to sea and their deaths.

For Ellis J. Brandywine, hell had no fury like a demonic bully hoodwinked.

For Charlotte, apparently a mother's love defied the laws of mental and emotional abuse.

For me, I was not buying it. I couldn't.

I was convinced Charlotte had to have had help getting away. Possibly help from her family. Maybe from someone working at Brandfield. Maybe from someone I didn't know about yet, or maybe, *maybe* she had gotten help from someone I had just spent more than two hours with today.

I closed my eyes and sighed, depressed at the idea of having to turn Gwen in as an accomplice to kidnapping and/or murder—and all because of a single moment on her front porch and her genuine concern for me.

I opened my eyes, slipped the report into the envelope, and carried it to the register, where I paid the check and left a big tip for my friendly waitress. Stepping from the cool, comfortable air of the truck stop into the glare of the afternoon sun and the heat gave me a jolt but not one strong enough to lift my mood. I pulled my keys out and went to my SUV feeling like a recidivist fourth-grader on his way to the principal's office again.

I opened the driver's side door and tossed the report across to the passenger seat. I climbed in and went through my normal routine of windows down, AC up, and waiting for the lingering hot air to be forced out.

While I waited, I thought about Gwen sharing with me her determination to return to the States after she had gotten well. She needed, she had said, to step away from her old life completely and start fresh, including with a new name. She said she could not bear to be called "Aubrey" anymore because she heard echoes of Ellis's smooth, slithery voice whenever someone addressed her by her given first name. And having to explain to people that "Guin" was short for Guinevere seemed pretentious. So, she became "Gwen Phelps" until Quinn and Ben had entered her life, changed her last name, and made her whole with their love.

It was an uplifting ending to a horrifying story, and I was glad I had stayed to hear it. But it was getting late by then, and it was time for me to leave Fort Collins. I had picked up the envelope from the table and thanked Gwen for seeing me, thinking how relieved I was to be able to rule her out of any involvement with the drowning of the twins or Ellis Brandywine's impending death.

We had said our goodbyes as we walked to the foyer. Gwen had opened the front door and stepped outside with me. But before I could leave, she had taken my hand and, like Charlotte, had imparted a warning.

"Be careful, Dev," she had said with her dark eyes boring hard into mine, "and be done with and as far away from Ellis as quickly as you can. And whatever else you do, stay away from Brandfield, because people who go into that ugly place don't always come back out. At least not as who they were when they went in."

Then she dropped my hand, stepped back inside, and closed the door.

I had made my way in a daze down the flower-lined walkway with the slow, shuffling footsteps of a zombie. I'd gotten into the SUV and started the engine feeling sick and numb except for the fear that had prickled the back of my neck. I had dropped the windows, kicked up the AC, and sat stunned by the clear, perfect vision I had gotten at Gwen's touch, an image I would have given anything not to have seen.

And now I was sitting in my vehicle again in the parking lot of the busy truck stop, phone in hand, about to call Jonah, when my cell buzzed with an incoming text. It was from Jo, saying he was taking a break and spending the night with Angie.

Good, I thought, and exhaled a long, slow breath.

I put the windows up and the engine in gear, and left the parking lot. As I hit the highway and merged into the late streaming traffic, I decided not to bother Jonah with a response other than *okay*. Nothing that had happened to Gwen at the hands of Ellis Brandywine was ever going to change. Neither was the devastating image I had seen.

The bad news could wait until morning.

Chapter Twenty-Two

I was up early on Friday and fulfilling my vow to hit the gym. Jonah was not home yet, so I placed the Deckard and Drew file in the middle of his desk and left.

The unusually overcast morning I woke up to felt heavy with the cloudy threat of a summer shower and matched the dark mood I had awoken in. Although I had slept well, I could not shake the despondency I felt over my certainty that Gwen was somehow mixed up in Brandywine's looming demise—and, maybe, the deaths of the twins, too.

After the gym, I drove home in a spattering rain and a slightly better mood. I had done a brutal, fast-paced circuit on the machines that had left every large muscle of my body screaming for mercy and the small ones whimpering like beaten dogs. The addition of some pounding cardio on the treadmill had left me lathered like a racehorse after ten furlongs on a muddy track. I had finished with time in the steam room to sweat the last of my glum thoughts out through my suffering pores and then punished myself with an icy-cold shower.

When I got home, Jonah was at his desk, reading through the report. I got myself a cup of coffee, came back, and took a seat at the desk across from him.

He looked at me.

I looked at my coffee.

I thought of Gwen and what she had suffered at the hellish hands of Ellis Brandywine and his morbid doctor. Of Mecklan Personal Services studiously digging up the dirt that would be used to bury her under a possible felony-murder charge and blow a hole the size of a meteor through her beautiful family. I also thought about that last moment on Gwen's front porch and decided that, sometimes, life and my "gift" really sucked.

I brought my eyes up as the despondency I had worked so hard at the gym to exorcise washed over me again like an implacable black wave and left me slumped in my chair.

"Shit," I said.

"Tell me," Jonah said.

And I did.

Starting with a description of the flower-lined walk that led to the Smiths' front door, the home that bustled with kids, happiness, and love, and about Aubrey, who had been lured into hell as an innocent young lady and had clawed her way back as Gwen, a strong, marvelous woman. A woman who would do anything, I believed, to protect the life she had remade and the family she fiercely loved.

When I was done, Jonah asked, "Did Gwen give you any reason to believe there's a tangible threat from Brandywine to her or to her family?"

"No," I said, "but ..."

Jonah sat back in his chair. He was looking at me with his cop eyes now, and everything about him was cool, patient, and assessing.

I drank some of my coffee, hoping the caffeine would jolt my depressed thoughts into a working, coherent form. I chewed my bottom lip for a moment before I sighed and coughed up what I couldn't keep down anymore.

"I can't rule out revenge," I said. "God knows Gwen has plenty of reason to want Ellis Brandywine dead and to see him suffer horribly on his way to the dirt farm. What I can't see is her having the means or the opportunity to do it."

Jonah looked at me as if he were about to deliver bad news.

He was.

"It's here," he said, indicating the report spread on the desk between us. "Maybe not her opportunity but certainly the means."

"Bullshit," I grunted, feeling a defensive rush of emotion for Gwen and her family. "I looked at that material, Jo, and three quarters of it are things we already knew. Besides, Gwen is too smart to hand us the knife you and I'll use to stick in her back."

Jonah continued to look at me.

Screw those cop eyes, I thought—and crumbled. But I added another long sigh to make sure he knew I was doing it grudgingly.

"So, what was in there that I missed?" I said.

"It wasn't in the report, Dev. It was on it. The name."

"Deckard and Drew," I said. "So what?"

"So not just anyone can afford to hire them. And even if you can, they're selective about their clientele."

I considered that and said, "Jo, we already knew Gwen came from a wealthy family."

"But you need money *and* very special connections to get this outfit to consult for you," he said, bookending the word "consult" in chopped air quotes.

I shook my head, still not understanding why this was a big deal to him.

"I hate to repeat myself unless I'm drunk, but, again, so what?" I said.

Jonah reached for the report, shuffled it into a tidy stack, and set it back down on the desk. When he looked at me now, the cop eyes were gone, and an air of shut-up-and-listen had replaced them.

"When I started MPS, Dev, there were rumors floating around about an organization that did a certain kind of work. Out of curiosity, I looked for it. After a couple of months of searching, all I had found was the name of the company, Deckard and Drew. I couldn't find employees or clients, or track down ownership or investors. No one. For all I knew, Deckard and Drew themselves could have been a couple of ex-military guys or high-school friends or old drinking buddies. Or maybe the organization was named after somebody's pet giraffes.

"But most likely, a very smart person or persons picked a name out of the air—one having no particular association with anyone at their company—and slapped it on a letterhead so curious guys like me would be handed a wild goose chase to an ultimate dead end. And not just any dead end but an innocuous, hide-in-plain-sight dead end that was such an ass-load of work to get to that it discouraged most people from pursuing it further."

"But you weren't most people," I said and sipped my coffee.

"You're right," he said. "Now I was determined."

"Of course, you were. You hate dead ends," I said.

"More than kale," he verified and went on.

"After a few more weeks of searching, I learned that Deckard and Drew began as a company that specialized in kidnap-victim returns. Alive or dead, you got a body back. If the victim had been killed and the body was unrecoverable, you got details."

I thought about that.

"Scam?" I said. "Kidnap. Return. Pocket the ransom and the fee?"

"That was my first thought, especially when I heard about the fine print in their contracts that said the kidnappers don't always get turned over to the authorities."

"You mean they kill them," I said. "Clean up the loose ends."

"Nobody knows, Dev. It seems that some of the bad people Deckard and Drew crossed paths with were so bad that they ceased to exit. Any history—birth, school, medical or police records—that proved they were ever alive was being scrubbed away as if they were so evil they never should have existed to begin with. And Deckard and Drew was rumored to be doing the scrubbing."

Which made me worry where this story was going.

"These people don't screw around," I said.

"But they do reach out to determined private detectives," he said, and my breath seized in my chest as if I had gulped lead instead of caffeine.

"And?" I managed to croak.

"And when they did, I made a new acquaintance," Jonah said, as if that were a good thing when it came to these people.

I continued to breathe lead, but now I felt like I had a head full of helium, too, because the thought of inadvertently bringing ourselves to the attention of an organization with that kind of power was terrifying. All I could do in the moment was hope that my fear level would drop and I wouldn't experience the whole periodic table of elements before Jonah got to the end of his story. I knew neon was not considered toxic, but I was not sure how Mrs. K or Melvin might react if I showed up to cut the grass with glowing red eyes.

"Your new acquaintance—was he threatening or dangerous?" I said, surprised that I didn't sound like a chipmunk.

"*She* was stunning," said Jonah.

"You mean drop-dead-gorgeous stunning or fuck-me-she's-got-a-taser stunning?" I said.

"I mean beautiful, Dev. About five seven, mid-thirties, athletic build. A whisper of Asian ancestry shaping her eyes and showing in her bone structure. The morning we met, she had kind of a business-casual look going on. You know, jet-black hair pulled up in a complicated knot thing on her head, tailored gray suit, light touch of makeup that, believe me, she did not need."

Jonah paused, and we stared at each other.

He was smiling. I wasn't.

I spoke. Slowly.

"Let me get this straight. You're telling me, Jo, that you met a pretty associate from Deckard and Drew, and she did what? Threaten to dazzle you to death if you kept looking into their frighteningly powerful company?"

"You're not even close," he said.

"But you are," I warned him, wondering if impatience had atomic weight and what the blast range was going to be if he didn't get to his point soon.

Jonah ignored my impatience and went on.

"Around that same time, I had been hired by a guy to find an ex-girlfriend from their DU college days. He figured he hadn't been able to connect with her online because he wasn't tech savvy, and, the last he had heard, she had married, and he assumed she had a new last name. But he was going to be in town for a seminar and said a mutual friend had told him she might still be living in Denver. He sent me a picture of his long-lost love and a list of places they used to go. I checked him out. Everything looked on the level, so I took the job. I figured I could work the internet, make a few calls, put on my cycling gear, and make the rounds of the places on his list."

It was the perfect cover, too, I thought, because downtown Denver was swarming with cyclists. Jonah would be just one more guy on a ten-speed. He was also very good at starting casual conversations with strangers that elicited answers or leads.

"Next day, Dev, I'm up, on it, and out the door. My first stop is a little coffee joint. I bump into a woman coming out of the place. She drops her purse and spills her coffee. I feel like a clumsy jerk, pick up her purse, and offer to buy her another coffee."

"So what happened?" I asked, as what felt like freon began filling my veins and cooling my blood into slow-pumping worry.

He shrugged.

"I bought us both coffees," he said.

"And what? She slipped something in yours?"

"Better than that, Dev. When I handed her the new coffee, she said, "Thank you, Jonah," in a voice that breezed over me like silk floating over satin."

"But you hadn't told her your name," I said.

He poked a finger at me and said, "You should be a detective."

"And you should be dead. Why aren't you?" I said.

"Because I think she liked me," he said.

"How could you tell?" I asked.

"Because she paid me a compliment," he said, and I stared at him like I would the village idiot.

"That's what this long-winded story is all about, Jo? A damn compliment?"

"Sort of," he said.

I glanced out the window. The rain had passed, and the sun was already drying up the moisture we had been gifted earlier. I felt the lead in my chest dissolving and the helium in my head leaking away, but the damn freon was making a stand. I slid my gaze back to Jonah.

"And this compliment was what? She liked your ass in those tight bike shorts or something?"

"My skill and tenacity, Dev. She said *very* few people got as far in their search for them as I did. But she made it clear that it was far enough."

"And that didn't scare the living shit out of you?"

Jonah shook his head.

"I was too impressed to be scared. Besides, she was smiling when she said it."

"I'm not," I said.

"I noticed," he said.

I looked down and noticed my coffee cup was empty. I considered smashing the heavy porcelain on his thick skull but opted instead to run a scenario by him.

"Any chance, Jo, this conversation we're having could be part of a devious plan? Like your new acquaintance figured someday you would tell me this long, drawn-out story knowing I would probably snap and kill you halfway through it and save her the trouble of having to make you disappear?"

"Maybe," he laughed. "But I also got a consolation prize for playing."

"Which was?" I asked.

And now, it was *his* turn to glance out the window. When he looked back, there was a change in his expression sober enough to make me wonder if I wanted to hear what he was about to say.

"My new acquaintance showed me a picture of another long-lost love. Only this one had been murdered. Turns out my client had dabbled in some kinky sex with a few coeds during his college days. He was planning to run for public office in a few years, and he was making sure there would be nothing disqualifying found in his past. He had made a hit list. The woman who was murdered and the one he had hired me to find were on it."

"Son of a bitch," I said, shocked.

"Yeah. Son of a bitch," Jonah said, and our eyes held.

"Was that the end of it?" I asked.

"Not exactly. When I pulled out my cell to turn the bastard in, my new acquaintance said not to bother. The authorities had received an anonymous tip that was going to lead to the man's arrest within the hour."

"And that was it?"

"Except for a dinner invitation that night, where she mentioned during drinks that any trace of my slight involvement in the matter no longer existed."

"And *that* didn't scare the living shit out of you?"

"I know it should have, Dev, but what can I say? She and her organization had saved me from being an accomplice to murder. Plus, she had let that long, silky hair out to play and was wearing a slinky, black dress that clung to her like it should have paid for the privilege. And she smelled great, too."

"Oh, well, as long as she *smelled* great," I said, but that was all the sarcasm I could muster. Even if their methods were terrifying, I owed Decker and Drew a debt of gratitude. I was not sure Jonah could have survived being complicit in the death of any innocent woman, unwittingly or not.

"Anyway," he continued, "I told you this story because you need to understand the level this organization operates on and that, if Gwen Smith had access to their services, it would explain two things—why we had trouble finding her and, if she wanted to kill Ellis Brandywine, they might have been her means. Deckard and Drew would have created the opportunity themselves."

"Shit," I said and slumped even more in my chair.

I leaned my head back and stared up at the ceiling. I could feel Jonah's mind working, his patience filling the space between us, hear his chair creak as he shifted in it before he went on.

"You told me you have no reason to believe there is a threat to Gwen or her family," he said. "And the wife and mother you described doesn't sound to me like a woman who would risk losing everyone she loved for something as base as revenge."

And as much as I wanted him to be right, it was not enough to save me from the black wave of despondency as it washed over me again, picked me up like bobbing ocean debris, and dumped me back on the Smiths' front porch, where I stood ready to leave, Gwen reaching out, taking my hand in hers and changing everything in an unmistakable flash.

"Dev," Jo said, "you've told me what you saw with your eyes at Gwen's home. Now tell me what you saw with your touch."

I sighed, peeled my gaze off the ceiling, and straightened in my chair. There was no putting it off, no changing it, so I braced myself and came clean with one word spoken on a short breath.

"Charlotte."

Chapter Twenty-Three

"When?" said Jonah.

"When I was leaving. Gwen stepped outside with me, took my hand, and warned me to be done with her ex-husband as soon as possible and to stay out of Brandfield."

"The same warning Charlotte gave you," said Jonah. "Maybe that's why you thought you saw Charlotte."

I shook my head.

"No," I said, not letting myself off the hook. "It was Charlotte."

Jonah stayed silent.

I stayed despondent.

The Deckard and Drew report stayed on the desk between us, glaring like an accusation.

"Damn it, Jo," I snapped, as my temper suddenly flared and a flame of self-loathing scorched through my guts. "God only knows the number of people Ellis Brandywine has abused or the lives he has ruined over the years. The guy's a monster. But here I am, aiding and abetting his cruelty and the game he's playing with Charlotte's mind. What kind of a monster does that make me?"

Jonah shifted in his chair and said, "You're not a monster, Dev."

"Don't patronize me, Jo," I said, refusing his absolution. "Charlotte and Gwen are in it together. I *saw* it."

"You saw *something*, Dev, not necessarily murder."

"What else could it be?" I said, the anger gone but with the bitter taste of betrayal left moldering in my mouth.

"I don't know that yet, but I will," Jonah said.

"How?" I asked, and he tapped the report.

"With this," he said, and I sighed.

"There's nothing in there to save Gwen from going to prison now or to free Charlotte, Jo. I looked at it."

"Exactly. You looked *at* it. I read it. Every damn word," he said, and my sluggish brain came to attention.

"You found something," I said.

"It's only a theory, Dev, but it involves Sunridge and Gloria Brite and whatever the hell Merrick Glandon was doing to the patients there," he explained, and I corrected him.

"Guests," I said, thinking of poor, fragile Rebecca. "Not patients. Dr. Morley addresses them as *guests*."

"They weren't 'guests' when Eleanora Brandywine was on the board. Back then, they were helpless," he said, a reminder I didn't need.

"So what do you think we should do?" I asked, my ego long past thinking I didn't need his advice.

Jonah checked the time and got to his feet.

"You look like you need a breather, Dev, and I'm hungry," he said. "We're going to get some lunch, come back here, and decide what you're going to tell Lana Troy."

"Crap," I muttered, getting to my feet. "I completely forgot it's Friday."

"Yeah, and considering that the morning is gone, I'm surprised she hasn't been in touch to complain," he said as we left the office.

We decided on a neighborhood eatery, figuring that a short walk in the rain-freshened air would help clear both our minds of worry for a while.

I was not hungry because the thought of having to speak to Lana Troy had destroyed what little appetite I'd had. But after the workout I had done, my body needed protein. I figured I could at least make myself eat a sandwich.

Jonah was closing the front door behind us when he said, "You know, Dev, you can't feel bad about yourself over this. It's this job. Everybody has secrets. And sometimes you learn things you wish you hadn't. It just happens."

"Yeah, well … " I mumbled, still feeling discouraged as we went down the porch steps.

But the heat of the early-afternoon sun felt good on my skin, while the strength of its rays began to evaporate the mist of despondency that hovered over me. Side by side, we made the turn in the direction of the restaurant, and, in a few steps, my despondency lifted, my mood lightened, and I found I had an appetite after all.

Chapter Twenty-Four

Lunch was quick and quiet, as we concentrated on eating rather than conversation. We returned to the office with our bellies full, our minds focused, and the determination to free ourselves from the tightening Gordian Knot our psychopathic employer had entangled us in. And with luck, I secretly hoped, we would find some evidence that would save Gwen and help free Charlotte, too.

Jonah and I worked out what I would tell Lana Troy. It was unlikely that she would ask if we had found anything concerning the whereabouts of the former Aubrey Brandywine. On the off chance that she did, I would lie and admit defeat in our attempts to locate her and reaffirm that we were proceeding with the belief that our mutual employer had been right all along. Charlotte was the likely culprit behind the poisoning.

I made a few notes while Jo and I talked. Needing something to drink, I took the notes and my cell phone to the kitchen. I'd had a burger for lunch, and the salty fries that came with it had made me thirsty; Jonah wanted to get back to his computer. He was curious about an entry contained in the Deckard and Drew report concerning a child they had tracked in and out of foster care.

I set my notes and my cell on the kitchen table and went to the fridge for a cold bottle of water. I stood hydrating and mentally practicing my lines for Lana Troy.

I glanced up at the clock.

The afternoon was drifting by, and the call was not going to make itself. I went to the table, pulled out a chair, and sat down. I set the water bottle next to my notepad, picked up my cell, and tapped in the contact number.

Alexander answered and told me in his snobby, disdainful voice that Ms. Troy was out of the office for the rest of the day. She had left instructions that I should put my weekly—and late—report in an email to her. He ended the call before I could say anything, smart-ass or otherwise.

I sat for a moment, annoyed that I was not at Brandfield, where I would be using Alexander's head for a speed bag right now. At the same time, though, I was relieved that I was not at the dreary mansion and that I had not had to speak to Lana Troy. But my stomach tightened when I wondered if she had left the office to make her regular visit to Sunridge and Rebecca. My emotions quickly cycled to relief when I reminded myself that neither Doctor nor Annalee Morley would allow anything to happen to Rebecca.

I picked up the bottle of water and chugged it empty, thinking that Jonah and I had to finish this case soon. If we didn't, I was convinced these yo-yoing emotions I was experiencing were either going to do permanent damage to my internal organs or would land me in a room at Sunridge.

I stood, tossed the empty water bottle into the recycle bin, and went looking for my laptop. Jonah, being Jonah, kept any and all of his electronics neatly organized in his office and always charging. I, on the other hand, had a laptop that I tended to be forgetful about. Jonah used to laugh and say that was okay for me, since I was a finder and could locate the damn thing by closing my eyes. But we both knew that was not true.

When we were in middle school, Jonah had gone through what I called his "mad scientist" period. He had become curious about my "touch thing," as he had called it, and he would run experiments on me by hiding something for me to find.

"Concentrate," he would tell me. "You can do it."

But I couldn't.

Then he would tell me what he had hidden—a candy bar or an orange or one of his dirty socks—and have me take another shot at it.

Still nothing.

Next, he would have me put my hand on his shoulder while he closed his eyes and thought hard about what he had hidden.

Another nothing.

He would sigh and open his eyes.

"Loser," he would say.

"Jerk," I would call him, and we would go outside to find something better to do.

And now I had to get going and find my laptop, which I did, on an end table in the living room.

I flipped it open and checked the battery level. It registered three quarters charged, which meant I didn't have to go looking for the power cord, too. I returned to the kitchen and my notes, sat down at the table again, and booted up the laptop. I typed up a short, phony email and hit "Send."

I closed the laptop not feeling bad about the phony email but feeling bothered by something else. It was like a roving itch in the back of my mind. When I tried to mentally scratch it, the damn thing moved. Automatically, my hand went up to rub the back of my neck as if I could pin the thought in place and massage it to the surface.

No luck.

I got up, made my way from the kitchen to the front porch, and sat down in Connie's rocking chair. I looked around marveling, as always, at how fast the semi-arid climate in Denver dispatched the aftermath of rain. The sky was already clear, and the streets were dry. If I had slept through the light rainstorm this morning, I would never have known it had happened.

Just as I would never have known of Gwen Smith's involvement if she had not touched my hand yesterday as I was leaving.

Son of a bitch, I thought, popping up to my feet so fast the rocker remained whipping back and forth behind me, as if I'd left a toddler-ghost version of myself there, and it was trying to rock itself madly to sleep.

I swept back into the house and straight to the office. I stood in the doorway, vibrating with excitement, waiting for Jonah to finish what he was doing.

"What?" he said when he felt my presence and looked up.

"Do you remember your 'mad scientist' period when we were in middle school?" I asked, and he grinned.

"Loser," he laughed.

"Jerk," I said, and his head tilted a fraction.

"What made you think of that?" he asked.

"Guess," I said, and it took him only a second.

"Son of a bitch," he half-whispered as the light went on.

"Yeah. Son of a bitch," I confirmed as I crossed the room in a couple of quick steps and sat down opposite him again.

"And you were right, Jo. I saw *something* when Gwen touched my hand."

"But not Charlotte," he said.

"I couldn't have," I said.

"Because she isn't *lost*," Jonah said, becoming excited, too.

"She isn't even hidden," I said. "Hell, the whole country knows she's in prison," I laughed and saw Jonah's eyes change to cop mode.

"Tell me again what you saw," he said. "Exactly."

I did, beginning with Gwen's touch on my hand, experiencing that same, warm glow I had felt in Charlotte's presence and the flash image of a female on a distant shoreline, water lapping behind her on a building sea, her long auburn hair whipping around her shoulders in a blustery breeze.

"Charlotte's hair is short," Jo pointed out.

"It was long when she went to prison," I said.

"But like we said, Dev, she's in prison. Not lost."

"But someone we're looking for is lost. Someone we were told was dead. Someone who I got a glimpse of and assumed it was a grown woman who looked small because I saw her in the distance."

"Someone who was young and looked very much like her mother," Jo said.

"Nora," I said. "I saw little Nora."

"Son of a bitch," Jo said and sat back in his chair.

"Son of a bitch," I agreed and sat back in mine.

Chapter Twenty-Five

Then Newton's third law of motion kicked in.

For every action, there is an equal and opposite reaction.

Or *What goes up must come down*, and we came down with a crash.

Why did I see only Nora?

Why not Richie, too—if he was alive?

Why did I see Nora on the shore and not in someone's home?

What was the connection that made me see Nora when Gwen touched my hand?

Did it mean I was right about Gwen and Charlotte being in this together?

And what about Brandywine's slow-moving murder?

Had he been poisoned because he was getting close to finding the twins?

Could Nell—ever protective of Charlotte—be involved, too?

Or was her protection an act and she was Brandywine's mole?

Did this mean Ellis Brandywine had been right about Charlotte all along?

Could Charlotte actually be the person who had set his death in motion?

Were Nell and Gwen her tools for doing it?

Or did Charlotte have help from someone at Brandfield?

Help from someone like Laurence Glandon?

Could Glandon have fallen for Charlotte when she lived at Brandfield?

Could she have manipulated him into helping her get away?

Would the thought of Glandon touching her make me puke till I threw up my liver?

The possibilities kept coming. Our original flush of elation kept fading.

Jonah and I threw questions at each other like hard, straight fastballs until our brains were wrung out and our heads were squeezed dry of every last imaginable scenario. We went to the kitchen, where Jonah grabbed a beer, and I poured myself a bourbon. We took them to the front porch. Connie's rocker had stilled itself, and so had we. We stood sipping our drinks and watching the occasional car drive by or nodding to a passing neighbor.

"I could go back to Fort Collins and confront Gwen about what I saw," I suggested, but Jonah shook his head.

"First of all, if you tell her you 'saw' a missing child in a vision when she touched your hand, she'll just think you're nuts. Maybe call the cops. Secondly, after everything Brandywine put her through, if Gwen is part of this and has kept quiet about it this long, she isn't going to crack now. Not even if *I* go and talk to her," he said, and we fell silent.

Jonah drank more of his beer while I sipped my bourbon and let my mind wander to the day at Brandfield when I had impulsively committed Mecklan Personal Services to this case. That had been only a couple of weeks ago, but it felt more like it had been a couple of months.

Back then, I had believed I was ready to take the lead on this and trusted myself to make the decisions on what had seemed like a sad-but-simple case. Now I didn't know *what* to believe or who to trust, other than Jonah.

I was so deep in thought I didn't realize the fingertips on my left hand were tingling or that I was running them under my thumb until Jonah nudged me with an elbow.

"What?" I said.

He glanced down at my hand. I held it up and looked at it as if I had not seen it in a long time. The tingling sensation was mild but accompanied by another one of those annoying, free-floating itches in my thoughts. I let my hand drop and closed my eyes. I relaxed and began roaming around in my mind, chasing the itch, feeling that I was close to something important if I could just nail down that one, damn thought. I must have looked off because I heard concern in Jonah's voice when he spoke.

"Dev?"

I opened my eyes. He had turned to me and was frowning.

"You okay?" he asked and bumped my bare arm with the back of the hand that was holding his beer.

When he did, the thought stopped floating and became an image. It hung there, clear, squalling, and painful.

"Jo," I said, "what were you working on when I interrupted you?"

He gave me a quizzical look.

"A hunch I have about Gloria Brite. I don't think she was only warehousing mental patients and misfits. I think she may have been selling babies out of Sunridge, too."

"What makes you think that?" I said.

"What made you ask?" he said.

"This," I said bringing up my left hand and waggling my fingers. "And this," I added, indicating my arm where he had touched it.

Jonah's eyes narrowed.

"You saw something," he said, and I nodded.

"The Deckard and Drew report. You mentioned they had also tracked a child in and out of foster care."

"Yeah. The child was only ever identified as 'Baby X.' I don't know if they ran out of time or lost the trail and the baby altogether. Why?"

I took a deep breath.

"I think I saw that child."

Chapter Twenty-Six

"**B**oy or girl?" he asked, going straight into cop mode. But I could not answer that any more than I could answer *why* I saw any of the images that I did. Or why some images came in a flash of insight and only once. If I was working and prepared, an image came into focus as more of a scene than a flash, allowing me extra time to see people or things around it. All of which Jonah knew and did not understand any more than I did or Connie had.

"It was a newborn, Jo. And I mean *new*. Two people in hospital scrubs. One was holding the baby, while the other was cutting the umbilical cord."

"What about the mother? Did you see her?" he asked, but I had to shake my head "No."

"It was like a bloody, obstetrical version of a *Peanuts* cartoon," I said, "where the focus was on the child. I never saw the face of an adult."

Jonah took in a breath and blew it back out.

"That child has to be significant. You wouldn't have seen it, and Deckard and Drew wouldn't have spent time looking for it if it wasn't," Jonah said more to himself than to me. He asked,

"What about the hands of the adults? Could you see anything identifiable? Gender? Race? Tattoos? Scars?"

That was another head shake.

"Latex gloves," I said. "Both people."

The two of us stood there, silent and mulling, as we finished our drinks. It was nearing dinner time, and traffic was picking up as neighbors returned from work. Jonah and I went inside. Neither of us was hungry yet after the lunch we'd had, so Jo went to his office and back to work.

I was too agitated to sit still, so I went up to my room, changed clothes, and headed out to the backyard. I went to the garage for gloves, snips, a rake, and a trash bag. Being outdoors and physically busy was relaxing for me, and we had a rosebush that needed attention. I put on the heavy gloves that would protect my hands from the thorns, picked up the tools and the trash bag, and left the garage.

We had a big Linden tree in a corner of the yard. It provided plenty of shade and the sturdy branches that Jonah and I had climbed when we were kids. But nearer the house was a stretch of fence that received more than enough of the direct daily sunlight needed for the rosebush planted there to thrive.

In the late Spring after Mike had been killed, Connie had encouraged Alyssa to return to gardening. The four of us had trooped to a nursery and come home with a carload of annuals and a single rosebush. Over the following months and under Alyssa's natural touch, the rosebush had taken hold and bloomed, producing huge yellow flowers that smelled heavenly.

Somehow during that summer, Alyssa had managed to interest me in the care of the rosebush. I would work alongside her, deadheading spent blooms and watering and mulching the base. She taught me when and how to feed and prune it, and to ignore Jonah when he laughed at me for playing with flowers. While she worked and taught me, Alyssa would tell me about her childhood and growing up in Denver. Jonah was drawn into what we were doing only when she talked about meeting Mike in high school and some of the things they had done together back then.

I went to work on the rosebush, thinking about the virtues Alyssa had told me were associated with each color of rose and remembering the mellow sound of her soothing voice. I smiled as my mind drifted to that first autumn after Mike's death when the Linden tree that Jonah and I had loved to climb all summer had become our enemy, dumping its leaves in loads that Jo and I had to clean up on weekends.

We were raking and grumbling one Saturday morning when Alyssa, wearing jeans and one of Mike's big shirts, had joined us in the backyard and turned the chore into a lesson. She had worked alongside of us, telling us about the mythology of the Linden, that many cultures considered it sacred, and that its presence protected you from evil spirits. To see one in your dreams meant that a loved one who had passed was watching over you.

While I pulled weeds and cleaned up dead leaves from under the rosebush, I thought more about Alyssa and the shimmering love I had witnessed between her and Mike on the day I had touched the side of her face. How she had stayed strong for more than a year, how Jonah and I were sitting on a low branch of the Linden the following summer, chewing gum and talking baseball, when Connie had come into the backyard with tears on her face and a police officer by her side.

Alyssa had taken flowers to Mike's grave and been found by a groundskeeper, huddled against the headstone, flowers spilling from her lap. He had told the arriving officer she had looked so peaceful that it had taken him a moment to realize she was not a mourner who had cried herself to sleep.

Jonah and I had stayed out of the Linden for the rest of the summer. But when Autumn came and the leaves began falling, we had cleaned them up without complaining and as if we were performing a last sacred duty entrusted to us by Alyssa.

And sometimes, I still see a Linden in my dreams.

I finished with the rosebush. I returned the tools and gloves to the garage and disposed of the trash bag. I left the garage and stood looking at the Linden, being cooled by its shade, the tips of its branches reaching out to me like encouraging hands, as if the spirits of Connie, Mike, and Alyssa were all there, watching over me and offering strength and direction.

I closed my eyes and took in a long breath through my nose. I exhaled slowly through my mouth, and, as I did, a clarifying light filled my mind. One more breath, and I saw Charlotte, along with the truth I had deliberately blinded myself to. I opened my eyes.

The leaves of the Linden ruffled their confirmation but couldn't ease the sadness that filled me in that moment of truth.

I went into the house, picked up my cell, and made two calls—one for a meeting to confirm a hunch I had and the other to put the power of our depraved employer to use.

Chapter Twenty-Seven

Once again, Annalee Morley welcomed me to Sunridge. Her husband had been surprised by my call late last night but said I was certainly welcome to return. He would, however, be meeting with the family of a potential guest this morning and unavailable to help me personally.

That was fine with me. I didn't need his help. I needed a few minutes with Rebecca Brandywine.

I followed Annalee down another sunny hall to a glass-enclosed garden room that looked out on the peaceful back lawn. The room was spacious and restful, and dotted with containers of green plants and cheery potted flowers. Guests were playing checkers or other board games at small tables with their neighbors or sitting quietly, reading books or flipping through magazines.

On my way to Sunridge, I had turned over in my mind Jonah's reaction to what I had told him after I had finished with the rosebush and gone into the house to make the phone calls. He thought the hunch that had brought me here today was plausible—if frightening—but worth following up. And he was going to be busy on Saturday, too.

Jo had told me that his hunch about Gloria Brite had taken an unexpected turn. It was important enough that he was going to make the drive to Arvada to meet with a retired detective to check it out. Neither of us had to explain more. We both sensed that we were close to finding the central pieces of this sickening puzzle that would allow us to fill out the rest of the picture, however the hell warped and ugly it might turn out to be.

I was surprised how well I had slept last night and how calm I'd been on the drive to Sunridge, because I had awoken this morning focused yet bothered. Instead of being excited by the possibility of resolution and being done with Ellis Brandywine, I had the uneasy feeling that the longer we searched for the twins' bodies and the closer I got to finding Brandywine's killer, the more danger Jonah and I were in.

Annalee and I made our way through the garden room and stepped outside. She raised a hand to shade her eyes from the bright sunshine that flooded the cloudless sky and warmed the late-morning air. She looked about for Rebecca and her baby, who had been invited to a picnic by her neighbors.

"There they are," she said and pointed to where the three of them were sitting crossed-legged on a red plaid blanket near a pond.

Annalee dropped her hand, and we started along the walkway toward the little gathering.

As we walked, I wondered if this moment was going to feel as anti-climactic for me as it had for Jonah, when, five years after Mike's murder, his killer had been identified by a jailhouse snitch. As it turned out, the low-life scum was already behind bars for two other robberies and another murder. But before the bastard could be tried for Mike's death, he was murdered in prison himself.

"Good morning, everyone," Annalee said as we approached the picnickers. "Are you enjoying your day?"

I waited while Annalee chatted with the small group and fussed a bit over the "baby"; Rebecca preened like a proud parent.

Then Annalee said, "Rebecca, I have a friend with me today who has visited us before. You might remember him. His name is Devon West."

"Hello, Rebecca," I said as her eyes rose to meet mine.

They were lovely and innocent—and empty of recognition. I smiled to put her at ease while paying close attention to the delicate bone structure of her face, to the edge of her graying hairline, and, most importantly, to the shape of her mouth.

"You have a beautiful baby," I said, and she beamed with love and happiness.

"Thank you," she said, smiling broadly at me with her full and very distinctive lips, an exact copy of which she had passed genetically along to her daughter, Lana Troy.

Chapter Twenty-Eight

"**H**ow is that even possible?" Annalee said after recovering from the shock of receiving that information from me.

We had left Rebecca and her neighbors to their picnic and were stopped midway down the hall we had passed through earlier.

"When I met with your husband, Mrs. Morley, he told me that Rebecca had disappeared for a period of months shortly after Ellis Brandywine had brought her to Sunridge," I said, and I could see her mind working, slipping three decades back in time, wondering what she had missed.

"Yes, I remember that," she said, and I went on, sharing with her as gently as I could Jonah's theory.

"My partner thinks Gloria Brite may have been selling babies as a sideline to the warehousing of patients here."

Annalee blanched.

"Mr. West, are you saying the former director realized Rebecca was pregnant when she got here, hid her until her until baby was born, and then sold the child?"

"Sadly, yes," I said.

"Oh, my God," Annalee said and pressed a hand to her stomach as if she were going to be physically sick. "How could anyone be such a monster? How could John and I not have known?"

"First of all, you and your husband weren't in charge when Rebecca came to Sunridge," I said, trying to alleviate some of the guilt rippling across her face. "As for monsters," I said as we began walking again, "I'm afraid there are more of them connected to Rebecca, her own daughter being one of them."

We reached the end of the hall and crossed through the lobby. We stopped in the high-ceilinged foyer, and Annalee looked at me with eyes full of pain and worry.

"Mr. West, you said Ms. Troy is one of the monsters. John and I have always thought her strange, at the very least, but she's never given us any reason to think she might be dangerous. We would never have let her near Rebecca if we had. Do we need to keep her away from Rebecca now?"

"I think that would be a good idea until you hear from me again," I said, and she gave me another pained look.

"You have my word," she promised and said goodbye.

I drove back to Denver satisfied but not elated. Making the connection between Rebecca Brandywine and Lana Troy was what I thought it would be—confirmation, not revelation. And although it was some explanation for Lana Troy's peculiar visits to Rebecca, it served only to generate more questions for me.

If Gloria Brite knew Ellis Brandywine was the father of Rebecca's baby, why had Lana Troy ended up in foster care and not growing up at Brandfield?

What had gone wrong with what had to have been Gloria Brite's plan to sell her back to her billionaire father?

Also, adoptees or abandoned children often searched for their birth parents, but how had Ms. Troy made it through a succession of foster homes to an important job at Brandfield, working for her father?

Why hadn't Ellis Brandywine told me that she was his daughter?

Why be secretive about that?

Had she not told Ellis she was his daughter, something that could be confirmed with a DNA test if Brandywine had been skeptical?

And where did Laurence Glandon fit in?

The smarmy s.o.b. obviously had played a part in this, but was it an important one?

Or was he just an observer, content to watch and laugh while Ellis pulled the strings on Mecklan Personal Services, the two of them betting on how long Jonah and I could be kept searching for children who were never actually meant to be found?

I stopped for some groceries in Denver. It was too early to start dinner when I got home, so I put the perishables away and went up to my room to change into shorts and old gym shoes. I thought the grass could use a trim, and working on it would keep me busy and my mind occupied until Jonah returned. I dragged the mower from the garage, fired it up, and went to work on the shaggy front lawn, feeling productive but anxious.

Nothing at Sunridge had set my fingertips tingling, so it was not worry or fear that was eating at me. It was more a feeling of agitation—how a thoroughbred jittery with pent-up energy must feel trapped behind the race gate, waiting to explode onto the track.

I had finished the back lawn and was returning the mower to the garage when my cell phone rang from a pocket of my shorts. I pulled it out and checked the caller ID.

"Hey, Jo," I answered it.

"Are you home?" he asked.

"Yeah," I said. "Just finished cutting the grass. I was going to wash up and start the grill."

"Good. We have to talk," he said.

I had closed up the garage and was headed for the house when he asked, "What about your hunch? Were you right about Rebecca and Lana Troy?"

"Yeah," I said. "How did things go on your end?" I asked, and there was a pause before he answered.

"I was wrong about Gloria Brite, Dev," he said as I went inside and grabbed a bottle of water from the fridge.

"You mean she wasn't black-marketing babies?" I said.

I twisted off the cap and drank.

"I mean she wasn't Gloria Brite," he said, and I yanked the bottle away from my mouth.

"She *what?*"

"She was a phony, Dev. A working girl who had stumbled onto a golden opportunity and had the smarts and the guts to go for it."

"Well, son of a bitch," I said.

"Son of a bitch," he agreed and added, "Listen. I'm about twenty minutes away. Get the grill going, and I'll tell you the rest over dinner."

"There's more?" I said.

"Plenty," he said and hung up.

Chapter Twenty-Nine

"**H**er real name was Cloris Jean Hefflewhite," Jo began as soon as we sat down at the patio table to eat. "The first time she got busted for prostitution, she was twenty years old and using the alias 'Jeanine White.'"

An old copy of Cloris's rap sheet had told Jonah half her story, while the retired detective, Les Wolcott, had related the rest.

Raised on a farm in northwest Indiana, the adolescent Cloris had had big plans for herself, and none of them involved marrying someone who drove a tractor for a living and smelled like manure. She had been picked up as a runaway twice—once on her sixteenth birthday and again on her seventeenth, trying to hitchhike to Chicago.

Upon her unhappy repatriation the second time, she had made it clear to her family that planting-for-dollars, canning fucking peaches, and putting up goddamn pickles was not going to be her future. Her parents got the message. For her eighteenth birthday, they gave Cloris what cash they could and a ride to the Amtrak station. The first train leaving was going to Denver. She bought a one-way ticket, flipped Indiana the bird, and never looked back.

Les, who had been a patrolman when he tagged Cloris in that first arrest, had checked her background. He found her record as a runaway but no reason for why she had run. There was no history of physical or sexual abuse by anyone or any of drug dependency. What he did find was that Cloris Jean Hefflewhite had greed, cunning, an above-average intelligence, and enough ambition to power a rocket launch to Venus. What she lacked was any sign of a conscience or a willingness to go straight.

Les told Jonah that his next contact with Cloris came about six months later. He had been sent to a hospital to take a report from an assault victim who turned out to be Cloris. Apparently, while testing the waters of expansion, Cloris had dipped her avaricious toes into another hooker's pond. The old pro had warned her twice. The third time, Cloris had gotten a brutal beatdown from the hooker's pimp and dumped on the sidewalk as an object lesson.

At the hospital, Cloris had admitted to Les that she knew she had been running a risk by not having her own pimp. But the idea of "handing her earnings over to a vicious prick too lazy to fuck for a living himself" had really pissed her off. She also knew she could not go back to the street now without one, so she decided it was time to change her game. She put the word out that the old hooker was cheesy with syphilis, ratted out the pimp who had beaten her, got hired on at a high-end escort service, and left the street for good.

"But Cloris being Cloris," said Jonah, "that didn't last long, either. About a year later, the owner of the escort service, a woman named Brenda Lazlo, caught her in a restaurant having dinner with a rich client she was working off the books. There was a confrontation that went from screaming match to fistfight. That ended up in a trip to Denver County for both women, where Brenda was heard vowing to kill Cloris if she ever saw her again. Cloris had confided to Les that she was not worried about Brenda. The rich client had given her a line on an interesting job, and she figured it was a good time to take it."

Done with our dinner at this point, we cleaned up the patio table and went inside, where I poured a bourbon, Jo grabbed a beer, and we made ourselves comfortable in the living room while he finished the story.

"Les said he heard nothing more about Cloris until a few years after he had eventually made detective. He and his partner had been sent to a motel in Denver, where the shaken manager had let them into one of the rooms, where a woman's body was marinating in a bathtub full of bleach. The manager said the renter's name was Alice Heffle, but what was left of her face had told Les it was Cloris.

"Three motor-vehicle licenses were found in her purse. One in the name of Alice Heffle, another in the name of Jeanine White, and a third in the name of Gloria Brite. Les remembered the second name as one of Cloris's old aliases, but a check on the 'Gloria Brite' name came back as the director of the mental hospital in Evergreen."

Wondering how a former hooker had ended up as a director of anything, Detective Wolcott told Jonah that he and his partner had gone to Sunridge to see if someone there could tell them. The new director had never met the old director, but a young shrink who worked there identified an early mug shot of

Cloris as Gloria Brite. He said he didn't know anything about Gloria Brite's background or how she had got the job. He had also seemed shocked—though not terribly surprised—when he was told about her murder, but he was unable to be of any more help than that.

During the ride back to Denver, Les remembered what Cloris had said about a rich client giving her a tip on an interesting job. On a hunch, Les had looked up Cloris's old medical record from the beating she had taken. Her night nurse had been the real Gloria Brite. The nurse's credentials and name were what Les figured Cloris had used in a bit of identity theft to get the directorship at Sunridge, although he had never been able to figure out why she had wanted it.

"That's when I told Les about Cloris's patient scam," said Jonah, "which didn't surprise him. He said beds for cash sounded like a Cloris-type scheme. But when I suggested that she was selling babies, too, he said 'No way.' He said Cloris liked a quick, sure payoff. She was too impatient to wait nine months to collect her money, and the possibility of a miscarriage or prospective parents changing their minds and leaving her with nothing wouldn't be worth her time or effort."

"Did you tell him about Rebecca?" I asked.

"I did. And he conceded that, based on the timing of Rebecca's disappearance and return, along with Cloris's almost immediate departure from Sunridge afterwards, it was plausible that Cloris may have sold Rebecca's baby. But he also said there would had to have been a hell of a lot of money involved for Cloris to have waited that long to collect."

I sipped some bourbon and said, "Did Les think selling a newborn daughter back to her filthy-rich father might be worth the wait?"

"He did. He said it also explained something else for him: why Cloris had returned to Denver, knowing Brenda was still in business and her death threat was still standing. He guessed that Cloris was there to sell the baby, but her past with Brenda caught up to her before she could close the deal and be on her way."

"Which could explain how Lana Troy ended up in foster care to begin with," I said. "Maybe whoever killed Cloris couldn't bring themselves to kill a baby and left it someplace where it would be found."

"Or sold the baby to someone themselves," Jo said. "Although neither scenario explains why Lana Troy was shuffled through a series of foster homes. As a newborn, she should have been easy to place."

I thought for a moment, remembering that Jonah had never had the amount of direct icy interaction with the frost queen as I'd had, which had left me unable to picture Lana Troy as ever having been anything else.

"But what if, Jo, even as a little girl," I suggested, "Lana Troy was as almost as cold and frightening as she is now? What if someone who couldn't adopt legally had bought her and got buyer's remorse when they realized they had purchased a baby Maleficent instead of a sweet little Sleeping Beauty? With the adoption being illegal, maybe they dumped her and walked away."

"And set her scary little feet on a long path to Brandfield? Possible," said Jonah and drank some of his beer.

I drank more of my bourbon, mulling over everything Jonah had related. I couldn't admire what the former Cloris Jean Hefflewhite had done, but I did have to admit to being a little amazed by the destructive accomplishments of one greedy, amoral farm girl.

"What do you think happened to the money Cloris made running Sunridge? You think it might still be in a bank somewhere?"

"Could be," said Jonah, "and still collecting interest. But I don't care about the money. I think it's what happened to the baby that matters."

"And how that baby ended up at Brandfield working for her father," I said.

"And whether or not she could inherit his estate," Jo said. "Especially with the twins out of the way."

"Which would be a motive for murder and to help Charlotte flee," I said, depressed about what I still needed to do.

"So, what's the next move?" I asked. "Drive out to Brandfield and confront her?"

Jonah shook his head.

"This is still a working theory, Dev. We're going to need real proof before we do that, because I don't think Brandywine is going to accept being told he was wrong about anything—even the identity of his own murderer. And we know Lana Troy is smart. If she's behind this, she'll have covered her tracks well."

"So, more digging?" I said.

Jonah nodded. He was holding his beer bottle by the neck and swirling the last of the dark liquid around. He was getting that "mission directed" look on his face, and I knew he was going to be up all night.

I finished my bourbon knowing that Jonah was right about Brandywine. He would not like being told he was wrong about the identity of his killer, but it was going to feel damn good to me when we did it.

"Are you still going to the prison tomorrow?"

I nodded and let out a breath that I felt like I had been holding since I had stood in the shade of the Linden the day before.

"No choice," I said. "I have to warn Nell."

Chapter Thirty

I was surprised that my fingertips were not tingling when I parked at the Denver Women's Corrections Facility the next day. It was one o'clock on Sunday afternoon, less than forty-eight hours since I had made that phone call to Brandfield on Friday evening, yet, here I was, at a federal prison, being escorted to a private meeting with a convicted murderer, a meeting that had been arranged for me as easily as a casual lunch date.

Maybe my fingertips were not reacting, I considered, because I had become numb to the insidious reach of Ellis Brandywine's terrifying power. Or maybe I was just fed up with being intimidated by him. But as I followed a guard to the interview room, I knew it was more likely because of the depression that had landed on me that morning like a heavy, wet blanket that was smothering my feelings and making my footsteps drag.

The guard let me into the interview room and closed the door behind me. Charlotte was sitting at the table, with a single chair across from her, as I expected, but instead of Nell standing sentinel at the back of the room, she was seated next to Charlotte, wearing street clothes and a stony expression.

I trudged to the table, slid back the empty chair, and sat down.

"Hello, Charlotte," I said, and she gave me just enough of a smile to make my breath catch.

"And thanks for coming on your day off, Nell," I said, and she gave me just enough of a glower to make my testicles sweat.

"I was going to ask how you got my cell number," the prickly guard said, "but then I remembered you're a dick."

I ignored the dig and replied, "Jonah's the PI. I'm a finder."

She stabbed me with a look and said, "There's a difference?"

"Sort of," I said, too depressed to flinch.

"Well, you're both working for Brandywine, so I don't give a good goddamn what you call yourselves. As far as I'm concerned, you two are a couple of assholes neck deep in an ocean of shit that you should have stayed the hell out of," she said, and the edge in her voice was as sharp as the look in her eyes.

I was wondering if I was going to leave the prison feeling slashed and bloody when Charlotte intervened.

"Let him speak, Nell," she said, and I did.

"Please understand, Charlotte," I began, "that I agreed to work for Ellis before I knew what he was. And once I did, it was too late. There was no ending the contract."

"Bullshit," Nell spat and glared at me like I was the biggest pussy she had ever met.

Maybe I was. But pussy or not, it didn't make me any less determined to face the truth and do whatever was necessary now to paddle my way out of that ocean of shit she had referenced.

Charlotte studied me with her beautiful eyes and frowned.

"Ellis threatened you," she said.

"And everyone I care about," I said. "As I'm sure he did Nora and Richie to control you."

"Then you understand why I had to do what I did," said Charlotte, and the ache in her voice pierced my heart like a stinging little arrow.

"Some of it," I said and forced myself to go on.

"I know, Charlotte, that you wouldn't have stayed anywhere there was danger for your children or be with someone who was evil enough to harm them."

"And Ellis is nothing but evil," she whispered softly.

"He's also running out of time," I said. "Which is making him more dangerous than ever."

"And that's why you're here today," said Charlotte, with a tired but knowing look in those eyes.

"Yes. I came to warn Nell," I admitted, and the glower Nell gave me now was as hard as the grip she had once put on my forearm.

"Well, *finder*, in case you haven't noticed, women don't stay here for the amenities. This place is a fucking fortress. If that shitbag Brandywine wants to kill Charlotte, he'll have to get past me. And that isn't going to happen," she said.

"I believe you, Nell," I said. "But taking Charlotte's life has never been the goal for Ellis Brandywine. If it had been, she would have never left Brandfield alive."

Nell bristled and slammed the table with her hand.

"Then what *is* the goddamn goal?" she demanded, her voice full of anger and climbing. "Charlotte has lost her children. She's going to be in prison for the rest of her life.

How much revenge does that prick need to get before he gives up the goddamn ghost and dies?" she said, and I laid it out for her.

"This is not about revenge, Nell. Ellis is playing a game. He's been toying with Charlotte all of these years, believing that winning was a matter of time. But it's time he now no longer has."

"Then why the fuck is he still playing?" she said.

"Because Charlotte is," I said, and Nell's mouth fell open.

She sat stunned, looking at me like the oxygen had been seared from her lungs with a blowtorch. When she was finally able, she closed her mouth and turned to Charlotte, the prisoner who was also her friend.

"What in the hell is he talking about?" she said, and Charlotte answered her calmly.

"Ending it," she said.

"Ending what?" said Nell, and Charlotte looked to me to explain.

"The very last game that Ellis Brandywine is ever going to play," I said. "The game that Charlotte was made part of almost a decade ago before she could understand what was happening or what was at stake."

"And what was at stake?" Nell asked.

"Her sanity," I said. "I believe the goal of this game, as it was with his first wife and whatever the sick instigation for it, has been to drive Charlotte out of her mind. I think if Ellis doesn't put *her* in Sunridge, too, he loses."

"And Ellis never loses," said Charlotte, sounding as sad and discouraged as I felt.

Charlotte and I retreated into silence, while Nell crossed her arms over her chest and retreated into thought. When she was done, she uncrossed her arms, straightened in her seat, and said, "Okay, finder, how do we stop him?"

"By remembering that Ellis Brandywine has been playing this game since he was a little boy, a game he's been able to pride himself on always winning—until he matched himself against Charlotte," I said. "She hasn't beaten him, but I'm betting that, in all of these years, she's the only person who has ever played him to a draw."

Nell shrugged.

"Who cares if she has? If Brandywine is failing as fast as you say he is, he's not just standing at death's door—he's got one foot over the damn threshold. Why not sit tight and wait for him to take the other step?"

"Because Brandywine won't wait. He'll make another move, and he'll do it soon," I said, and the guard in Nell zeroed in on that.

"What kind and how soon?" she said.

"Most likely, he'll have someone Charlotte cares about, someone like you, crippled or killed within the next few days, knowing it would cause her immense pain and guilt, enough pain and guilt, over time, to finally drive her out of her mind and, someday, into Sunridge," I said.

"Even if he doesn't live long enough to see it?" she said.

"Even if he doesn't live long enough to see it," I repeated, watching her struggle with the level of evil that entailed.

"You know, finder, I had pegged that arrogant fuck as an abusive control freak. So when one of his previous goons said something about Charlotte and Sunridge, I just figured that's why there was never a divorce. Brandywine getting her moved there might be a way for him to push the law out of his way and put her back under his thumb. But that wasn't it, was it?"

"Not even close," I said.

"So are you telling me …?"

"That in essence, Ellis Brandywine is so vindictive, he will be playing his game with Charlotte even after he's dead. Unless Charlotte ends it now, as she tried to six years ago," I said, looking Nell straight and hard in the eyes.

It took a moment for the meaning to sink in. When it did, it hit Nell like a slap across the face that set her head whipping back and forth between Charlotte and me like a weathervane in a thunderstorm.

"Oh, no. No goddamn way," she said, shoving her chair back from the table.

She shot to her feet and began pacing the small room.

"Nell, it's the *only* way," Charlotte said, her voice soft but firm.

But the angry guard was not having it.

"Forget it," she snapped, her voice brittle and her face set like granite. "I'll throw you in the hole first."

"But, Nell," Charlotte pleaded, "Ellis can't be allowed to hurt any more people. Not because of me."

"I said *forget it*," she repeated, still pacing and without an ounce of budge in her tone. "You've lost everything you ever cared about because of that evil prick. You're not going to lose your life, too."

I stayed quiet, letting Nell pace off a few more steps of her anger before I spoke.

"But Charlotte hasn't lost everything," I said.

Nell stopped pacing and looked at me.

"The twins," I said. "Only one of them drowned."

Chapter Thirty-One

"I'm sorry," said Nell. "I know you believed all of this time that she was innocent."

We were standing at the edge of the prison parking lot. I was staring west at the mountains and feeling deflated.

"It's not your fault, Nell. Charlotte never lied about being a murderer."

"Don't judge her, finder. Not for being a mama bear protecting her cub."

But I was not judging Charlotte. I was judging myself for being a world-class sap who saw only the beautiful blue in Charlotte's eyes and not the maternal fierceness.

"Listen," Nell said, and I looked at her.

She had turned and was facing me squarely, hands planted on her hips.

"We both know the whole score now. Charlotte has promised us time, but Brandywine won't give us another goddamn minute. So stop feeling sorry for yourself, get your ass in gear, and end this sick fucking game of his before she does."

"I'm not sure that I can," I said and was instantly sorry I had, as she drove an iron finger into my chest and hammered me with a command.

"Do it—or Brandywine will end us all," she said and marched off to her vehicle while I dragged myself to mine.

Sadness, stupidity, anger, fear—all took turns battering me on my drive home, until they melded into an overwhelming sense of hopelessness and left me feeling like I was back at Brandfield the day I had barged in only to stand paralyzed at the bottom of the staircase, unsure whether to run for safety or keep going and fight.

My driving drifted from lane to lane as my mind drifted back to the prison and to Charlotte and what she had shared.

"Do you recall when I told you Ellis was a handsome devil? I learned quickly that he was a maniacal one, too. As soon as we knew that I was pregnant, his behavior became unpredictable. Excited one moment. Annoyed the next. Looking back, I think he was anxious to get on with his game but was not allowing himself to play it until after the birth. But once the twins arrived, the real hell began."

And the game Ellis began with Charlotte was similar to the one he had played with Gwen back when she was still Aubrey. It was the game he had played since childhood—draw them close, and then push them away, toying with the victim's love and trust, wallowing in their hurt and smiling at their bewildered reaction. Some of the details differed. Where Ellis and Aubrey had battled over using Glandon as her doctor, Ellis had left that decision up to Charlotte, as if it were not important at all.

Listening closely as Charlotte had related more of her story, I realized something I should have picked up on when I was with Gwen in Fort Collins—something important that I was only realizing now. There had been a much larger household staff in previous years than I had seen at Brandfield. All of whom had responded to Charlotte but reported to Ellis. Some days, Charlotte said, she had felt in charge of them, and, other days, she felt they were her jailers. She also believed they were Ellis's accomplices in gaslighting her.

In the beginning, it was small things. A book she was reading or a brush she used would go missing and then reappear in a place she would never have left it. Lunch dates were canceled by friends, who left understanding messages for a speedy recovery when she was not ill. Leaving her cell phone to charge all night yet finding the battery dead the next day. And as the weeks went on, the tactics intensified.

When Nora and Richie were a year old, Charlotte went to the nursery one morning to find Nora gone. She had rushed from room to room in a panic, shouting for Ellis, yelling for help from the staff, who looked at her like she was crazy, only to rush back to the nursery to find both babies sleeping peacefully.

After one missing-baby incident that happened while Ellis was away on a business trip, she had returned to the nursery, where she found him home and holding the missing twin ... and smiling. She had begun sleeping in the nursery after that, but, even with the door locked, she said, she never had another night of rest at Brandfield.

And on it went.

Ellis, cold and indifferent for days and then suddenly warm and attentive, proposing a family trip, only to change his mind at the last minute and send Charlotte off—with one child.

And like any proud parent, Ellis had invited his in-laws to visit after Nora and Richie were born. During their stay,

Ellis had presented so perfectly the image of loving husband and father that Charlotte knew that no one, not even her own mother, would ever believe he was anything else or understand the subtly structured, psychological terror that loomed over every minute of her life.

And always hovering at the edges was Glandon, his morbid presence an added element of pressure, another layer of fear, watching the twins with a greedy light in his eyes, hungry to get them away from her and down into his hospital, where so many of the staff went and never returned.

The twins were a year and a half old when Charlotte knew that she could not go on living this way, that her marriage wasn't over—it had never actually been—and that she had to take her children and leave Ellis before her sanity left her.

That same afternoon, while Nora and Richie were napping, she had gathered her courage, marched into Ellis's study, and demanded a divorce. She had found Glandon there with him, her skin crawling from the look the two of them had exchanged, confused at first when Glandon had taken a twenty from a pocket of his slacks and handed it to her gloating husband. Charlotte was stunned and horrified when she realized that she had been part of a bet, nothing more than a playing-piece in an insidious game Ellis delighted in and controlled.

She had almost fainted from the desperation that had hit her in that moment, overwhelming her with the certainty that Ellis would never let her go, that it was only a matter of time until he broke her, until her children slipped into Glandon's greedy medical clutches, and Brandfield swallowed her up like a black hole and claimed whatever was left of her mind.

"I'm not sure when I crossed the line from living to existing and wondering how long I could hold on. Then one day, Ellis sent me to a spa in Denver. The twins were three years old, and he said keeping up with them seemed to be wearing me out. He decided I needed some rest, but how was I to rest anywhere away from Brandfield knowing my children were left with those monsters in that dark, ugly lair?"

Charlotte said she had sat alone in the changing room that day numb and defeated, unable to think or function, helpless as her mind slowly loosened its grasp on the sadistic reality of her present and the untenability of her future.

She had no idea how much time had elapsed while her sanity had eddied about her and slowly away, or why it had come floating back on a wave of words, clear and strong, full of encouragement and a plan for saving herself and her children. She had registered the words, but the details had seemed impossible. The glimmer of hope they gave was cruel.

Just the sort of game Ellis would gleefully play with her mind.

"He sent you," Charlotte had said to the woman who had materialized out of nowhere, sat down beside her, and spoken those words with unwavering confidence. A woman whose description matched that, Dev realized, of the dark-haired acquaintance from Jonah's encounter with Deckard and Drew.

"No," the woman had replied. "But he has been on our radar."

"Then she put an arm around my shoulders, and I was suddenly no longer tired or afraid. And I knew that it would not be easy, but, with her help, I could deal with Ellis and end his terrible game."

Chapter Thirty-Two

And now I believed that I could, too, until I arrived home and found the front door open. Not open far enough to be noticeable from the street but too much to be an accident.

My fingertips tingled as I placed a hand on the door and slowly pushed it the rest of the way open.

"Jo?" I called out and stepped inside to silence and the living room as I had left it.

No furniture overturned.

No sign of a struggle.

No reason for alarm.

"Jonah," I called louder and made a beeline to his office, where, again, there was no Jonah and no sign of a struggle or anything that told me to panic.

My pulse jumped anyway, and my heartrate zoomed as I whipped across the room and behind his desk. My hands shook as I threw papers around, hunting for a note or a message, something—anything—that would tell me where he was. When I found it, my body went cold, my knees buckled, and I dropped into his chair like a sack of wet mud.

My cell rang.

"You're dead," I answered it with my eyes welded to the spot on the desk where Hank Spitball's silver medallion lay.

"Please contain yourself, Mr. West," said Lana Troy. "Hasn't anyone taught you that histrionics are not only tedious but juvenile, too, and serve only to expose the speaker as impotent?"

"Go to hell," I said through gritted teeth, my whole body thrumming with anger.

"If there is one," she replied tartly, and I had to bite my tongue almost to bleeding to contain myself from calling her what she was.

"What did you do to Jonah?" I said.

"Only what was necessary," she answered.

"Necessary for what?"

"To change his mind," she said. "Mr. Brandywine wanted a meeting with the two of you to discuss your progress, but Mr. Mecklan insisted there wasn't a need for it. He had to be convinced otherwise."

"If you've hurt him …" I said, and she laughed.

"Don't be dense, Mr. West. Of course, we've hurt him. How much *more* we hurt him will depend on how long it takes you to get here," she said.

"Listen, you sick bitch," I started, but she cut me off with another laugh.

"Name-calling? Really, Mr. West? I thought you had learned your lesson about wasting my time," she said, scraping the memory of Hank Spitball's death and the humiliation that followed it over my ego like a cheese grater.

"Fuck you," I snapped.

"And Mr. Mecklan, too?" she said, landing the punch I should have seen coming, the one that painted an ugly picture in my head of what they were capable of and drove the air from my lungs. I closed my eyes and sat fighting for breath, cell crushed to my ear, fingertips stinging, the image of Hank Spitball and his broken neck exploding in my head, and my chest tightening with the fear of causing that or worse to happen to Jonah.

"Still there, Mr. West?" she said, poking like a brat with a stick at the nerves she had made raw and bloody.

But rather than causing another useless outburst, her taunting forced my mind into focus.

I opened my eyes, knowing I was caught up in a game but not sure now whose game it was or which opponent was the more dangerous, Ellis Brandywine or Lana Troy. What I *was* sure about was that the next move was mine.

"One of the twins is alive," I said and got a sharp gasp and an earful of ice in response.

"You're bluffing," she hissed.

"Am I?" I said and started counting.

I was almost to ten and the end of my rope before she replied.

"I'll let Mr. Brandywine know."

"And that's all he'll ever know if Jonah's not breathing when I get there," I warned, feeling the odds swing a sliver in my favor along with a slim chance of getting Jonah out of Brandfield alive.

"You're wasting time," she said coldly and ended the call.

I dropped my hand to my lap, and my cell phone slipped from my fingers. I felt drained and lucky. But not lucky like a guy who has won the lottery. Lucky like a guy behind the wheel of a speeding car that has skidded out of control up to the edge of a cliff and whose brakes caught at the last second before going over.

I closed my eyes again and pressed the heels of my hands against the lids, pushing back on the pressure that was trying to push them out of my head.

I lowered my hands and forced myself to take long, deep breaths, one after another, until my pulse beat normally again, my fingertips stopped stinging, and the pressure behind my eyes was gone. I felt better, but better was not a plan.

I opened my eyes, still on the edge of the cliff, teetering between hope and helplessness, not knowing what to do next, wondering if there was enough good in the world to offset the profound evil of an Ellis Brandywine or a Lana Troy, when the answer came to me, floating in images that I wrapped around myself like armor.

Connie and Jonah. Mike and Alyssa. Mrs. Koselke. Rebecca. Gwen and Charlotte. And Richfield James Brandy-wine Smith—deceptively tall for his age, who played soccer, knew sign language, had saved the world countless times, and for whom Charlotte had sacrificed her freedom and murdered his twin sister to keep him safe from her and his father, and away from the darkness of Brandfield forever.

I opened my eyes, picked up my cell from my lap, and called Nell. It went to voice mail, and I left a short message about what had happened and where I was going. I warned her to watch her back and to watch Charlotte closer than that.

I set my cell down next to Hank's medallion and pushed Jonah's chair back from the desk. I knelt down to the small gun safe Jonah had installed under there and punched in the code to open it. As a former cop, Jonah was more comfortable with firearms than I was, but I was not going to Brandfield unprepared. And I figured that, if Jo was conscious and able, he might be in the mood to shoot someone.

Unlike me, who planned to find Lana Troy and strangle her.

Chapter Thirty-Three

The late afternoon sun had lost its glare, and the hottest part of the day had baked off when I turned onto the grounds of Brandfield for what I had decided was going to be the last time.

Unlike my previous visit, there had been no blinding fury on the long drive here or rage upon my arrival. Nor was I tense or nervous as I drove up the weathered gray ribbon of asphalt in front of the dark-brick monstrosity and parked.

Of course, the 9 mil I had tucked under my seat and Jonah's Glock in the shoulder holster I was wearing may have had something to do with my feelings of calm and confidence. That and the knife I had slipped into the pocket of the windbreaker I had donned to cover the gun and holster rig, along with the last-resort-if-everything-suddenly-goes-to-hell small canister of pepper spray I had strapped to my left ankle. I also had a hot ball of avenging anger doing a slow, smoldering burn in my belly and fueling my determination.

I killed the engine but left the keys in the ignition, laying odds on the probability of a fast departure, especially if only one of us were able to leave Brandfield alive. I got out of the SUV and went up to the door.

It opened before I could knock, and there stood the disgruntled housekeeper with her trademark surly expression and her right hand pressed protectively against her chest. The hand was so heavily bandaged it looked like a gauzy, white paw, and her eyes looked red and swollen, as if she had been crying hard.

"Follow me," she snarled, and I did.

We wound up going a different way from my last trip here, through the main-floor rooms to the staircase, and, this time, I ascended without hesitation. I was disappointed that Glandon and his smarmy attitude were not waiting for me at the top. After all, I had to locate the bastard before I could pound him into paste.

Halfway up the stairs, my grumpy escort began an angry, mumbling monologue about "Glandon" and "fire" and some other weird shit that didn't make any sense. When we reached the landing, she stopped, turned to me, and said something that made even less.

"Eleanora could have stopped him, you know. She could have told that damn doctor not to let Alexander hurt me. I begged her, but she wouldn't listen. That bitch wouldn't help me. No one here ever does. So this time, I'm gonna show her. I'm going to show them all. You'll see!"

But all I saw was crazy, so I gave her a consoling look and a solemn nod to get her moving.

It worked, and we traced the path I had followed with Glandon through Brandywine's bedroom and into his study, where the charm-school reject halted and jerked her head toward Brandywine's office. I left her in the study, scowling and mumbling in front of Eleanora Brandywine's life-size portrait and shaking her left hand in a fist at it.

"Devon. Glad you made it," Glandon greeted me, with his smile oozing that oily smugness that set my teeth on edge. "Ellis understands from Lana that you have some good news for us."

"Fuck you," I said, cutting off his Fred Friendly crap, as the ball of anger in my gut glowed white hot and began burning at the edges of my self-control.

Brandywine gave me a sharp look.

"There's no need for rudeness, Mr. West," he reprimanded me.

He was parked in his wheelchair behind his huge desk, buried under his usual mound of blankets, the oxygen tube snaking up over his shoulder and hissing air into his pinched, papery nostrils.

"You're understandably upset, but we can still conduct our business as gentlemen," he said, the words wheezing from him like an old accordion leaking air and time.

I considered that and decided he was right.

"Fuck you, *gentlemen*," I said. "Where's Jonah?"

Brandywine sighed.

"Come now, Mr. West. Did you really drive all the way out here believing I would hand him over to you so easily? After all, what's to prevent the two of you from leaving with the information you said you have once I do? I could never allow that," he said and looked at me sadly, as if I were still that dull schoolboy he had first encountered.

I returned his look with a flat one and said, "It doesn't matter what I believe, and I don't give an exploding case of bottled shit what you think you will or won't allow. I get Jonah. You get the information. End of contract. Goodbye."

Glandon gave a throaty chuckle and shook his big head.

I stayed calm and waited.

Brandywine glared at me and said, "I'm afraid that's not how this is going to work, Mr. West."

"It is if you want to know who really poisoned you," I said, and Brandywine went still.

Glandon dropped his smile.

Their eyes flicked back and forth between them like snake tongues testing the air before they slithered their gazes back to me.

"Which I'll tell you when I see my partner," I said and pulled out the loaded Glock and pointed it at them.

"Well, well," said Glandon with an eager, greedy light in his eyes. "You certainly are an interesting specimen."

"But unacceptably impudent," said Brandywine.

"Like I give a damn," I said and reiterated the deal. "You give me Jonah. I give you your information. We're done."

"Far from it, Mr. West," Brandywine wheezed again. "I have plans for you."

And the look he gave me this time goosed my lizard brain into warning mode but half a beat too late as something stung me in the side of my neck.

In a single breath, my muscles turned to jelly, the Glock slipped from my hand, and my eyes rolled back in my head. The last thing I remember were my eyelids fluttering shut as I pitched forward and fell a long way down into darkness.

Chapter Thirty-Four

When I opened my eyes again, I was flat on my back, with a wide, droopy-eyed face inches from my own.

"He's awake," said the face. "Now what?"

I blinked a couple of times and recognized the gardener. His breath smelled like peanut butter and jelly, and he was leaning in close, studying me the way a curious child with a dime-store magnifying glass would study a bug.

"Thank you, Morris," said Glandon. "You can go now."

Morris plodded out on his heavy-booted feet, and I took in my surroundings along with my situation, which was anything but good.

I was in a brightly lit hospital room, strapped into a bed by a webbed belt pulled tight over my thighs. The safety rails were raised, and my wrists were tacked to them on either side of me with padded Velcro restraints. I felt weak and dizzy, and my stomach felt queasy, aftereffects, I assumed, from whatever I had been drugged with.

I did a slow, careful turn of my head to the right and saw Glandon. He was humming to himself while he searched through cabinets and sorted through drawers, choosing syringes and vials, and adding them to a tray that, with a painful squint, looked to me to be holding items used for a blood draw.

Glandon bounced a glance off me and stopped humming.

"The discomfort you're feeling will pass soon. As for your cell phone, gun, and knife, there's no need to worry. Ellis had the housekeeper put them someplace safe," he said, reassuring me as if I were a child concerned about some misplaced toys rather than a kidnap victim trapped in a medical dungeon at the mercy of a mad physician.

I straightened my head, lifted my eyes to the ceiling, and lay listening to myself breathe. Although my head felt heavy and my mind was groggy, I was alert enough to note that Glandon had not mentioned the pepper spray. I wiggled my left foot and felt the small canister still strapped to my ankle, but, with my hands restrained as they were, it may as well have been someplace safe, too.

And Glandon was wrong.

I did need to worry.

But first I had to find Jonah.

I lowered my eyes from the ceiling and turned my head to the right again. I tried to speak, but my tongue felt thick, and my mouth tasted like I had been drinking glue.

I peeled my lips apart and said, "Where's Jonah?"

Glandon made a face and *tsked*.

"I'm afraid your friend got bruised up a bit when Lana and Alexander went to fetch him," he said. "Broken left forearm, too, unfortunately. I didn't bother to set it, but I did give him a good dose of morphine for the pain. When he's conscious, I'll get his arm into a sling and have him join us."

"And Brandywine?"

"Resting before Alexander brings him down."

"In the meantime?" I said.

"In the meantime, Devon, you and I are going to get to know each other better," he said and brought his completed tray to a table beside the bed. "You know, we haven't had anything interesting going on at Brandfield since Charlotte left us. Things were getting pretty dull until Ellis became ill. It's been a challenge keeping him alive these last two years, but even that's nearly at an end."

I gave that a half-second of thought and realized that, as much as I wanted to see Ellis Brandywine dead and on his way to the hell he deserved, I had not considered what the aftermath for those left here would be.

"What will you do when he's gone?" I said and recoiled as Glandon leaned over me.

He ignored my question, took my chin in one of his big hands, and turned my head from side to side. He let go of my chin and brushed his fingers along my brow. He hit a tender spot near the hairline, and I winced.

"You banged your head pretty hard when you went down," he informed me and used the bed's lift control to bring me slowly up to a sitting position. "You had me worried. Concussions can be a nasty business."

"Nice to know you care," I said as he picked up a penlight from the tray.

He clicked the penlight on and drifted the narrow beam back and forth across my eyes.

"How are you feeling now?" he asked.

"Recovered and ready to leave. You can send the bill to my insurance company," I told him, and he chuckled.

"That's the spirit," he said, clicked off the penlight, and set it back on the tray. "Have any questions while we're waiting for Ellis?"

"As a matter of fact," I said, my stomach going from queasy to tight as he pulled on a pair of latex gloves, "what's the story on this place?"

"What do you mean?" he said and took hold of my right arm at the elbow. He lowered his big head to examine the area inside the bend.

"I mean Brandfield is a big place. But I've seen only a handful of people working here. How do you run it with such a small staff?" I said, something I had been curious about since my first visit.

"Lana," he said. "She's an absolute demon of efficiency and discipline."

And of silence, I thought, guessing it was my efficient and disciplined point-of-contact who had snuck up behind me and made contact to the side of my neck with a short-needled Mickey Finn.

I was an idiot for not thinking of something like that happening, but I was an idiot who learned fast. Somehow, I was getting out of these restraints and finding Jonah. And when we made our break, I didn't want to have any other unaccounted-for employees sneaking up or popping out to stop us. And as much as my increasing level of fear made me want to shout and swear and thrash against the restraints, I knew I had to stay calm and keep probing, buying time, and getting answers until I could find Jonah and a way out of this damn place.

"But what about when Eleanora built Brandfield? Or when Charlotte was here? Weren't there more staff back then?" I said.

"Quite a few. All relatives, by the way," said Glandon and gave another *tsk*.

The restraint on my wrist and the resistance I was giving were making it difficult for him to position my arm for the draw.

"What happened to all of them?" I asked. "Quit, fired, or lurking?"

Glandon stopped twisting my arm. He lifted his ghoulish eyes to mine with the corners of his mouth lifted in a livery smile.

"No one *quits* working for Ellis Brandywine, Devon. I thought you would have figured that much out," he said, lowering his head again, and began tapping on the crook of my arm, probing for a vein.

He was right. I had figured that out, but now I had to figure out how to distract him into making a mistake I could exploit.

"So what happened to them?" I pressed.

Glandon kept tapping and said, "It used to be called *the family curse*, but I call it *genetic attrition*."

I stared at the side of his head, hypersensitive to his gloved touch on my arm but curious about his answer.

"What's 'genetic attrition'?" I said and was glad I did. He let go of my arm, and his big head came up again, looking not just pleased that I had asked but as if he had been waiting decades to tell.

He had.

"It's the name I have given to my life's work," he said with the disturbing pride of the medical psychopath that he was. "It's also something of a long story, if you really want to understand."

I shrugged my shoulders as much as I could with my hands strapped down and said, "It's not like I'm going anywhere," although the tips of my fingers were going crazy.

My pulse was also tap-dancing in my neck, and my blood was surfing like a tsunami through my ears, while Glandon stood with his wide mouth puckered into a fat purse, nodding to himself and deciding where to begin.

"For the sake of time," he said, "let's start with what you already know about the history of the Brandywine family."

Which was fine with me, as long as one of us was talking.

I forced my thoughts together and gave him an encapsulated version of what Jonah had dug up about Eleanora being descended from Romanian twin brothers, ending with her meeting his uncle Merrick in college and the relationship that developed between the two of them after the dorm fire.

When I was done, Glandon looked impressed.

"I see Lana was right to hire your service. You really are quite thorough," he said.

But screwed if I can't get out of this bed.

"Your turn," I said, and one of his eyebrows went up.

"Oh, Devon, you have no idea how right you are," he said, and his words landed on my ears like a chilly warning rather than a simple response, making that pulse in my neck dance even faster.

Now I was not sure what had me worried more—what he meant by that or Ellis Brandywine's plan for me. What I was sure of was that neither thing was going to be good and that both were going to happen soon.

"So, what about this family-curse stuff?" I said to keep him talking and away from my arm.

Glandon smiled as if he knew what I was up to but went on anyway.

"Well, Devon, for that, you have to go back more than a hundred years or so to the family patriarch, a Romanian count who was, by all accounts, a brutal character. Exceptionally ruthless and thoroughly evil. As the story goes, he heard about a Romani caravan that was camping near his castle and that one of the women had a beautiful daughter with unusual gray eyes. The count decided he wanted her, so he raided the camp with some of his men and took her. The poor girl was barely fifteen and died within the year giving birth to twin boys. When she did, the mother went insane with grief and spent years trying to kill the count and his twin sons while he tried to kill her, a deadly game they played between them for years.

"Eventually, the count grew bored of it and sent the twins to America to keep them safe from her revenge. But according to the family legend, before they left, the mother put a curse on the count. She said his descendants would live in a poisonous shroud of distrust and untimely death until the line withered to nothing and their evil was consumed in a final inferno."

"That's quite a curse," I said.

"The Brandywines are quite a family," he said.

"No kidding," I said, and he gave another one of those damn chuckles, a habit that was getting under my skin, which was already crawling from his touch.

"But I don't understand what that has to do with the number of employees here," I went on.

"You don't?" said Glandon, watching me closely, waiting for me to work it out.

When I did, the tips of my fingers tingled even more, and the hair on my arms stood up.

Because I knew then what Eleanora Brandywine and Merrick Glandon had been doing in the intense isolation and gloomy seclusion of Brandfield.

I knew why they needed Sunridge.

Why the housekeeper looked like a near-copy of Eleanora and why the gardener had the same big head as Laurence Glandon.

"They were trying to clone themselves," I said, and Glandon nodded.

"You see, Devon, my uncle was absolutely mad for Eleanora. Couldn't bear the thought of being parted from her. They both knew about the family-curse business and thought it was silly until Uncle Merrick looked into it and realized that it seemed to be true. The count never had another child that lived, and his descendants from his twin sons never even made it close in age to their seventh decade. If they weren't all fighting amongst themselves and knocking each other off, they had a stroke or a heart attack or some other medical catastrophe and dropped dead usually no later than their mid-fifties, with only a few making it to sixty. They eventually stopped killing each other, but they tended to marry late, propagate poorly, and went on dying relatively young.

"When my uncle decided to look for a genetic cause, Eleanora built Brandfield to give him a private place to do his research. She hunted down the count's remaining descendants and lured them here over the years to live and work and be studied. But when they continued to die off early, my uncle decided that what was needed was an injection of fresh genes into the family bloodline and a wider scope of research. And that's when Eleanora became involved with Sunridge."

"And turned the patients there into a steady supply of lab rats," I said, repulsed and thinking of the records Dr. Morley had found after Merrick Glandon's sudden death.

"Gloria Brite," I said. "How did she fit in?"

"A lucky happenstance," he said and loosened the restraint on my right wrist.

He rolled the inside of my elbow up and applied the rubber-band tourniquet to my upper arm. He dabbed a wipe with alcohol and swabbed it over the area, where a vein looking as big as a fat worm had raised.

Lousy traitor.

"Make a fist," he instructed, and I hesitated. But I needed him to go on talking and forget about the loosened restraint, so I restrained myself from telling him what he could do to himself and did.

"As I was saying, when Uncle Merrick couldn't find a genetic cause to modify, he switched his efforts to cloning. He would harvest eggs from Eleanora periodically and also kept an impressive sperm bank. When Ms. Brite took over the directorship at Sunridge, need met greed, and ..."

"And Gloria Brite supplied the wombs to grow the fertilized eggs in," I said, hating them all and sickened enough to gag.

Glandon eased the draw needle into my arm and began siphoning blood into the attached vial. I watched and went on talking.

"Obviously, your uncle and Eleanora weren't successful."

"But they did come close a few times," he said.

"The housekeeper?" I guessed.

"Noreena," he said, concentrating on his task. "They had great hope for her. She looked so much like Eleanora and even had her dreamy penchant for pyromania. Unfortunately, she was reckless as a child about the fires she set. Always sneaking into rooms forbidden to her and setting little blazes. The only way my uncle could keep her from burning Brandfield down to nothing was to punish her severely if he caught her so much as looking at a match, a still-necessary task that our Alexander helpfully took over, by the way. Lucky for Noreena, she was born with a culinary gift. The original cook here was one of the women brought in from the New York branch of the family. When that woman died of a cerebral hemorrhage at fifty-one, Noreena replaced her."

"And Morris?" I said.

Glandon changed vials.

"Born abnormally strong and frighteningly violent. I was told that, even as a toddler, his tantrums were wildly destructive. Uncle Merrick had seriously considered scrapping him."

"What stopped him?" I asked, chilled by the casual way Glandon said "scrapping him."

"My uncle discovered that Morris, at five years old, already had an amazing talent for forgery. After Uncle Merrick lobotomized him, Morris became as gentle as a lamb, and his skill and strength became useful."

"And he hasn't dropped dead."

"Uncle Merrick was, genetically, his father, and one of the women from Sunridge was used as the mother, so there are no Brandywine genes complicating things in Morris," he said. "Relax your hand," he ordered, and I did.

"But your uncle died kind of young, too," I said, and his look went glacial.

"My uncle wasn't just mad for Eleanora. He was actually mad—and a fool, too. Eleanora, on the other hand, was never a fool. She lived fully in the present and never believed in cloning. But she had an unfortunate weakness for Uncle Merrick going back to the fire in her college dorm room, where they recognized something special, shall we say, in each other. Ever since then, she indulged his silly, wasteful whims while he frittered away valuable resources and completely ignored the more-serious issue that was plaguing the Brandywine family."

"So you scrapped your uncle and took his place," I said, not surprised at what was apparently a Glandon family trait.

Glandon gave his big head a confirming bob and then switched to the last vial.

He removed the rubber-band tourniquet one-handed and dropped it on the tray.

"What was the more-serious issue? How to get rid of all the bodies?" I said, taking what I was afraid might be one of the last opportunities I would ever have to be a smart-ass.

"Actually, Devon, we have our own incinerator. Morris loves flowers, and, as a joke, Ellis told him the ashes make good fertilizer for his geraniums," he said and gave another damn chuckle.

"Funny guy, that Ellis," I said, long past tired of that chuckle and remembering the little building puffing dirty smoke at the edge of the parking area. "So what's the more serious issue?" I prodded, wanting to do to Glandon what Alexander had done to Hank Spitball.

"The end of the Brandywines," he said, his look back to warm and his voice back to chatty. "Not only do they die early—this last generation was born sterile. The twins may not have been. But they were too young for that to be determined before Charlotte snatched them away."

"Which made finding them …"

"Invaluable to my research and the extension of the family line."

"What about your boss?" I asked, and the glacial look returned.

"Exceedingly selfish and as wasteful as my uncle. Scrapping any fetus that wasn't perfect and never allowing me to touch the twins, viewing them only as playing pieces in one of his incessant games."

Glandon finished the blood draw, removed the needle from my arm, and covered the point of insertion with a cotton ball and a bandage.

"Tell me, Devon, do you believe in the existence of evil?"

"Yes," I said, knowing there could be no other answer. Not since the day I had first set foot in Brandfield.

"Me, too," he said, as he straightened the vials into an even row of dark liquid on the tray. "And by living here all of these years, I have had the opportunity to study both good and evil closely."

Which made me wonder where the hell he'd found any good around here to study until I remembered that Ellis had married it three times.

"And what did you learn?" I said, and he turned to me with that eager-to-tell look again.

"The first thing I learned was that good is industrious. Always needing *to do*. Feed the poor. Shelter the homeless. Save the children. Be kind. *Smile*, and all sorts of other wasteful nonsense," he said with a dismissive wave of his hand.

"Disgusting," I said. "What about evil?"

"Well, Devon, that's where the research got interesting," he said, and there was something about the way he said it that made my stomach go a little queasy again.

"And?" I said.

"And," he continued, "I've found that, while some evil is learned, some evil is."

"Is what?" I said.

"Not *what*, Devon. Some evil *is*," he repeated, as the air in the room changed, and the tips of my fingers suddenly burned.

"And here it is now," he said and turned to the doorway, where, framed like a portrait of virulence, sat Ellis J. Brandywine in his wheelchair, smothered in blankets, his oxygen tube snaking up over his shoulder, and smiling.

Chapter Thirty-Five

The smile was gloating, and the hard glint from my first encounter here with him was in his eyes again. Behind him, stood Alexander, whose look, I thought, was pretty arrogant for a guy whose job involved hurting a middle-aged housekeeper and having his ass whipped for fun. But then again, he wasn't a guy who was dumb enough to have gotten himself roofied and velcroed to a bed.

Paying closer attention to Brandywine's condition now than I had upstairs, I realized that Glandon was right. Brandywine's hands and face were even more patchy and inflamed, while the sickly pallor beneath had turned a pasty gray. The layer of skin that stretched across his scalp had shed so thin I could see the blood pumping like a tired afterthought through the narrow veins beneath it. I got the feeling that, if he gave one good sneeze, he would blow himself out of the little that was left of his birthday suit.

And Brandywine knew it, too, which is why he had made this move on me and Jonah. He was finishing the game while he still could.

"Ellis, perfect timing," said Glandon as Alexander pushed the wheelchair into the room.

"I hope, Laurence, that Mr. West hasn't been any more of a problem," said Brandywine, his words coming out as barely more than a sigh.

"Not at all. As a matter of fact, we've been having a nice chat about the family history," said Glandon as he removed the latex gloves and dropped them onto the tray. "If you'll excuse me, I need to take these blood samples to the lab room and check on our other patient," he added and left.

"You may go, too, Alexander," Brandywine wheezed.

Alexander gave me a smirk and glided out. In the silence that followed, something occurred to me.

"You're pretty old for a Brandywine," I said.

"Yes, and who knows how much older I may have gotten if I hadn't been poisoned. Which you were meant to prove Charlotte had arranged and have obviously failed to do," he said, his voice weak and whispery but still strong enough to hold an edge.

I gave him a long sigh and my best bored-employee look.

"If you're dissatisfied with my work, sir, I'm afraid Mecklan Personal Services doesn't have a Human Resources department. But you can call our office and speak to Mr. Mecklan. He handles all complaints."

I could see Brandywine was dying, so to speak, to fire something ugly back at me but was frustrated that he was too weak to do it. He settled instead for snorting oxygen and looking angry enough to spontaneously combust, so much so that, for a moment, I thought I actually smelled smoke.

But next to fear, there's nothing like anger to get the adrenaline going, and his anger gave him enough strength to speak.

"Tell me which twin you located," he demanded.

I kept my look bored and my eyes on his while I wiggled my wrist in the loosened restraint that Glandon had forgotten to tighten.

I knew I could be free in about four seconds flat, but I didn't want Brandywine or Glandon to know that yet. Not as long as I didn't know where to find Jonah or if he was conscious enough to walk.

I was weighing the need to be patient against the satisfaction I would get if I freed myself, went to Brandywine, and shut off his oxygen, when I saw the glint in his eyes flip from hard to sure.

"You found Nora, didn't you?" he said, which I found curious.

"Why do you think it was Nora?"

"Because Nora was the stronger of the two," he said, sounding pleased not because he thought she was alive but pleased because he thought he had won another bet. But being pleased seemed to be exhausting for him, too, because his eyes fluttered shut, and his shallow breathing slowed to a hint.

I waited, not sure if he was resting or comatose, thinking about all the pain this one monster had created for so many people and wondered if it was worth getting out of the restraints to send him to hell—a place where he would probably feel right at home.

And then I thought about Charlotte and the end of her story—of being "allowed" one day to visit her mother in New York, gnawed by anxiety and terrified that Ellis might, at the last minute, change his mind about her going or about the twins leaving with her.

But when he didn't, Charlotte had known her chance had come, that, somehow, the enigmatic woman from the spa would use this opportunity to set her freedom and the safety of her children into motion, even though complete freedom and safety meant Charlotte would have to find the courage to be as ruthless as her husband in order to do what she knew had to be done.

I tilted my head back and stared at the ceiling while I considered the ruse of the boating mishap and why it made sense. There could be no land "accident" with bodies burned or mangled beyond recognition because you can't change the DNA, especially the Brandywine DNA that Charlotte had been horrified to see manifesting in her daughter, beautiful little Nora, who had been a perfect baby. Almost never crying even when she was sick or cutting teeth, but by two years old was hurting her brother with pinches and slaps or pulling his hair. By three, it had become a game—snatching his favorite toy away and watching him cry or showing him affection one moment then ignoring him the next.

Charlotte had wanted to believe the behavior was normal sibling rivalry and something that, like Jeremy Brandywine had believed about Ellis, could be worked with and changed, until the afternoon she had caught Nora trying to push a heavy vase off a table and onto her brother's head while Ellis watched and smiled. It was then she knew the evil her womb had bred and that her son would never be safe as long as he lived at Brandfield or while his sister was alive to torment him.

And as hard as it was to believe that it was only hours ago that I had been sitting across a table from Nell and Charlotte, it was just as hard to wrap my head around the double-cross Charlotte had found the courage to perpetrate on Deckard and Drew—and herself.

I heard a noise and brought my gaze down to see that Glandon had returned. As promised, he had brought Jonah with him, and it was obvious that the "bruising" he said Jonah had sustained was more severe than a few purple splotches. Along with the broken arm, Jonah had a split bottom lip and dried blood crusted on the side of his head from a wound that could have come only from a blow with something hard enough to break the skin. Just the same, a wave of relief washed over me seeing that he was alive until I saw the pain knotting his face, and noted his drugged, shuffling footsteps.

My heart sank, and what was left of the hot ball of anger in my belly burned out. No way was Jonah in any condition to make a fast break for it, and I sure as hell couldn't carry him. But I had not returned to Brandfield to give up and leave without him, so while Glandon led him to a chair across the room, I did what I knew Jonah would do—I forced myself to stay calm and look at other options.

My first thought was to grab Brandywine and use him as a hostage to get us out of here. But even if Morris and Noreena were too mentally defective to understand that our escaping meant the end of Brandfield and prison for everyone here, it was a sure bet that Glandon, Lana Troy, and Alexander weren't. And Brandywine was so close to death anyway, it would be like trying to trade road kill for a ticket to Disneyland, a deal none of them was going to make.

And even though I knew I could get myself free, grab the pepper spray from my ankle, and neutralize Glandon with a quick blast, I knew everything else would go slow after that.

I would have to dump Brandywine from his wheelchair, get Jonah into it, and then figure out where the hell the elevator was. After the ride up, I would have to contend with Lana Troy and Alexander while maneuvering Jonah around on the borrowed wheels through the twisting layout of this damn, dark place. That, of course, would be like playing hockey with those two freaks on blades and me trying to beat them to the exit on the Zamboni.

And even if I could locate the elevator quickly, manage to get us back upstairs, slip us through Brandywine's office, his study, and his bedroom undetected, I would have to somehow bump Jonah down a flight of stairs in the wheelchair without crashing to the bottom and past the angry housekeeper, who might find us and mutter the alarm.

Okay. Maybe not a last resort but not a first choice, either.

Yet logic dictated that, although Eleanora had designed Brandfield to be a maze of lunacy, she had also been smart enough to design another way up and out of the basement besides a single elevator. But I knew it would take longer than we had to make Glandon tell me where the other way out was, longer still on my own to find it while dragging an injured and half-zonked Jonah around with me, and, worse, I would have no idea where in this hulking mausoleum it would lead us.

So another "No," I thought, as fear prickled the back of my neck, and I choked on the irony that Jo and I were running out of time as fast as Brandywine was.

I closed my eyes. I was not throwing in the towel, but, to be on the safe side, I said a prayer that, no matter what happened, I would, at least, get the chance to tell Jonah I was sorry that I had gotten us into this mess.

And while I prayed, the fear prickling the back of my neck spread through my body and ate into my gut, making it churn at the thought of Connie's boys becoming a couple of Glandon's guinea pigs when I heard Jonah moan.

I opened my eyes and looked across the room.

Jonah's head came up, and, when his eyes met mine, he winked.

Chapter Thirty-Six

"**S**on of a bitch," I said, realizing we had both been waiting to make a break for it until we had each found the other.

"Son of a bitch," said Jonah, grinning through his pain as he realized it, too.

Glandon stood looking blocky and smug and not realizing anything.

"Jerk," I said to Jonah.

"Loser," he said to me.

Glandon said nothing, but his smugness shifted to alarm when I pulled my right hand free, yanked open the restraint on my left wrist, and popped the catch on the webbed belt that tethered my legs.

The grating rip of the Velcro separating startled Brandywine awake. When it registered with him that I was out of the restraints, he joined Glandon at the deer-in-the-headlights party.

"Tell him," I said to Jo and grabbed the pepper spray from my ankle.

Dropping the right safety rail, I swung my legs off the bed and stood.

When Jonah stood up, too, Glandon flinched like he had been jabbed with one of his own needles and took a long, oozing step away from him.

"Tell me ... what?" wheezed Brandywine.

"Your third wife didn't have you poisoned," Jo said.

"Liar," Brandywine hissed.

"He's not lying. Lana Troy did this to you," I said, feeling all the satisfaction I knew I would at this moment and right up until Glandon shocked us all.

"Don't be ridiculous," he said. "My daughter was studying him."

"*Your* daughter?" said Jo and I together.

Talk about a mic drop.

"Yes," said Glandon beaming like a lab-coated lighthouse.

Brandywine looked stunned, while Jonah and I looked at each other and then back to Glandon for an explanation. Which he was more than proud to give, and paternally so.

"You see, gentleman, decades ago, during my first visit to Brandfield, Uncle Merrick asked me to make a donation to his sperm bank. He must have used the sample to inseminate Rebecca. I can only guess that it was unfortunate timing after that. Ellis sent Rebecca to Sunridge before my uncle knew if the procedure had been successful, and I scrapped my uncle before he mentioned it."

"But ... there were ... records," rasped Brandywine.

"Most of which were damaged in one of Noreena's fires and some, like Rebecca's, were destroyed," Glandon said.

Which made me wonder what kind of punishment that one had cost the angry housekeeper, while it explained the records

John Morley had found stored at Sunridge. Uncle Nutjob had moved them there for safekeeping.

"And without the medical records or the uncle," said Jonah, whose tone had shifted solidly to cop mode, "Gloria Brite assumed the same paternity as we did. That's why she left Sunridge and took a chance on returning to Denver."

"And made a phone call that could have only sounded to you like another one of her greedy scams," I said.

"Exactly," said Glandon. "Until years later, when as an adult, Lana became curious about her past, searched for her birth mother, and found Rebecca," he continued and turned to address Brandywine.

"Lana came here one day when you were away on a business trip, Ellis. I met with her and was skeptical about her claim of Brandywine parentage, and she agreed not to press the matter with you until I did a DNA test. You can imagine our surprise at the result."

But it was obvious that surprise was not what the dying billionaire was imagining.

"You ... told me ... Lana ... was mine," he huffed on seething bursts of wispy breath.

"I did because Lana is a brilliant chemist and has an advanced degree in biomedical research," replied Glandon, sounding as arrogant as Brandywine never would again. "When I learned about her degree, I knew immediately that she would be of tremendous help with my work.

"Unfortunately, Ellis, you were as rigid as Eleanora had been about using only blood relatives here as employees. For that reason, I was concerned that you would reject Lana out of hand. Hence, the little deception," he finished innocently and smiled.

But learning what I had from Glandon himself, I was throwing a flag on that line of self-serving crap.

"Bullshit," I said, and Glandon turned away from Brandywine and back to me. "You did it because you were tired of your boss wasting your resources, and you were sick of the games he was constantly playing. Lying about Lana Troy's paternity was a chance for you to get something you wanted and play a game of your own with him. A game you won every day."

Glandon raised an eyebrow and gave me that "interesting specimen" look again.

"Very perceptive of you, Devon," he said, and the malicious triumph in his voice was so deep it made the tips of my fingers tingle.

I checked to see how Brandywine took that and went with *not well*, based on how badly the veins on his pasty scalp were throbbing.

"But I ... still have ... a daughter," he panted.

And all I could do was stare because, even as he hovered inches from death, Ellis J. Brandywine chose to spend his last minutes on Earth not donating his fortune to charity or apologizing for past bad behavior but immersed in a twisted game and refusing to concede he had lost.

I shook my head and delivered the truth.

"Not a daughter, Brandywine. A son. A living, breathing *good* son that Charlotte sacrificed everything for to make sure he would be safe from you and all of the other evil in this malignant place," I said, and it was a toss-up who looked more shocked, him or the doc.

"No … not … possible," Brandywine croaked, and I almost laughed.

"Not only possible," I confirmed, stepping closer to his wheelchair, "but done, and all without Charlotte losing her mind. Which means she beat you, asshole. Game over," I said, and Brandywine blanched.

Then the three of us watched without an ounce of mercy as his raw, patchy face flushed with rage, and his weak, watery eyes bulged and blackened with hate. His wasted body stiffened beneath the mound of blankets while his bony hands twitched, and his peeled head snapped backwards over and over in sharp, jerky spasms.

His thin, bloodless lips pulled back in a snarl as his mouth stretched in a desperate effort to speak, but it was no use. All that came out was a phlegmy gurgle before his jaw went slack, his head dropped sideways, and whatever was left of the evil that he was descended slowly down into death. For several seconds, the only noise in the room was the sound of the oxygen hissing. His eyes went blank and filmy, and the shroud of blankets encasing him collapsed on itself.

I was the first to move, and that was in a quick step backward as the weight of the collapsing blankets forced an oily odor up and out through his dead, gaping mouth and filled the room with an eye-watering stench.

"What in God's name is that smell?" I said and backed farther away.

Glandon's eyes gleamed as he answered.

"That I believe, gentlemen, is the putrefied soul of Ellis Brandywine. The evil that inspired his games and celebrated the destruction that he caused," he said, too enthralled by his patient's death to see that Jonah was blasting him with a look that could scorch concrete.

It was a look I had never seen on my brother's face before, and I braced myself for an explosion. But Jo was able to stay calm enough to speak, although, when he did, his voice was low and dangerously tight.

"Tell me," he said, "did either of you pieces of shit ever give a damn about any of your victims?"

Glandon shrugged.

"Ellis chose the women and the games. I'm a scientist. My role was to observe and document," he said, as imperious and cold as I was betting his insane uncle had been.

Glandon didn't realize that he had just waved a red flag in front of a seriously pissed-off bull.

This time, Jonah did make a move toward Glandon, set to throttle him one-handed, but I had first dibs on the smarmy bastard even if I hadn't called it. I also had questions I wanted answered before one of us thumped him into putty, so I held up a hand, and Jo stopped.

"Brandywines usually do an early exit," I said. "Why didn't your boss?"

"Well," said Glandon, the twisted pleasure in his voice making my fingertips tingle again, "after decades of study, it's my conclusion that the Brandywine evil was a congenital condition that grew in the ones born with it until it reached a level too powerful to contain. As I explained to you, Devon, the body then suffered a medical catastrophe and expired. In Ellis, the level of evil was high, even for a Brandywine. It's my theory that, as he played his games, its organic strength grew but was diluted at the last, crucial moment by a win."

"Because a win was what for him?" I asked.

"Masturbatory," he replied. "The climax that siphoned off the excess amount that would have normally killed him."

Managing not to vomit at that imagery, I said, "So, what was different this time?"

"The opponent," answered Glandon. "You see, it's Lana's theory that, as the game with Charlotte dragged on without a win and the needed release, rather than kill Ellis, the excess evil mutated and became something akin to an autoimmune disease that spread slowly through his body, necrotizing each of his organs, a single cell at a time, in such a way that, put in simple terms, caused Ellis to rot to death from the inside out."

"Jesus," I said.

"Christ," said Jonah.

"Indeed," said Glandon and tucked his hands into the pockets of his lab coat.

He stood there, looking like an oversized nerd waiting in front of his junior-high class to be commended by the teacher on a perfect presentation and added, "It's been an amazing process to observe."

"No," replied Jonah. "It's amazing you and Brandywine were never caught and sent to prison. Which is where you're going now," he promised, but Glandon didn't look worried. He just did his annoying chuckle and spoke.

"Not likely, Mr. Mecklan, or may I call you 'Jonah'? Regardless, it's you two who aren't going anywhere," he said and pulled his hands from his pockets, a short syringe held in the left one. He flicked the protective plastic cap off and brought it up to strike.

I raised my hand with the canister of pepper spray, set to give him a blast, but stopped when I heard Jonah snort.

"What?" I said.

"Pepper spray? Really, Dev? You came here to rescue me with pepper spray?"

"Well, no. I mean, yes, but I also brought—oh, fuck you, Mecklan. Do you want to get out of this goddamn dungeon or not?" I said, which is why Jonah was distracted and looking at me when Glandon lunged and hit him hard in the chest with the flat of his right hand.

Jo tripped backwards over the chair. He went down cursing and trying to protect his broken arm as Glandon rounded on me with the syringe held high and ready to strike. I dropped him to his knees with a quick shot from the little canister and left him coughing and choking, while I rushed over to Jo.

"What do you think of the pepper spray now?" I crowed.

"Shut the hell up, or I'll tell Angie about it," he said and groaned as I helped him to his feet.

Chapter Thirty-Seven

J onah and I had both been unconscious when we'd been brought down here, but that was not going to stop us from finding the way back up. All it took was the threat of another shot of pepper spray, and Glandon led us to a set of elevator doors, while his eyes ran water, and his nose ran snot. I hit the button to open the doors, and we loaded in. Jo and I pressed into the back of the compartment for the ride up, tucked as tight as possible into the corners behind Glandon and the spit and mucus he was coughing and spewing.

I didn't know where we would be when the elevator stopped, but, at least, I hoped, we would be somewhere above ground. When it did stop and the doors opened, I blanked for a second until I realized we were in Brandywine's office and had ridden up in the concealed elevator Gwen had told me about. It had been disguised with a faux panel on the far wall behind Brandywine's huge desk.

And if that wasn't disorienting enough, I thought for a moment that I heard the *pop* and *whoosh* of flames coming from another room. I blinked and saw someone standing on the other side of the desk. It was Noreena, swirled in a cloud of smoke, her eyes glittering like two shots of hundred-proof madness. She had ripped the gauze off her right hand, exposing a raw, bloody burn on the back of it and a dangling broken pinky. She was holding the Glock in front of her with both hands.

"You!" she screamed at Glandon and pulled the trigger.

The weapon kicked. The supersonic report boomed. Glandon slammed into the back wall of the elevator. I smashed the button to close the doors and send us back down.

"Who the fuck was that?" yelled Jonah.

"Housekeeper," I barked as Glandon slumped to the floor, clutching his abdomen.

I dropped to a knee and peeled his hands away.

Jonah stared at the gunshot wound and looked grim.

Glandon rolled his head and moaned.

When the elevator stopped and the doors opened, Glandon grunted, "My lab," and we pulled him to his feet.

He tossed his head to the right, and we helped him stagger in that direction down a hall. At the end was a room with medical supplies and linens. To the left was his lab, where he collapsed and lay gasping and sweating on the floor.

Jonah hurried back to the supplies room and returned with a towel that I folded into a tight compress. Glandon moved his bloody hands, and I pressed the compress hard against the burbling wound. Glandon brought his hands back and held it in place.

"Over there," he said and jerked his chin toward a narrow bank of tall cabinets across the room.

I rushed over to them, and he said, "Middle door. Press the knob."

I did, and the cabinets swung inward, revealing a set of steps that ascended to a wide landing.

I went back to Glandon. Jo and I got him to his feet again, and we helped him, bleeding and panting, up the stairs.

We smelled more smoke when we hit the landing, which turned right to a second set of stairs. It was a short flight up to another landing and a door.

"Wait," I said and pounded up the stairs.

Smoke was seeping in around the door, but when I touched the knob, it wasn't hot.

I knew Glandon could not make it up here on his own, and Jonah was flagging from his own pain and injuries. Rather than call out to them, I pounded back down the stairs, where the three of us gulped what air we could and stumbled our way up to the top.

When I opened the door, we were hit with a blast of super-heated air and the terrifying crackle of nearby flames as dense black smoke flooded into the stairwell and attacked our lungs. My eyes burned and watered, but, squinting, I could make out a row of filing cabinets and recognized the waiting area beyond.

"C'mon," I shouted and directed them in a rush for Alexander's office and the way out.

I had three seconds of giddy relief believing we were going to make it until we bolted through the arch and into a room-sized oven of broiling heat and gruesome death.

Noreena, the firebug housekeeper and cook, had beat us here and set a blaze that was racing up the walls and licking at the ceiling. A trail of blood led from Alexander's desk to his crumpled body, where it lay blocking the door. He was stabbed full of holes, and the knife I had brought to Brandfield was buried to the hilt in his neck. A tendril of fire had danced along the ceiling, flitted down onto his head, and pirouetted his sandy-colored hair into a crispy cap. The smell of his charred scalp would have been sickening if there had been time to gag.

There wasn't.

Jo and I backpedaled fast and spun around to see Glandon gripping his bloody abdomen and lumbering into my point-of-contact's office.

We dashed after and found him bent over Lana Troy, who was sprawled dead on the carpet in the middle of the room. She had been pumped full of so many bullets from the Glock that I was surprised there had been any left in the handgun when Noreena had pulled the trigger on the doc upstairs.

Glandon moaned and dropped to his knees.

Under different circumstances, I might have felt sorry for the bastard, but there was no time for pity or a wake. The blaze behind us was roaring like a voracious beast and spreading fast through the arch into the waiting area, gorging its relentless way forward and consuming everything in its path like a fiery glutton at an all-you-can-burn buffet. The smoke it belched was getting thicker, and its scorching heat had us soaked with sweat and fear. We had to find another way out. *Now.*

"Glandon!" I shouted.

He looked up, pulled another syringe from his pocket, and raised his hand to use it. But before he could flick the plastic cap off the needle, his eyes rolled back in his head, his hand dropped, and he collapsed across his daughter's bullet-riddled body.

I darted over to him, knelt down, and checked for a pulse on his neck. I didn't get one, but I pocketed the syringe—just in case. Eleanora Brandywine's pyro clone was still on the loose somewhere, and who knew what she might come at us with next?

"That way," I yelled, and Jonah and I sprinted through the door at the back of Lana Troy's office to the elevator she and I had ridden up at the beginning of this whole goddamn nightmare.

When the doors opened this time on Brandywine's office, I dove out, ready to crash into the mad housekeeper and take her down. She was gone, but she had left Brandywine's boat-sized desk a blazing postscript in her deranged and vengeful wake.

Jonah came out of the elevator slower, the pain from his injuries pinching his face into a tight mask. I knew he was functioning now on determination alone, while the adrenaline that had kept me going had morphed into panic. My heart was pounding like a jackhammer, and my blood was roaring in my ears as I hustled us toward the study. As we passed, we saw the room engulfed in flames and another body on the floor.

It was Noreena, crushed to death beneath the burning portrait of her nemesis, her angry face peeking out from the upper edge of the heavy gilded frame. She had died with her eyes open and glaring, her left hand flung above her head in a burned and bloody fist, as if she had been in the middle of one of her mad mumbling tirades when the painting had crashed down and killed her.

I swung my head away and saw the double doors to Brandywine's bedroom flung open, the curtains and bed alight. I turned Jonah in that direction, and we charged through the room, dodging flames, slapping sparks off each other's backs, and knocking whirling embers from our hair.

We kept going in the searing heat and burning danger until we reached the landing at the top of the wide staircase, where Glandon and his smarmy smile had once waited for me and where we now stared down into a raging pit of deadly black smoke and fast-spreading fire.

Jonah and I looked at each other and knew we had no choice. He took a grip on the railing and the two of us descended into the heart of the blazing inferno that Brandfield had become.

I was already dazed from fear and the dwindling level of oxygen, and when we hit the bottom of the staircase, I froze for an instant, paralyzed with the sudden terror that I would not be able to find the way out through the smoky maze of dark rooms down here.

"Which way?" shouted Jonah over the roar from the building flames.

At the sound of his voice, I snapped out of it and looked around. When I did, I realized the flames that surrounded us were also lighting the way out. My lizard brain snorted a punchy laugh and goosed me into action.

I grabbed Jonah's right arm and pulled it around my neck. I circled my left arm around his waist and hauled us through the broiling labyrinth and out the front door. I didn't stop until we had stumbled down the concrete stairs, past my SUV, and across the driveway to the wide, sloping lawn where the two of us collapsed, weak and woozy with relief. We lay on our backs, gulping air and staring at the smoke-darkened sky while Brandfield continued to blaze, and the bodies we had left behind baked into ash.

I closed my eyes and slowed my breathing. The roaring in my ears faded as my nose filled with the noxious smell of my singed hair. As my heart rate came down, my nerve receptors woke up and began sending out dozens of stinging messages from the burns on my arms, face, and the back of my neck.

"Are you guys okay?"

I opened my eyes and saw Morris. For all of his age and physical size, he stood over us looking as frightened as the mental child that he was.

"We're fine," I said and sat up.

A couple of more deep breaths, and I was on my feet.

I looked down at Jonah. His face was tight and pale beneath a smatter of blisters and burns. The wound on the side of his head had opened, and fresh blood was trickling from it. Sparks had left a spray of small burns all over his right arm and had eaten holes through the sling on his broken left one.

"Could you give me a hand, Morris?" I said, and we helped Jonah to his feet.

"Now what?" asked Morris.

Before I could answer, there was an explosion from inside the mansion, and we all jumped as the windows across the front blew out and spit glass and fire in our direction, as if Brandfield was making one last grab for our lives.

"Go," I yelled, and we loped to the SUV as fast as Jonah could move.

Morris got into the back, while I helped Jonah into the front passenger seat. I dashed around to the driver's side, yanked open the door, and hopped in. I slammed the door shut, kicked the engine on, and cranked the AC as cold as it would go.

"Police," said Jonah.

"Hospital," I said.

"Goddamn it," snapped Jonah.

"Shut up," I said.

"Don't fight," Morris whimpered.

"We won't," I said and slipped the short syringe from my pocket, flicked off the cap, and popped Jonah in the neck with it.

"Loser," he said when the needle pinched his skin.

"Jerk," I said as his eyes fluttered shut.

I threw the engine in drive, and Morris asked, "Is he okay?"

"Just sleepy," I said and smashed down hard enough on the gas pedal to make the SUV buck and the tires squeal.

As we sped away, I glanced in the rearview mirror and saw Morris looking back over his shoulder.

"What about my flowers?" he asked.

"I'll get you new ones," I promised.

"Okay," he said and settled into his seat.

When I reached the end of the property, I stopped.

The sun was hanging low and glowing in the sky, and the dusky view before me was soft and gently calming. I had just enough time to pull in a breath and exhale the last dregs of the smoke from the fire that had nearly consumed us before my adrenaline level dropped and my body began to shake.

I waited for the tremors to pass and then moved my foot from the brake to the gas pedal, turning the steering wheel as I did, pointing us west toward Denver and home and the mountains I had thought I would never see again.

I drove away from Brandfield in silence, grateful that Jonah and I were alive and praying that evil burned.

Chapter Thirty-Eight

The next couple of weeks went by in a bubble of emotional detachment for me. Some days, I was clear and focused. Other days, I did everything in a blur.

And sleep was a crapshoot.

On the long nights when I didn't dream that I was surrounded by roaring flames and in a desperate fight for my life, I dropped into a deep, black void of nothingness and floated in a state of nonbeing. I woke up drained each morning and did whatever needed to be done that day, shuffling through the hours like a zombie and caring for Morris until evening fell, and I fought or floated through another long night again.

The easiest part after the fire had been the drive to Denver and the hospital. Jonah spent most of the ride unconscious, and Morris had spent the time quiet and awed to see there was a world beyond Brandfield. I had spent the drive wondering how I could possibly explain what had happened there.

But if a writer could boil a four-hundred-page novel down to a one-page synopsis, I figured I could boil a terrifying brush-with-burning-death experience down to a believable paragraph of bullshit.

I was questioned several times by different authorities in the days that followed our near incineration. And each time, I told the lie that Jonah and I had just arrived for a client meeting with Brandywine when the fire had broken out. I emphasized that we had not been able to find anyone else in time to save them and were lucky ourselves to get out of Brandfield alive—which was not a lie.

The people who questioned me remained skeptical until they talked to big, innocent, droopy-eyed Morris and he backed me up with the housekeeper's history of setting fires.

The fracture in Jonah's arm had been worse than we had realized and bad enough to need surgery. I had refused treatment on our arrival at the ER until Jo was half loopy with sedation and on his way to an operating room. After he was gone, I borrowed a security guard's cell phone to report the fire and the deaths, and to call Angie. I was being treated for smoke inhalation and burns when she had arrived. I must have been a pretty pathetic sight because she took one look at me and said she would be taking over Jonah's care for a while.

I didn't argue.

I'd had to park Morris in the waiting room while all of that was going on. I had been worried that he would be frightened by the unfamiliar surroundings until I remembered that he had spent his entire lobotomized life in a similar setting. When the emergency-room doc had finished with me, I went to collect the big guy and found him happy and eating a small bag of chips someone had given him and absorbed in an infomercial on the waiting-room TV.

Morris and I hung around until Jo's surgery was done and he was in recovery. While we waited, Angie cornered me and demanded to know what in the hell had happened. But by that point, both my mind and body were beyond exhausted, and I was functioning on autopilot. All I was able to do was shake my aching head with its smelly, singed hair, and give my concocted story. I could tell she didn't believe a word of it. Just the same, I knew she would make sure Jonah's story matched mine, just as we both knew she would get the truth from Jonah later.

It was after two in the morning before Morris and I had gotten home. He was hungry and ate three peanut-butter-and-jelly sandwiches and drank two glasses of milk before he was ready for sleep.

I chugged a bottle of water and longed for the shower I couldn't have because of my ointment-slathered burns. I got Morris settled in bed and then went to the bathroom, where I stripped and threw everything I had on into the trash. I ran the sink full of water and washed up as best as I could before crashing into my own bed and a fitful sleep.

I tossed and turned that night, trapped in a nightmare of being chased by demons and death and roaring flames until I stumbled and fell blindly into a patch of darkness and safety. But in the end, the fire found me. I cringed as it blasted me in the face with its heat, and its fiery brightness forced my eyes open to the sight of a giant looming above me. I almost screamed before I realized the brightness was daylight and the giant was Morris.

"Now what?" he had said.

"Coffee," I had mumbled and dragged myself out of bed and downstairs to the kitchen to make him breakfast.

Jonah spent forty-eight hours in the hospital getting used to his cast and being watched for signs of concussion. Angie had delivered him back to me after three days at her place, during which time, she had gotten the real story from him. When she left, I said "Bye," but she said, "Pepper spray?" and laughed all the way to her car.

I had turned a red face to Jonah and said, "Fuck you, Mecklan," and he had laughed like a drunken hyena.

Ungrateful snitch.

Sometime early on, Mrs. Koselke had stopped by with a big plate of cookies. I introduced Morris, and they liked each other right away. I couldn't tell if he liked her because the cookies were peanut butter or because of the gentle vibe she gave off when she recognized a stray. Either way, Mrs. K instinctively knew we were both in need and had kept us supplied with meals, goodies, and comfort over the next several days.

I also introduced Morris to the backyard and Alissa's yellow rose bush. He spent most of every day there admiring the large, scented blooms or sitting in the cool, deep shade beneath the Linden. Sometimes Melvin, furry and fat as ever, would join him, and they would nap together under the big leafy tree.

I spent a lot of time in the backyard, too, mostly mornings with my coffee. But no matter how much caffeine I ingested and sunlight I absorbed, I continued to wade from hour to hour in a fog of exhaustion and emotional detachment.

I had taken it as a good sign that my fingertips had not tingled since the harrowing escape from Brandfield. But it had taken Jonah to recognize that I was dropping into depression. It had helped to understand what was happening to me and to believe the darkness would pass. It eventually did, but, in odd moments, I would feel a wisp of sadness drift over me like the shadow of a deceased loved one passing by or a warning of pain to come.

Jo had gained strength each day, and we had gotten busy tying up loose ends. While he had straightened up the office—literally, one-handed—and touched bases with clients, I had made calls.

Before leaving the hospital after Jonah's surgery, I had left a message with the borrowed cell on Nell's phone, telling her the Brandywine nightmare was over. Replacing my cell phone had been at the top of my priority list and the only task I had been able to handle on my first day with Morris. I had texted the new number to Nell and gotten a message from her later in the day.

Thanks for letting me know, Finder. Don't forget us.

How could I?

Because Ellis Brandywine had traveled under the radar and been out of the public eye for so long, his death and coverage of the Brandfield bonfire had made only a blip on the evening news. I called Gwen to learn if she had seen it. I let her know that she and her family were safe and that Jimmy could go on sharing his smile, playing soccer, or saving the world from destruction.

God knows the world would always need it.

I got in touch with Judge Halliday and told him he could put a match to the beach house in Antigua. He had laughed and said he was going to sell it instead. There was a boys' home that could use the money. He also said to call him if there was ever anything he could do for me or Charlotte.

A week after the fire, I called John Morley. I told him what had happened at Brandfield and about Morris. He assured me Morris was welcome at Sunridge. He also said that he'd had a visitor recently about whom he thought I would be interested to hear.

The next day I packed up the clothes and things I had bought for the big guy, and the two of us made the drive to Evergreen. As much as I had wanted to, I didn't stop at the Mexican restaurant for lunch as I had before because, other than the food Mrs. Koselke made, I hadn't been able to get Morris to eat anything but peanut-butter-and-jelly sandwiches.

Morris had become a little anxious when we pulled up to the tall, spike-topped gates of Sunridge, but once on the beautiful grounds, he relaxed. I parked and had to prod him up to the front door because he kept stopping to stare at the flowers. But I finally got him inside, and while Annalee had taken him for a walk around the peaceful place, John Morley and I had made ourselves comfortable in his office and talked.

Dr. Morley had some questions about the fire and Lana Troy. I knew he was not the kind of person who would have wished that death on her, but I was not surprised when he admitted that he was glad she and Ellis Brandywine were gone and that Rebecca would never have to leave Sunridge.

I had asked about making arrangements to pay for Morris's care. He told me the cost would never be my concern because of the visitor he had mentioned—a woman whose description matched that of Jonah's acquaintance from Deck-ard and Drew.

Dr. Morley said she had appeared at Sunridge a few days before and handed him a certified check made out in an eye-popping sum. Stunned by such a large donation, he said he couldn't help but ask why she had chosen to give the money to Sunridge. My fingertips couldn't help but tingle when he said she told him it was only right that the money came back to Sunridge, since it was where Gloria Brite had made most of it.

Dr. Morley and I had left his office after that and made our way outside. We found Annalee standing beside Morris, who was kneeling, not surprisingly, by a bed of brightly colored flowers, his big hands moving from one lovely bloom to the next, gently cupping each in turn for a fascinated inspection. When Dr. Morley and I approached, Morris stood and looked at me with his droopy eyes.

"Now what?" he said.

"Would you like to live here, Morris?" I asked.

He bobbed his big head and smiled.

And when he did, I knew he would be as safe and happy here as Rebecca was and always would be.

Chapter Thirty-Nine

A month after the fire, Jonah's head wound was pretty well healed, and his broken arm was nearly mended. Before long, he would be out of the cast and into physical therapy.

Our burns had also healed, most without scarring, except for an ugly one on my right shoulder—an angry swatch of puckered skin and a permanent reminder of how close to death I had come. Summer had moved along from the pleasant warmth of June into the soaring heat of July. Mecklan Personal Services had picked up two new clients, and our lives were approaching the intersection of Normal and Good.

I still loved the bright, clear Colorado sunshine, but, every now and then when it pushed the thermometer up toward triple digits, my nerves went a little jiggy and my hands began to shake. Rather than admit to heat-triggered flashbacks and seeking help, I sought air conditioning and waited for the anxiety to pass.

Hey, I'm a guy. Don't judge.

There had been only one item left on my list of things to be done, and I was doing it now.

The death of Ellis Brandywine had meant a lot of things, including the end of his influence at the Denver Women's Correctional Facility. No more picking up the phone and having a meeting on demand. That's why I'd had to wait so long for this visit with Charlotte.

Nell had managed to get access one last time to the private room. We talked as she escorted me to it. She said that Gwen had written to Charlotte and sent pictures of Jimmy. It was touching how much the tough guard softened as she spoke— sounding like a proud aunt rather than her scary, arm-crushing self.

I had written to Charlotte, too, and told her that I had contacted a lawyer on her behalf. The lawyer said that, with Gwen's testimony and Ellis Brandywine's history of psychological abuse, she could make a case for appeal based on diminished capacity due to mental battery. And even if she could not get Charlotte's conviction overturned, she believed she could at least get her sentence reduced.

Charlotte had written back and thanked me for trying. But she said nothing could undo the fact that she had taken her daughter's life and that she was where she deserved to be. She also told me not to worry about her, that she was at peace and working with a prison program that helped non-lifers learn the skills they would need to cope successfully with life on the outside.

Nell and I reached the private room. She unlocked the door, and when we entered, there was Charlotte, seated at the table, her hands resting in her lap, waiting for me. When our eyes met, my breath caught. I was not sure I would be able to do more than stand and stare until she smiled, and the aura of peacefulness that surrounded her expanded like warm, loving arms and drew me forward.

I heard keys jangle as Nell locked the door behind me. I made it to the table and sat down while Nell crossed the room. But rather than taking up station there, she surprised me by leaving through the other door and closing it behind her.

Charlotte and I held each other with our eyes, and once again that poker-face-that-I-didn't-have betrayed me.

She read it easily.

"Please don't be sad, Dev. Everything is okay now," she said, and the words sounded so true coming from her that I almost believed them.

"Not everything," I said, and she studied me for a moment.

"What's hurting you?" she asked, and I wasn't sure that I could answer without feeling worse than I did.

But I had to say it.

"You are. Or, rather, you still being in here is. I feel like I failed you, and I'm sorry," I said, and Charlotte smiled.

When she did, the room brightened, and my heart did that little flutter.

"You haven't failed me, Dev. My son is safe now. That's what matters. That's all that has ever mattered. So there's nothing for you to be sorry about."

"It still isn't fair," I said, stubbornly clinging to the last bit of hope I had that she would change her mind and let me help her.

"Not much in life is, but that doesn't mean you have to be unhappy," she said. "And the work that I do here is important. I hope you understand."

"I do," I said, understanding with an aching reluctance that her sentence and her work here were her penance and her redemption. I couldn't give her freedom to her. She needed to earn it herself for it to be true.

"I only wish, Charlotte, that …"

"I know. I wish it, too," she said, which was so much better than saying goodbye.

But it was goodbye, and we both knew it.

"If there's anything you ever need," I offered.

"A letter or a visit would be nice now and then."

"Of course," I said, about to leave, until I thought of one more thing.

I placed my hands open and waiting on the table.

Charlotte gave me her beautiful, glowing smile and placed her hands in mine.

And for a lovely, ethereal moment, the walls and the bars of the prison surrounding us shimmered into mist and noth-ingness, and I saw that Charlotte was right.

Everything was okay.

END

Acknowledgements

Many thanks and a special gratitude to my beta readers and writing support corps—Andrea Burrow, Marian Brennan, Nancy and Dan Hoffman, my son Scott Griffin for his willingness to discuss with and encourage me through the challenges of writing along with his patient tech support, and to Amy Schiel, my daughter, reader and head cheerleader for team Brandfield.